MY MURDER

ALSO BY KATIE WILLIAMS

Tell the Machine Goodnight

YOUNG ADULT NOVELS

The Space Between Trees

Absent

MY MURDER

Katie Williams

RIVERHEAD BOOKS
NEW YORK
2023

RIVERHEAD BOOKS
An imprint of Penguin Random House LLC
penguinrandomhouse.com

Library of Congress Cataloging-in-Publication Data

Names: Williams, Katie, 1978– author.
Title: My murder / Katie Williams.
Description: Hardcover. | New York : Riverhead Books, 2023. |
Identifiers: LCCN 2022039803 (print) | LCCN 2022039804 (ebook) |
ISBN 9780593543764 (hardcover) | ISBN 9780593543788 (ebook)
Classification: LCC PS3623.I558265 M9 2023 (print) |
LCC PS3623.I558265 (ebook) | DDC 813/.6—dc23
LC record available at https://lccn.loc.gov/2022039803
LC ebook record available at https://lccn.loc.gov/2022039804

International edition ISBN: 9780593714690

Printed in the United States of America
1st Printing

BOOK DESIGN BY MEIGHAN CAVANAUGH

For Fia and Frank,

I'd clone you if I could

MY MURDER

1

I WAS SUPPOSED TO BE GETTING DRESSED FOR THE party, the first since my murder. Instead, I was messing around with the shower drain, which was running at a creep, leaving the inside of the tub scaled with soap and peppered with dirt. So I wasn't dressed, not a shoe, not an earring, not a panty. I was naked, in fact, and crouched in the tub, sending an unwound hanger down the drain after a wad of another woman's hair.

The hanger scratched the wall of the drain, scratched again, but then (gotcha!) sank into something soft.

"I have pants!" Silas called through the door.

At his voice, the hanger twisted in my fingers, the end of it surfacing with a small puff of drain gunk. I cursed.

"Now socks!" he called.

I sent the hanger down again. Was it silly to feel sorry for the bathtub, holding all of that water, letting all of that water run through it? Surely after all the washing that went on inside it, the poor thing might hope to be left clean.

"I'm tying my tie," Silas said. "It'll take one minute. Two."

This was Silas. This has always been Silas. When we're late, he'll announce each of his preparations as he makes them. He becomes a ticking clock of toiletry, my husband.

"I'm just stepping out of the shower!" I called back.

Actually, I'd done no such thing. But I almost had it now. I could feel the small suck of resistance as I pulled the hanger up and out. And there it was, a dark knot of hair, glistening in its placenta of soap. It was the size of a mouse. I poked the hair with the end of the hanger. This was my hair.

This wasn't my hair.

This was her hair.

A knock.

Silas opened the door before I could answer.

"Wheeze? You okay in here?"

He never used to do that, barge in on me. But I decided I'd leave it alone, at least now, at least for tonight, because I knew how he worried, always worried. And he was careful, so very careful, like I was a glass of water filled to the brim that he must carry from room to room, searching in vain for the person who'd asked for a drink. But then there were these other times when his worry made him not careful at all, the opposite of careful in fact, like just now with the door.

Silas leaned in farther. It took him a minute to spot me in the tub with my gobbet of drain hair. What else was there to say but: "Yuck."

"It's not my hair," I told him. And it wasn't. The minute I'd gotten home from the hospital, I'd gone to the stylist and had her cut my long hair down to the nape. A woman cutting off all her hair to demonstrate how her life has changed. A cliché? Sure. But that wasn't why I'd done it. I'd done it because I loved the feel of air on my neck.

"Not mine, either." Silas ran a hand over his head and showed me his teeth.

Once upon a time, Silas's hair had been long enough to brush his shoulders, long enough to stop up a drain, long enough to fall in my face during sex. Now he wore it short, and if you stood in a certain spot, in a certain light, you could see the glisten of his pate.

"It's *her* hair," I told him. "Your first wife's. What an animal she must have been! Did she even own a brush?"

Silas pushed a smile onto his lips. I knew he didn't like my jokes about his "first wife," but I couldn't help myself. I'd stop as soon as I could help myself.

"Okay," he said. "Good job. But do you think . . . ?"

"I know, I know, I'm about to get dressed."

Silas looked down and away, and I remembered my own nakedness. Since the commission had brought me back, I'd become aware of my own body in a way I'd never been before, not even when I'd been pregnant. Now I was aware not of how my body looked or what it could do or what it contained, but of what it *was*, the fact of it. I could feel it even now, the gum of my earlobes, the knot of my belly button, the whorl of each fingerprint. I was in my body. I was my body. I was alive. And I thrilled and fizzed to the very edges of myself, as if I'd been poured in, poured full. I stood, the last drops of water sending themselves off of me.

"It's just that Travis is weird about parties," Silas was saying. Travis was his coworker, the one having a birthday, which was a round one. Thirty? Forty? I couldn't remember the number. "He expects everyone to arrive on time like it's work."

"Well," I said, meaning, *Isn't it?*

Silas held out his hand to help me out of the tub.

"Hey." He lifted my hand to mouth level, like he might kiss the back of it. "We could cancel."

"We couldn't."

"We could stay home, watch a movie. Order pizza. All the things."

"All the things we've been doing every night since my murder, you mean?"

Silas winced. "My murder"—this was the other thing he hated for me to say.

"I'm only saying, if a party's too much—" he began.

"It's not too much."

"If it's too soon—"

"Don't make a big deal. It's only a party."

He leaned in to kiss me lightly. I kissed him back how he wouldn't expect it, long and deep. His lips were familiar and slightly chapped, a hard row of teeth just behind them.

I drew back. "I want to go to the party."

"I believe you," he said, blinking at the kiss.

My screen chimed. "Babysitter's here."

While Silas went downstairs to let in Preeti, who left crumbs of chips in the dip and took secret pictures of me to send to her friends, I got dressed. I pulled out a pair of stockings, untangled them. I *did* want to go to the party; that was the truth. I'd been murdered, but now I was alive. I wanted to do every last inch of every last thing. I wanted to eat until my spoon scraped the bottom of the bowl. I wanted the prickle of air on the back of my neck. I wanted to laugh and fuck and unclog the bathtub drain. I wanted to feel the skim of these stockings over the skin of these legs.

Damn. I'd put a fingernail through the stockings, the cobwebs. I balled them up and dropped them down to the baby, who was in her carrier on the rug by my feet. Nova brought the stockings to her mouth and proceeded to suck a toe. I went to the closet and found a pair of pants instead, yanked them up, belted them. And there it sat on the closet floor, the green canvas bag, the one I used to take to the gym. It was packed full, zippered closed.

Nova made a small sound behind me. A coo. She had the foot of the stocking all the way in her mouth. A wire of shame slid down my spine. Stockings: a choking hazard. And I'd given them to her. I should've been thinking, watching, alert.

"Sorry, Pudge. Gotta take those back."

I swooped the baby out of her carrier and divested her of the stockings now damp with her spit. She was so big now, a large girl, a lovable Pudge, two full armfuls. Nine months old. She'd been outside me for as long as she'd been inside me. (Not me.)

Stockings gone, Nova began to squirm in my arms. Then, suddenly, she was crying, full-throated, like it was her only passion in life.

Before my murder, Nova never used to cry, not much, not at all really. She'd made plenty of other noises, frequent and reassuring: she'd burbled and suckled and farted and smacked her gums, which were glistening to the point of startling, like a thing that should be kept under wraps, a wet pink secret. Sure, she'd fussed sometimes, mostly in her sleep, like maybe something in her dreams was annoying her, her little features drawn into the center of her face like a cloth bunched in a fist. But she hadn't cried. *Babies cry*, everyone said. Except Nova hadn't. Until I'd disappeared on her, and then reappeared months later, like the most terrifying game of peekaboo ever. Now she cried every time I held her, cried and nothing else.

Silas was back, eyebrows raised at the wailing baby. The wire of shame down my spine again, this time electrified: I'd left the closet door open behind me, the green canvas bag right there on the floor, if he peered over my shoulder he would . . . I shuffled back and nudged the door closed with my heel.

"Give her over here." Silas stepped toward me, arms open. "You can put on a shirt."

"I thought I'd go like this."

"Happy birthday to Travis." He reached out. "Give her over."

Silas is a wonderful man; everyone agrees on this point. He has a good head; it rests upon his shoulders. But I didn't give the baby to him. Instead, I bent over her. Her squall grew more frantic now that she was surrounded by her most detested person, a.k.a. me. I pushed my face against the top of her skull, the bones of which had finally fused together, thank goodness, thank god. When Nova was first born I'd been worried I was going to put a thumb through her soft spot, like the boy in the nursery rhyme with the plum. I'd been afraid I'd accidentally step on her rib cage and shatter it like the bulb of a wineglass. I wasn't scared of those things anymore, not now that I knew all the other ways in which I was sure to fail her.

"It's okay," I told her. "It's okay, Pudge. Hush." To Silas, "I must still smell like the hospital. That's why she's crying. Babies and dogs can smell things we can't, right?"

"Dogs and bees," Silas said. "Fear."

"Dogs and bees fear what?"

"No, that's what they can smell: fear."

"Then probably babies can smell hospitals."

"They've all been there, I suppose." Silas was careful not to put his thoughts on his face, but I knew what he was thinking anyway: I'd been home for three months; whatever hospital smell there might've been was long gone.

Silas frowned. "Wheeze—"

"It's okay," I said before he could say any more. "It's okay if she cries. Really." I put the baby in her carrier, where she immediately quieted. "Look. She's stopped."

"Are you sure you don't want to—"

"We're going to that party." I shrugged on a blouse and began buttoning each button with decisive snaps of my fingers to show him that I meant it. "Take the baby down to Preeti. I'll meet you in a minute."

Once I heard Silas's steps on the stairs, I returned to the closet. The bag was still there. Where else would it be? I unzipped it a few inches, revealing a layer of gym clothes. Hidden beneath these clothes were my passport and my Social Security card and some other necessary items, a bracelet Dad had given me when I was eight, and an envelope with the remnants of Nova's dried umbilical cord.

When I'd first packed this bag, a few weeks after Nova was born, I'd told myself it didn't mean I was going to leave my family. Packing the bag was simply an exercise to manage the unnameable, all the feelings I didn't feel, the wobbling socket of dread where the feeling of motherhood—that steady, nurturing joy I'd been assured I'd feel—was supposed to be. Packing the bag had soothed me, folding the clothes into tidy squares, hiding the treasures beneath, and hushing the zipper over the lot of it. Since then, I'd been murdered and cloned, undone and remade. And now I could see the packed bag for what it was: a near miss, an almost fuckup, a terrible, terrible mistake. My Nova. My Silas. How could I have ever thought of leaving them? I pushed the bag farther back in the closet and shut the door. I'd unpack it tomorrow. Silas never had to know.

He was waiting for me now, downstairs. I doubled back to the bathroom for mascara and lipstick. Powder. I stopped with the powder brush held to my chin and stared at my face, peered closer and closer still, until the tip of my nose bumped the glass.

"I'm here," I said to myself. "I'm here and I'm going to a party."

STRANGERS

THE YEAR BEFORE MY MURDER WAS THE YEAR OF being recognized by strangers. The phenomenon started at the beginning of my pregnancy, Nova only the secret curve of my belly. People on the street began staring at me, even turning their heads as I walked by. Ticket-takers would smile at me and say, "Hello again!" Waiters would tap their chins and ask, "Where do I know you from?" A mystery to me. Had a clutch of distant relatives moved into the area? Was there a newly famous actress with my face?

Then one afternoon in the middle of my second trimester, my boss, Javier, had turned up at the house vibrating with energy, even his mustache a-twitch.

"Javi, what on earth?" I asked, stepping onto the porch.

He took me by the shoulders. I'd never seen him like this. Javi was always relaxed, always loose and beaming. His managerial style consisted of throwing compliments out his open office door.

There on the porch, Javi was someone else altogether, wide-eyed and tight-jawed. He'd been downtown, he told me, and had seen on a screen, out of the corner of his eye, a news report about one of the murder victims. He'd mistaken her for me. Even after he'd looked again and realized that the woman's face was only similar to mine and her name not mine at all, still he hadn't been able to shake the feeling that she was me. He'd needed to see me in person, he said. Then he'd pressed his palms to the sides of my head and sighed in relief, as if he'd been afraid his hands might go straight through my skull and clap together.

So here was the answer to the mystery. This was the person I'd reminded strangers of, one of the women crumpled here and there across the city, one of the women who'd been haunting the news reports, one of the women with her shoes lined up next to her body, as if waiting for her to step back into them.

After Javi left, I stood in front of the hallway mirror, brought up her picture on my screen and compared our faces, pale ovals on glass. We were both white women with long dark hair, somewhere around thirty. She was prettier than I was, though, this murdered woman, this Fern, bright where I was dull, delicate where I was blunt, symmetrical where I was askew. But slowly, if I turned my head at a certain angle and narrowed my eyes just so, I could see what the strangers saw. We resembled each other.

I dumped a bottle of dye on my head, a red hue verging on purple. The color left a pink stain along my hairline like a burn. And it made not a lick of difference. Still strangers stopped me. Still they squinted and tapped their fingers against their chins. Still, they couldn't quite place me. I learned to stand there patiently and let them cycle through their various grade-school classmates and local weather girls. I learned to smile and say, "I just have one of those faces."

2

AND THEN I WAS AT THE PARTY, DIM LIGHTS IN AN
unfamiliar living room, scent of dusting spray and tea candles fog-
ging the air. I'd wanted thumping music and strangers and dancing.
Instead I'd landed at a wine-charms-and-chitchat type of affair. The
guests swirled around me. They touched my arm or they didn't.
They approached me in twos or threes, like I was the punch bowl,
like I was the cheese tray, like I was the stack of tiny napkins fanned
just so. I hadn't been around this many people in months. Their attention unnerved me, the accidental eye contact, the murmurs that
might have been my name. I even thought I heard someone humming that rhyme, the one children use for their clapping games:

Edward Early, Edward Early, hunting in the dark
Edward Early, Edward Early, left Angela in the park.

Fern he dropped in the shopping cart.
Jasmine he laid on the street.
Lacey he spun on the merry-go-round.
Louise he left with bare feet. Louise he left with bare feet.

I looked around for Silas, who, for all his worry and fuss before, had now disappeared on me. I had no idea where to. Well, not true. I was pretty sure he'd snuck into the backyard with Travis for a smoke. I fled for the kitchen and found something purple to pour into my glass.

When I turned around, the partygoers had found me again. There were four of them, Travis's girlfriend (whom I secretly called Already Tipsy), a couple draped on each other like they might otherwise collapse, and a lone woman who kept sniffing sharply, from either a cold or disapproval, I couldn't tell.

There were those people who objected to the replication commission, whether because of religious reasons or last year's scandals. And then there were those people who objected to me specifically, who believed I didn't deserve to be brought back, because who was I anyway? Some nobody, some stranger. It should've been their favorite singer or favorite grandmother instead.

"Lou!" Already Tipsy cried out, true to her name, a drunken flush across her nose and cheeks. "We're so happy you're here!"

I wasn't sure if by "here" she meant at the party or, well, alive. Also, I couldn't remember her actual name. So I lifted my glass and said, "Happy birthday to Travis!"

"No," said one side of the leaning couple, "happy birthday to *you*!"

"Oh, it's not my birthday," I told him.

"In a way it is, isn't it?" the other side of the couple replied.

"Maybe we could call it a *re*birthday," the first one said. He took the wine bottle from my hand and raised it into the air. "Happy rebirthday to you!" He swigged.

"Let's just toast Lou," Already Tipsy interjected with a warning look at her friends. She reached out and touched my sleeve. "Right, everyone? Here's to Lou?"

"To Lou!" the group cried raggedly.

I raised my glass in return. They all cheered.

"So tell us," the man said, as the cheers trailed off.

"Tell you?" I asked.

"What it was like!"

"What what was like?"

"Being born, of course!"

Already Tipsy said the man's name, but she didn't stop him; also, she didn't remove her hand from my arm.

"Come on," he said. "I don't remember *my* birth. Do you remember yours?"

"Of course not," Already Tipsy replied. "I was a baby."

"Well, *she* wasn't!" the man pointed at me. "She was . . . like she is now."

I looked past them for Silas, who was still nowhere to be found. The partygoers were watching me with the obsessive focus the drunk can have, a wavery unwaveringness. I considered making a run for it. I could shout out an excuse as I went. *Bathroom!* Or *Doorbell!* Or *Fred!* Who was Fred?

But then I thought something else. Then I thought: So they want to know what it was like? So they want to be told? So tell them. So I did.

"The first thing I remember was a rushing in my ears that I thought was water."

The partygoers looked around at each other, then back at me. "Water," one of them repeated faintly.

"Now what waters these were, I didn't know. My own blood? The kitchen sink? Waves in the ocean of being and unbeing? As it turned out, they weren't waters at all. As it turned out, it wasn't the sound of water I'd heard, but the sound of my skin against my skin, my palms rubbing against the tops of my thighs. And *that's* when I discovered I had palms! And had thighs!"

Here they laughed. It was a funny thing, I suppose, to have a body. Or maybe it was a funny thing for me to have this body, the arm of which Travis's girlfriend was still touching, maybe elated, maybe disappointed, maybe both, that it felt like nothing other than a regular arm.

"When I opened my eyes," I went on, "I was sure I was underwater all over again. Everything was either a blur or a smudge, a smudge or a blur. And I thought: *Someone has come along and mushed the world all up.* But then I blinked, and I realized it was my tears. Just my tears that were making the world into a great big mush. And the second I knew them for what they were, they ran away down my cheeks."

"You were crying?" someone asked.

"Only technically. The doctors had loaded my eyes with fluids to keep the membranes wet. When I blinked, everything came into focus."

"What did you see?"

"My husband and child. Now *Silas* was crying. But then, Silas cries at everything, cries at credit card commercials and furniture left by the side of the road, cries at the *mere thought* of his grand-mother making soup."

They chuckled at this, their coworker, stoic Silas, crying over the thought of his grandmother's soup.

"Did you know them?" someone asked.

"Of course I knew them. I still had my memories. Otherwise, what would I be? Not me! Just a body. Just a great big mush."

The partygoers laughed again, uncomfortably this time. Already Tipsy glanced at her hand, still on my arm, but in the end, she left it there. Maybe later that night she would rub her finger-tips together and feel she'd come away with some silt of me, some flake, when really she'd only be feeling herself upon herself.

"What else do you remember?"

"I remember the smells. I smelled the hospital: disinfectant, the plastic wrappings my bedsheets came in, and something some-one was calling lunch. And the aftershave Silas uses. Lemon and leaf."

"You smelled your family."

"Yes, my family."

The partygoers smiled even wider at this and took simultane-ous sips of their wine. Already Tipsy finally lifted her hand from my arm in order to hug herself to herself. It comforted them, this story. Out of oblivion we come and into oblivion we go, tra la la la la. They wanted to believe what everyone did, that once the tears were all shed and the casket lowered, once they opened their eyes to whatever was after that, their family would be the first thing they would see.

I didn't tell them the rest of the story. It would make for poor party conversation. I didn't tell them about the tug of a catheter being pulled from between my legs; the mole on the doctor's chin, a blot showing through her powder like an eclipsed sun; Silas's voice saying, "Can she—?" and the distant realization that "she" was me. *Can she what?*

I didn't tell them about the pain, not transparent and glass-tipped like you'd think pain would be, but itchy and formless and unbandageable, like a badly burnt tongue, like the hole in your mouth where your tongue used to root.

I didn't tell them about the indignity of waking to find a team of doctors peering at and discussing, both in great detail and at great remove, the precise shape of my vulva.

And I didn't tell them about the time I didn't like to think about, when Gert had come to my hospital room, along with some fellow from the replication commission who kept adjusting the sleeves of his suit like he didn't want anyone to glimpse his wrists. They'd sat in chairs alongside my bed, and Gert had told me that I both was and was not the woman I believed myself to be. That woman had died, she'd explained. Had been killed, the replication commission fellow had finally ventured to say. Had been mur-dered, no one said. And me, I had been grown from a sampling of her cells. I was, in truth, a copy of that woman, the first and original Louise. But I should never think of myself as that, they were quick to amend, as a copy. When they said it, their eyes moved across my face, back and forth, like the glowing arm of a copy machine.

So that was my birth. The partygoers also asked about my death. Actually it was just one of them, the sniffing woman who lingered after the others had dispersed. The whole time I'd been talking about my birth, she'd been waving away crudités and assessing her reflection in the window behind my head.

"My death?" I repeated. "Oh, no. I don't remember that."

I tapped my temple, the same gesture Gert had made when she'd told me. In the hospital, Gert had had lipstick on her teeth. Well, tooth, just the one. I'd been relieved by that, relieved that she wasn't slick.

"Short-term memories don't survive the process," Gert had explained to me, as I now explained to the woman, "Also, you know, trauma."

"Oh, I *know.*" The woman put a hand to her breast. "I mean, I don't know *myself.* But I've read about that: trauma. It sounds just awful."

"Well. Yes."

"So you're saying you don't remember anything at all? Not one thing?"

"Not one."

"That's too bad."

The heat came into my face then, from the wine, not from the wine.

"It's too bad I don't remember my own murder?" I said, but she didn't seem to hear how my voice had changed.

"I mean, aren't you curious? I'd be curious."

"Curious? No. I've been told what happened."

"You have?" She leaned forward eagerly, the wine in her glass swirling to its golden rim, frothing to hear it.

I don't know. I try to be good and nice, nice and good. But sometimes something comes over me.

"He told the detectives that he'd staked out my running route," I said. "He said that he'd followed me for days, that he'd made notes about me in a small notebook reserved specifically for this purpose."

"How frightening!" the woman said.

"He said he was waiting in the trees, that he'd memorized the sound of my sneakers, that after I ran past, he stepped out onto the path behind me, grabbed me by the ponytail, and twisted it around his hand."

"How awful!" she said.

"He told them this was perfect—perfect for him, I mean— because the motion yanked me back and exposed my throat so he could slit it."

"How terrible!" she said.

"He told them it was quick."

"And painless," she whispered.

"Painless?" I looked at her. "Why would it be painless?"

"No, I—"

"A slit throat would be pain*ful*. He had to cut through my skin, my tissue, my trachea. And then I was breathing my own blood.

Can you imagine how that would feel, trying to breathe your own blood?"

She put a hand to her throat.

"Well, and you know the rest," I went on. "You've read the articles, seen the news reports. So you know he left me for dead. But I wasn't. Not yet. Somehow I ran, or probably I crawled, through the trees. They found me three days later in a rain ditch. I was trying to get to the road, they think, to flag down a car. But I didn't make it. Instead, I died. But . . . I don't remember any of that," I finished. "Like you said: too bad."

The woman's face had blanched. I had drained her of her blood. At first it felt good to have hurt her, then it felt terrible, and then it became no feeling at all. I stepped past the woman and out of the kitchen. I felt like I was watching myself from over my shoulder, watching the dark back of my head, as I walked straight through the party, down the hall, and into Travis's bedroom, the room where I knew no one would be.

I stared at the heap of guests' coats on the bed. No hands protruded from their sleeves, no heads from their collars, no chests rose and fell. Bodiless bodies. I lay down on the bed and burrowed right beneath them. I pulled the sheaths of wool and cotton and nylon over my chest, over my face, until I was covered in a crowd of empty fabric, arms and backs and shoulders that had no people in them.

I stayed there for a minute. Minutes. After a while, I could hear the partygoers in the other room singing a creaking rendition of "Happy Birthday." Someone must have brought out the cake. I even caught a whiff of wax when the candles were blown. That man had been right after all, the one who'd asked me about my birthday. I had two birthdays now, the one and the other. But I didn't sing along. No, I didn't feel like singing.

The door opened and someone stepped into the room.

"Lou?" Silas said. A pause. I waited for him to see my feet. "What are you doing?"

"Nothing much. Being a coat."

The mattress dipped. Then the sleeves and shoulders were lifted one by one from my face, and Silas appeared above me. He gazed down, his forehead puckered, his mouth a line. He didn't say anything about the coats, didn't say how we should've stayed home, didn't say he'd told me so. Like I said, he's a good man, everyone agrees on this point. I agree on this point.

He reached down and touched my cheek. "You okay?"

"Me? I'm great. I'm silk-lined and brass-buttoned. I'm double-breasted. I've got a pack of gum in my pocket. I'm ready for winter."

He made a face. "Too soon for a party?"

"Maybe a little," I admitted.

"I'm sorry I left you. I thought you were okay."

"I was," I said. "And then I wasn't."

"And then you were a coat."

"Brass-buttoned."

"What would you have done if someone had come in here to get their coat?"

"I don't know. Gone home with them?"

Silas shook his head, but he was almost smiling.

"Maybe," I said slowly, "I'll go home with you."

There. Smiling now.

"Maybe?" he said.

"Not maybe. I will."

He offered a hand, the coats falling away behind me, as I was lifted up, up to my feet. "Let's go home," he said.

BIRTHDAY

THE FIRST BIRTHDAY I REMEMBER IS EITHER MY THIRD or my fourth, one of those dim early ones. Someone—almost certainly Dad—had decided that I loved swans and had bought me a cake baked in the shape of one. We'd lived in a planned community back then, my dads and me, and a pair of swans bobbled on the pond at the community's center.

The truth was I didn't like those swans, not even a little. In fact, I was scared of them. They canted their necks and hissed like cats and fouled the small pond with plumes of green shit. Once, I'd gotten too close to the birds, and one of them had chased me. After that, I pointed and cried out whenever I saw them. That must've been where the cake idea had come from, my fear mistaken for delight.

Even if it was shaped like my nightmare, the cake was a confectionary wonder, with white chocolate curls and coconut shavings for feathers. I rarely got to eat sweets because my other dad, Odd, who was a nurse, believed children were trained to associate sugar with affection. Odd had a square jaw, square glasses, square shoulders, and a talent for avoiding nonsense, like it slid right off the edges of him. Which is why Dad, who had a sweet tooth and no practicality whatsoever, would've been the one to order the cake. Odd was probably right, about sugar and all the rest of it. But after Dad was gone, I regretted every single dessert he hadn't gotten to eat.

We did eat the swan birthday cake, though. And Dad got a big slice. I can see it now sitting before him, a wedge of white fluff. I can see his smile.

Me? Too bad. I'd caught the cold the kids in the community were passing around, and the whole front of my head was packed with mucus. It felt as if I wore a hot, itchy mask like a second layer of skin beneath my face. At the time, the cold had taken on tragic proportions. What were the chances, I'd lamented, of getting sick on this one day? *My* one day? Worse still, because of the cold, I couldn't taste the cake. Someone pulled out a candle for me to lick, I remember that much. The grain of the sugar and the whirl of wax beneath it, both of them one thing on my tongue.

3

"I HAD TO BREAK UP WITH HIM," ANGELA SAID. *HIM* was Angela's boyfriend. This was not news. Angela had broken up with the guy weeks ago, but she kept going over and over the decision, arriving at the same conclusion each time, like a hiker lost in the woods circling back to the same tree stump. The problem with the boyfriend was that he wouldn't let Angela out of his sight. A common reaction, Gert told us, given our situation. Angela grimaced. "But he wouldn't even let me close the bathroom door."

The serial killer survivors' group met on Tuesday afternoons. The replication commission had rented this meeting room from some limping family medical practice. Simpering, pastel, fuzzy— it was an old aunt's bosom of a room. The chairs were pin-tucked satin numbers. Weepy landscapes pocked the walls, views upon a world like a crouton left overlong in someone's soup. Up near the ceiling, the air vents droned without cease. I kept thinking one of the other women was humming under her breath. There were the five of us in the survivors' group: Angela, Jasmine, Lacey, Fern, and myself. The name was a lie. None of us had survived.

"He's still following me," Angela continued. "He's out in the parking lot right now. In his car. And I took the bus here. He drove behind it the whole way, stopping at all the stops." She wrapped one of her hands around her neck protectively.

Angela had a long neck and a small chin that she tilted upward as if she were constantly peering over a high shelf. This gave her a goose-like or—if I'm being generous—swanlike appearance.

Angela had been the first of us. She'd been found on a park bench by some dawn jogger or dog walker, her throat slit, her sandals lined up next to her bare feet. And did you ever notice how these are the people who are always discovering the bodies, these people whose lives are so orderly that they can rise early enough to find a whole other human being dumped on the ground?

"I've decided to just let him do it?" Angela said of the boyfriend. "It's just easier that way? Sometimes it's even . . . reassuring? Like, I'll get the feeling that someone is following me, and I'll sneak a look over my shoulder. And phew! It's just him."

"But isn't *he* the reason you have that feeling?" one of the other women asked. I didn't see who because I was distracted by Angela's use of the word "just," like a little cudgel hacking into the surface of all her sentences. *Just, just, just.* Angela was wrapping her hand around her neck in the exact same place her throat had been slit. I pictured the blood seeping between her fingers.

"That's what I'm saying," Angela replied. "When I see it's him, I feel relieved."

"Not *that* feeling. The feeling someone's following you. Maybe you have it because *he's* following you?"

It was Lacey who was speaking, Lacey who wore the darkest possible shade of lipstick, the rest of her face receding into the misty backdrop of her nightshade mouth. Lacey was the group contrarian; she liked to challenge what anyone else said, whatever they said. I couldn't be too hard on her, though. Lacey was the youngest of us, just twenty; she still lived with her mom. Lacey had been discovered on an elementary schoolyard merry-go-round, one leg dangling off the side, toe touching the ground, and a perfect circle drawn in the sand. That meant after he'd put her on the ride, he'd spun her around.

"I don't know about that," Angela said. "I might have that feeling anyway. Don't *you* ever feel like someone's following you?"

We murmured in agreement: We did. We all did.

I glanced at Jasmine, who was sitting next to me. Jazz was the oldest of us by nearly a decade, late thirties or early forties, her hair already streaked white, by age or dye or trauma. Jazz had been found in an intersection, lying flat on her back in the middle of the road. She was lucky she hadn't been run over. Actually, no. Lucky? Which one of us had been that?

"You see?" Angela exclaimed. "Everyone feels like they're being followed some of the time!"

"I still think it's more likely when someone *is* following you," Lacey said.

"You think I should ask him to stop? He won't stop."

Angela looked around at the rest of us one by one, as if taking a tally. When she got to me, she halted and her lips parted. I dropped my eyes, but it was too late. She'd seen where I'd been looking, at her hand on her throat. She flushed and her hand fell to her lap, where it twitched once. Shit. I'd mouth an apology, I decided, if she ever looked at me again, which she was not doing now.

"And how about you, Lou?" Gert asked exactly then.

Gert was not one of us, was not a murder victim, not a clone. Gert was a professional, specially trained. She'd come from the replication commission, moved out from DC to mid-Michigan, to run our support group, to balance the equations of our aftermath. Shortly after we'd been cloned, the rest of the commission, the scientists and the men in the suits, had moved on, but Gert was still here. And Gert was fierce. Gert was firm. She wore her hair in a tight, twisted braid that ran down the center of her head like the ridge on a lizard's back. She dressed in denim shirts, canvas pants, and work boots, as if our therapy would be like painting a house or tightening a leaky pipe. This was not so far off from Gert's therapeutic approach. *So what are you going to do with that?* Gert liked to say in response to our confessions and revelations. *How can you use that?* As if our lives were something we could simply take a screwdriver to.

Gert was still waiting for my answer. I wouldn't say what I really thought, which was that Angela should get rid of the guy, should break up with him once and for all, should tell him to fuck right off. I thought of the green canvas bag in the bottom of my closet; then I closed the door on that thought.

Instead, I said, "I think Angela should do whatever she wants with her boyfriend."

"Ex," Angela amended.

"If she wants to let him follow her, let him follow her."

"So we should all do whatever we want?" Lacey said. "That's hardly realistic!"

At the same time Angela said quietly, "I don't let him. He just does it."

"I wasn't asking you about Angela's situation," Gert said to me. "I was asking about your own. Would you like to tell us about your week?"

"My week?" I fumbled, at a loss. "I went to a party."

"And how was that? The party?"

I thought of the woman who'd asked about my death, her bloodless face as I'd pushed past her, the weight of the coats as I pulled them over me, one and then the next and the next, like shovelfuls of dirt.

"Loud. Crowded. I went home early."

"Riveting," Lacey murmured.

Gert gave her a look. "It's a good step," she said to me. "You left when you had to. You were aware of your needs . . ." And she went on about the power of positive self-talk and the importance of self-care. I don't mean to sound glib. It was just that I'd heard it all before, and none of it had ever worked for me. Telling myself that I was okay seemed like nothing but evidence that I wasn't.

"How about you, Fern?" Gert asked, turning to the one of us who had yet to speak. "Would you like to share?"

Fern tucked her hair behind her ears, an efficient gesture, and I got that glimpse I sometimes did of how she and I resembled each other, not like sisters or even cousins, but like an unpracticed artist, making sketch after sketch of the same woman's face.

"Not today," Fern said, which was what Fern always said, but wistfully, as if she were really saying, *Someday. Someday soon.* She was so pretty; she was probably often put in the position of making promises she had no intention of keeping.

"Not today," Fern repeated, like the refrain of a song.

Fern was the second victim, three before me, who was the last. Fern had been found at the edge of the Lansing Mall parking lot, tucked into a shopping cart, knees to her chin. The tackiest possible location, she liked to complain. She didn't even shop at the mall.

A MAN WAITED outside the clinic in a gold car he was driving himself and had parked to face the doors. He straightened when I came out, then slumped back down when the sun hit my face. Angela's ex-boyfriend, he must be. I'd imagined him with the weedy, petulant look of Silas's coworkers. In reality, he was soft and round with a prominent nose and close-set eyes, giving him an expression of dull surprise, the duck to Angela's goose.

And just then, as if my thoughts had summoned her, Angela emerged from the clinic and brushed past me. Well, not *brushed*, because her body didn't touch mine, only moved the air around it. She trotted toward the bus stop at the far curb, not even glancing at the gold car, though the driver watched her raptly.

I wondered if I should tell Angela that her ex-boyfriend was there, but of course she already knew; she'd said as much in group. Still, there was a stirring inside me, and I found myself calling out her name. Angela turned, but I couldn't make out her expression. Her eyes were black in the sun, as if they'd been pecked out.

"I'm sorry," I said. And what I meant to say was *for making you uncomfortable about your neck*, but what came out of my mouth was only the smallest, worst bit of this, "about your neck!"

I'm sorry about your neck.

Terrible.

Angela stared at me for a moment then turned back around and stepped beneath the bus stop, pert and motionless, like a gymnast on her mark. Meanwhile, the ex-boyfriend had swung his car into the slot directly behind her, leaving its engine to idle. The entire time, Angela hadn't so much as glanced at him. The entire time, he, whom I had fixed in the corner of my eye, hadn't looked anywhere but at Angela, not even when I'd shouted her name.

"Hey." Fern was at my elbow. She had a line of acne scars along her jawbone, visible only in the bright sun. Somehow even these were pretty on her, like the deckled edge of expensive stationery. "Want to go somewhere?"

I was surprised, then flattered.

"You mean like lunch?" I said.

"Sure. Like lunch."

"Just a minute," I told her. "I mean, yes. Yes, I do. But if you could wait a minute? Angela was just . . ."

"Angela was just what?"

"Sorry. Just a minute."

But Angela was gone. I scanned the length of the parking lot;

Angela was no longer there. I hadn't seen where she'd gone, but I could picture it in my mind, the forked road of possibility. On one side, the bus had come, its doors unfolding, Angela stepping up to be enclosed in its humming bulk. On the other side, Angela had stilled with the sense that someone was following her, his eyes fastened upon the back of her head, upon the nape of her neck. The feeling had grown until finally she couldn't stand it anymore. Until she'd turned, and there he was. There he always was. Until with a sigh, she'd traced the few steps back to where he waited for her, had lifted the shining latch and gotten in.

CRIME SCENES

ONE. Angela on the park bench, head tilted back, throat opened up, a pair of braided leather sandals on the ground in front of her toes, like she'd slipped them off for a minute to rest her feet.

TWO. Fern in the shopping cart outside the mall, knees bent to her chest, forehead resting against her knees, blood spilled and dried down her front, vintage pumps tucked into the fold-out portion of the cart, the place where you're meant to stow your child or your purse.

THREE. Jasmine under the traffic light, staring up at the sky, legs together and arms spread in a T, shoes laid out by one of her hands, as if she'd been carrying them while she'd walked through the city streets in bare feet.

FOUR. Lacey on the merry-go-round, curled on her side, boots in the toy's center, Lacey's leg cast off the edge, toe dragging, like she wanted to feel the sand, feel the spin.

FIVE. Louise at the edge of the park, collapsed in the rain gully off the side of the road, sneakers miles back through the trees, up on the trail, as if she'd kicked them off and tried to make a run for it.

4

"I CAN'T TALK IN THERE," FERN TOLD ME. "NOT IN front of all those *women*."

But apparently she could talk in here, in front of only me. Here was Bar None, a few blocks away from the college where Fern was studying something I couldn't remember, history or art. Maybe the history of art? The art of history?

"And then there's Gert," Fern went on.

"What about Gert?"

"It's like she expects us to be grateful, like *she* brought us back herself."

Bar None was the kind of industrial cube that filled with writhing bodies at night and scraped them all out in the morning. On a Tuesday afternoon, there was only a crust of customers in the place, only some crumbs. The night before, though, the bar must have been packed and running a special on glow-in-the-dark drinks, because, after serving us, the bartender took up his mop and resumed swabbing luminescent stains around the concrete floor.

Fern gave her scotch a swirl and a sniff. She took an experimental sip and promptly spat it back into the glass.

I laughed. "Not what you were expecting?"

"I had no expectations," Fern said. "I've never drank . . . drunk . . . drankened?"

"I believe the word is *drinkled*."

Fern smiled. "I've never drinkled scotch before. It tastes like someone made liquor out of"—she moved her tongue around the inside of her mouth—"their shoe."

"Want to switch?" I pushed my gin at her. "My husband drinks scotch. I've learned to endure."

"Husband? Jesus. I forgot you have one of those."

"Yep."

"And a baby, too, right?"

"She's at day care," I said hastily.

Fern gave me a look over the rim of the glass. "Well, I didn't think you'd left her by the side of the road."

"No, I know. It's just . . ." It was just that I hadn't thought of Nova in an hour, hours, not since I'd left that morning. That couldn't be normal, wasn't motherly. "It's just, I'll have to get her after this," I said.

Another lie, Silas was going to pick her up from day care on his way home from work. Silas always picked her up.

When Nova was first born, my nipples would dampen my shirt at the mere mention of her, a pure, embarrassing ache. I glanced down at my chest now. Dry, of course. These nipples had never dampened, had never fed her. After my murder, Silas had switched Nova over to formula. He'd bought the brand that came in those little pouches, each one labeled with the attribute it supposedly conferred upon your child—*fortitude, amity, sincerity*—like gifts from the fairies.

"So," Fern said, "you're a real, live adult."

A real, live adult. And how had that happened? Only a few years ago, I'd been like Fern, single, childless, with no one else to impinge or impede, my days an expression of my will and my whims. In other words, no dampened nipples, but then again, no dampened nipples. Was that what I'd wanted when I'd packed the bag?

"So?" I pointed between our drinks. "Switch?"

"Thanks, but I'm in it for the long haul." Fern lifted her glass in a tiny toast and took another reluctant sip. "Besides, I can't drink gin."

"Hangover?"

"No. Well, not how you mean it. It's that gin was *her* drink. *She* ordered it, so I don't. And she'd always toast with it, too. Every round, a toast in a different language—*bonne santé, salud, kanpai, prost*—like she'd been to those places, knew those words, like she hadn't just looked them up a second earlier on her screen." Fern wrinkled her nose. "Don't you think that's obnoxious?"

"I guess."

"Because she hadn't actually *been* to any of those places. She hadn't actually been *anywhere*." Fern took another sip of her scotch; she didn't wince this time.

"This is your ex-girlfriend?" I asked.

"Oh! Lou!" Fern burst out a laugh so forceful that her breath stirred the tiny hairs at my temples. "Oh, I love that you just said that!"

"Not your ex?"

"I meant me, silly. *She's* me. The me from before."

"You talk about yourself in the third person?"

"Not myself. *Her.*"

"But . . . you were the one who ordered the gin? The one who made the toasts?"

Fern ran a finger around the lip of her glass. "My other me did."

She went on to explain how she, like me, had woken up in the hospital without any memory of how she'd gotten there. Her parents and brother, who'd flown in from Arizona, each took a side of the bed, while Gert and some fellow from the replication commission explained what had happened to her: stalked, murdered, and cloned. Also like me, Fern had been assured that she was the same woman she'd been before, that she shouldn't think of herself any differently. But even though she was supposedly the same person she'd always been, her family wanted her to drop out of graduate school and move back to Arizona.

"But I didn't drop out of school. Or move back to fucking Arizona," Fern said. "Not that they could've made me. They're not my family."

"Not your—?" I stopped at Fern's look.

"They aren't," she said.

"I mean, *aren't* they?"

"That's not how I like to look at it."

"Then who are your parents?" I didn't know why I was pushing the issue, only that it bothered me. "The doctors? The replication commission? Gert?"

"Not *them*." Fern shrugged. "Maybe I don't have parents. Maybe I'm a self-made woman. Maybe I'm singing my own anthem." She set her shoulders back. "Tell me, have you ever sung your own anthem, Lou?"

"I don't know how to answer that."

She smiled. "Exactly."

The first thing Fern did, upon being discharged from the hospital, was to return to her apartment, where her not-parents had continued dutifully paying her rent. There, she'd emptied the closet of its bouquet of vintage floral dresses and embroidered sweaters, collected over the years by *her*, the Fern from before. Fern here, Fern now, wadded the entire precious bundle into a few garbage bags and dropped them at the curb. She didn't even turn her head when the garbage truck rumbled by the next morning. No, she'd already gone to a nearby store and bought seven sets of the same dark jeans and sweater, the same outfit she was wearing now, the same outfit she was always wearing, I'd noticed before.

What else? Fern moved her bed from the wall to the exact center of her apartment. She set her pillow where her feet used to be, her feet to rest against the headboard. She gave away the mystery novels stacked in the corner of her room and joined a fantasy football league. She became vegan. Instead of hot showers, she took baths in lukewarm water. "Like borscht," she said with a wink.

She even began to slip a coin into one of her shoes, a trick, she'd read, that a famous actor relied on to make himself walk differently for a role.

Just this past week, Fern told me, she'd adopted a cat and hand-fed it canned tuna until it adored her, never mind that she was allergic to cats and now owned nothing but dark clothing, all seven sets of which were covered in a confetti of yellow fur. She gestured at her fur-spattered torso as proof.

"Spoon has only ever known *me*," she said.

"Spoon is the cat?"

"I named him after the first thing I saw. *She* would've given it a lot of thought, *she* would've named him something like Francesca or Adelaide or Drusilla."

"Your other you would've named a boy cat Adelaide?"

"Probably. She wasn't very bright. Oh, and I had sex with Spoon's owner. His previous owner, I mean. When she came to drop him off. She didn't want to give him up, but her building doesn't allow pets, and the landlord heard him meowing through the door. She seemed pretty upset about it. Crying. Snot and all that. She was cute, even with the snot. And it was the least I could do."

The Fern from before had been one step removed from virginity. That one step had taken the form of a college boyfriend, a communications major named Wendell. "A communications major *because* he was named Wendell," Fern said. "That's my theory anyway. When we had sex, he used to ask me, and I am now quoting him, 'Can I enter you?'"

"Ew. He didn't."

"Can I enter you?" Fern repeated in an earnest voice.

I picked up my gin; my glass had gone empty. It had been drinkled. The bartender came over, the mop in his hand like some glowing sea creature, and asked if we wanted another round.

Fern gave me a conspiratorial glance and said to him, "Can I enter you?"

The bartender furrowed his brow. "What goes in that? Rum?"

I couldn't help it. I started laughing. And then I couldn't stop. I waved at the two of them apologetically, but I only laughed harder. I could feel the bartender and Fern watching me, first amused, then concerned, but still the laughter came and came, until it didn't feel like laughter anymore, but like my body was expelling something from deep inside itself.

Thankfully, Fern ordered another scotch, and the bartender beat a quick retreat. By the time he'd returned, I'd managed to get ahold of myself.

Fern took the scotch, tapped the side of the glass, and said to him, "I still hate this, you know. I'm not developing a taste for it. People say they do, but I, apparently, am not people."

"I already poured it," he replied. "You got to tell me before I pour it."

"No, no, I still *want* it. I'm just telling you that I hate it. In fact, since you're here, could I order another?"

"Another of the drink you hate?"

"Yes. If you don't mind."

The bartender didn't even wait to turn around before rolling his eyes. Fern beamed after him, whether oblivious of his annoyance or pleased by it, I had no idea. She turned to me and lifted her glass. "*Skoal!*" she said brightly.

After three scotches and no lunch whatsoever, Fern was drunk enough that I decided I'd better come with her in the auto, even though the computer would be driving. And a good thing I did, too, because I don't think she could've made it to her apartment by herself. The alcohol seemed to have bypassed her head and gone straight to her ankles, bending them sideways so that her feet dragged and tripped as I heaved us up the stairs.

Fern lived in one of the multifloor hives across from campus, rented out to the students, all bright paint colors and specious building codes. A hundred years and three flights of stairs later, we finally reached her apartment door. Whatever wobble disease had infected Fern's ankles had now traveled up to her neck; her head kept listing to the side as she tried to line up her eye with the door camera.

I took her head in my hands and held it steady. I felt her bones under my palms, the cartilage of her ears, and the hanks of her hair. I pictured her skull as a round hard bowl filled with life, as a terrarium curled with vines and caterpillars, as a nautilus with a pale glistening creature curled at its center.

The camera flashed in her eye, the bolt unlocked, and we stumbled through.

"Lights," I said. The apartment stayed dark. "Lights."

"It's cheap. You've got to yell at it," Fern said, and then shouted, "Lights! On!"

When the lights came on, I knew that the "before" Fern must have been a tidy person, because the apartment we were standing in was a complete and utter mess. There in the center of the room sat the aforementioned bed, but the path to it was strewn with beribboned, bemoused cat toys; cereal bowls spiked with spoons; and dark puddles of sweaters and jeans, as if Fern shed her clothes wherever she stood at the very moment it occurred to her to do so, which, now that I thought of it, was almost certainly what she did.

I waded through the mess, towing Fern along behind me. When we reached the bed, she fell straight into it, her wobbliness working in our favor. I set her feet in my lap and began yanking one of her boots. They proved difficult to remove, Fern's ankles still being drunk.

"What if I bring you a glass of water?" I asked once the boots were off.

She groaned in reply.

"How about a bowl in case you need to puke?"

No groan this time, which I took for a yes.

I found a mixing bowl on the kitchen counter, holding not the dregs of milk and cereal, but a stack of unopened mail. I set the envelopes to the side and returned with the bowl to find Fern rubbing her face against the pillow. When she finally stopped, the skin around her eyes was smeared with makeup like a bandit's mask. She stared into the bowl I handed her as if its bottom was far, far below, the deepest well.

"You won't tell them in group?" she asked in a small voice.

"Tell them what?"

"If I puke."

"I won't tell them," I promised, and brushed her bangs to the side.

She squeezed her eyes shut. "Lou?"

"Yeah?"

"They're still my parents."

"I don't—"

"What I said before? They're still my parents."

"Okay."

"You believe me?"

"Of course I do."

She lay back on the bed, the bowl resting on her stomach. "If you could not think of me as . . ."

I waited for her to finish.

"If you could not think of me as . . . ," she started again, and again she gave up with a tortured breath.

"I don't," I said. "I don't think of you as that." Though I had no idea what she'd been trying to say.

She gazed up at me and raised a hand in the air, curving her palm as if to cup my cheek, even though my face was nowhere nearby. Her eyes were half open, shining within the cages of her lashes. She was flushed and tousled and smelled deeply animal, of sweat and bedsheets and scotch. I thought about how our other bodies were somewhere else, hers and mine, somewhere below the ground, the insects working them into soil, and from soil up through the roots of the plants, and into the veins of the leaves, where, finally, they'd uncurl and receive the sun.

I sat with Fern until I was sure she was asleep, and then I crossed back to the kitchen. I took the envelopes from the mixing bowl and flipped through them until I found what I thought I'd seen before. Yes, there was the familiar logo: Smyth, Pineda, and Associates, the law firm that had defended Edward Early.

I searched through the rest of the stack and found two more

envelopes from Smyth, Pineda, and Associates; all three were sealed. I felt an itch on the back of my neck. I glanced back, half expecting to find Fern standing right behind me, breath on my neck, but she was still asleep in the bed. The itch remained. I looked up. A yellow cat peered at me from the top of the fridge.

I stared at the cat.

The cat stared back at me.

"Hello, Spoon," I whispered.

"Lou?" Fern mumbled from the bed.

"I'm here," I said.

"Thanks for taking me home."

"No problem."

"You'll go get your baby now?"

"What?"

"From the day care? You have to go get her."

"Yes, that's right. I'll go get her." I pocketed one of the three envelopes.

Fern's breathing deepened, and I tiptoed out. Just as I was closing the apartment door, I heard her say, "You must be a really good mom."

WHEN I GOT HOME, the house was empty, Silas still at the office and Nova at day care for another hour or so. I locked myself in the bathroom anyway, sat on the bath mat and cranked the taps so that if Silas came home early, he'd assume I was showering. I slid the envelope out of my pocket and tore open one side, extracting a single typed page.

The lawyer's language was polished and precise, like a font with tasteful serifs, which was, in fact, the font the letter had been printed in. The lawyer began with an acknowledgment of Fern's previous letters and an expression of sympathy for her situation. However, he regretted that he must, once again, decline her request to visit his client. After consulting with Mr. Early, the men were both in agreement that it was for the best, for reasons both legal and psychological, that Fern's name *not* be added to Mr. Early's approved visitors list.

I read the letter again, and of course it said the same thing the second time. Still I didn't understand it. Fern had insisted she was a new person. *Her*, she'd called the version of herself who'd been murdered, *my other me*. So then why did she want to talk to *him* of all people?

I tried to refold the letter, but somehow I couldn't follow the creases. I managed a hasty fold and rose, out of the bathroom, across the bedroom, to the closet. I pulled out the green bag, yanked the zipper open, and slid the letter inside. Then I zipped the bag closed again, pushed it to the very back of the closet, slammed the door, and sat against it.

What's the saying? My heart was in my mouth. But that's not where my heart was. My heart was not a metallic, velvet weight upon my tongue. My heart was all through me, all the way to the edges of me, my very outline crackling with the static of each heartbeat. My whole body was telling me to run from him. Was telling me to run.

EARLY

FOR A TIME, WE HADN'T KNOWN HIS NAME. WE'D wanted to, desperately we had. He was leaving women all over mid-Michigan, crumpled on benches, on roads, on playground rides, like a trail of silvered candy wrappers. He'd set their shoes alongside them so that we'd know that it was him, that they were his.

We had no name to call him, still we talked about him. How could we not? We woke and found him in the sweep of our morning newsfeed, the shock of him sending our eyes up to meet our family's eyes.

Another one?

Another.

He shivered by us in line at the grocery store, where we'd exchange a few grim sentences with a fellow shopper, both of us shaking our heads in mute agreement at the world's depravity. *How could someone—?*

He bubbled up at the office water cooler in that gurgle of displaced air. *I can't begin to imagine—*

And he was etched on all of our screens, so that when he wasn't in our mouths, he was in our eyes, constantly in our eyes, a mote, even though we'd never once seen his face.

We needed to know his name. We tried to find it. We traveled over the hills and furrows of the dead women's bodies, all to locate one whorl of his fingertip, one dab of his semen. We programmed algorithms and sent them tunneling through military records and HR complaints and credit card receipts. We snuck glances at the man walking a little dog (a prop?), at the man who interrupted us in the meeting (aggressive?), at the man who shared our bed (how well can you really know someone?). He was no man. He was any man. He was a man in a world that hated women.

His name, we eventually learned, was Edward Early. That sounds made up, but it wasn't. His mother had named him that, Edward Early, like something out of an old-timey ballad, strumming chords, a frayed voice, and a lamentable death.

I think about his mother sometimes. I didn't like to think about him, but for his mother, I find I can offer a thought. I know nothing about her beyond the court footage. I've read no articles, seen no interviews. I couldn't even tell you her first name. *Mother Early—* that's what I call her in my head.

Mother Early attended her son's sentencing. I've watched it on the screen. She sits in the first row of the gallery, just behind her son, and stands along with him and his lawyers when it's time to hear the number of years he will get. She isn't supposed to stand. The judge asks her to please return to her seat, but she shakes her head wildly, and in the end he lets her stay how she is. When they announce her son's life sentence, she nods, she knew. When they announce that the sentence will include forty years of benightment, which should be no surprise either, she presses her hands to her eyes, like a child counting while everyone else hides. Then she begins to sob.

I like to picture her sometimes. Well, maybe not *like*. Sometimes I picture her. It is simply something I do. When I picture Mother Early, she isn't a middle-aged woman standing in a courtroom with her pink-knuckled hands over her eyes. No, she's my own age, wearing a clean blue dress with buttons down the front. Why blue? Why buttons? I don't know. I've never owned a dress like that myself. In my imagination, Mother Early sits in a room in a chair with her hair falling across one cheek, a baby in her arms. Then someone opens the door, letting light in from the hall, and she lifts her face to see who it is. That's it in its entirety, the picture that comes into my head.

She named her son Edward, knowing his last name would be Early. Perhaps she liked the singsong of it. Sometimes I hug my knees to my chest and rock back and forth. Sometimes I think of what it would be like to never see your child again, not for the rest of your life, though the both of you are still alive. Sometimes I go out and walk as fast as I can walk without my toes pushing up into a run. Sometimes I picture her, that woman, raising her head at the sound of the door.

5

"AND HERE'S TROUBLE AT MY DOOR," JAVI SAID. HE
smiled at me like nothing could be more welcome.

Trouble. He meant me. It was the next day, a workday, and I'd
been standing in the hallway outside his office watching the shadow play of his outline through the fogged glass. I knew full well
why I'd been called in to talk with him; it was about what had
happened with Mr. Pemberton, about what I'd done. After hours
of waiting that were really only minutes, the Javier outline had
grown larger, and then the door had swung open to reveal Javi
himself, sweater-vested, a thin mustache on his upper lip like evidence he'd drunk the cream.

"There's trouble wearing a long face." Javi pulled his mouth into
an exaggerated frown. "Oh, trouble, what have you done?"

He was trying to make me smile. I would've worked one up for him if I could've, but there was little comfort in Javi's jokes, not when I knew, I *knew*, he was capable of smiling at me the entire time he was firing me.

Javi gestured me into his office, and I took the chair opposite his desk. He sat on his side of the desk and steepled his fingers. "Okay now. Tell me."

"Tell you what?"

"Yes, precisely: What? *What* did you think you were you doing?"

I didn't have a good answer. "Nothing. I don't know."

I'd returned to work a month earlier in my pretty yet sensible first-day dress. My coworkers had thrown a little party for me in the lounge. Javi had gotten chocolate cupcakes with frosting that spelled "Welcome" and vanilla cupcakes that spelled "Back," so you had to have one of each. Everyone was friendly. No one was weird. Benjamin complimented my dress, Zeus told me about his latest iguana, and Sarai did an impression of how Javi nibbled around the entire circumference of his cupcake before taking one giant bite into the center. After the cupcakes had all been eaten, Javi walked me over to my cubicle and set my helm on my head. As he lowered my visor, he said, "Glad you made it back to us, bubblegum."

And I felt like maybe that was what I'd done. No, I hadn't been murdered by a serial killer, selected by a government commission, and cloned by a team of doctors. I had simply gotten lost in a forest and walked among the trees until I'd spied the silver line of the road through the branches and headed toward it. Then my helm had blinked on, and I *was* back. My body was still sitting in my cubicle, but when I opened my eyes, I was back in my Room. My Room was in its default mode: a parlor, tastefully appointed, two sofas, and a fireplace. I sat on one of the sofas and clicked an option to make the fire light up. The flames crackled; the warmth touched my face. I was good in here. This was good.

The corner of my helm blinked an alert, a client in ten. The Room shifted for the approaching client, the shapes and colors of the parlor blurring and reforming into the dim greens of a hospice room. My shape and colors re-formed, too, and when I looked down at myself, I was an elderly man with knobby wrists and a round little stove of a belly straining at the buttons of his dotted pajama set. I got into the waiting bed. A middle-aged man came in. He climbed onto the hospital bed with me, and I held him, and when he burrowed closer and began to cry, I rubbed his back in slow circles like Dad used to do for me when I was sick.

My next client was a wispy woman. The room shifted to a sun-shot field and I to my standard work skin. The woman's eyes closed as I stroked the hair at her temples.

After that was a teenager who'd appeared in a skin that was half child, half cat. They remained still and watchful in my arms.

This was the job: holding people. Just holding them. Though I shouldn't say "just." You know as well as I do that it's not "just." If you do the work, you know it's like any other job, like cutting hair, like cooking food, like trading stocks; it requires experience and skill. You have to learn how to read people, to intuit when to loosen your embrace, when to clasp tight, when to let go entirely.

I'd been at the Room for a few years now, and I was okay at the work. Maybe even better than okay. Javi had started putting me on the busy shifts and assigning me the more difficult clients. My customer reviews were positive. I had a rotation of regulars. Well. The old me had had those things. *My other me*, as Fern would've said. The me here and now was in trouble.

"Did you forget the guidelines?" Javi asked now, back in his office, tapping his finger on his desk.

"I know the guidelines," I said.

Javi frowned. He'd given me an out, and I hadn't taken it.

"Maybe it was my hands." I stared at his. "Maybe they slipped."

Both Javi and I recognized this for the nonsense it was; what's more, we recognized each other recognizing it. He sucked in his lips, then puffed out his tiny mustache, a perfectly groomed afterthought.

"What do I do with you?" he sang softly. "What do I do with Lou?"

"You could fire me," I told him, so that I could be the one to say it first.

I imagined going home and telling Silas I'd been fired. I imagined how he would assume an expression of concern to hide his relief. Silas hadn't wanted me to go back to the Room. It wasn't the going back to work, he'd said, it was the work itself, the Room, the skins, the way I would have to set my own (*fragile*, he didn't say) self aside for the clients. I didn't tell Silas that this was precisely *why* I wanted to go back, that it would be a relief to be the one who was doing the comforting.

I'd brought up the idea of my going back to work at survivors' group, certain the other women would take my side. I'd felt sheepish about it even, like I was slumming for solidarity. But the women hadn't responded how I'd expected them to. Instead, they'd come back with a rapid fire of platitudes: *Take a break. You deserve it. You have your whole life to work.* Then Angela had cried above the others' murmurs: *Won't you miss your baby?* When we'd all stared round at her, she'd shrugged her goosey shrug. *If I had a baby, I'd love it too much to ever be away from it.* And I felt the shame press down through me to the soles of my feet, like if I were to get up and walk out, I'd leave a trail of damp footprints on the floor.

In a burst of certainty, which might have really been a fit of pique, I'd told Javi to put me back on the schedule. But obviously everyone else had been right, and I'd been wrong. Obviously I shouldn't have come back to work; I shouldn't have eaten Cupcake One.

"You could fire me," I said again, and waited for Javi to agree.

I thought of returning to the long days at home, days like dust motes suspended in sunlight, days when Nova would cry whenever I touched her, whenever I *looked* like I might touch her. The long days when I'd played the baby's lullabies on repeat. Not for the baby, for *me*. I played them on a loop for hours, until I could hear them even when they weren't playing, in the silence as Silas lay sleeping next to me, a low, ceaseless drone in my ear.

That very morning I'd been emptying my purse out in my cubicle, and one of Nova's tiny striped socks had been in there with my lunch and lipstick. *Oh! I did the same thing when I came back to the office,* Sarai had said, catching sight of the sock as she passed by, *I kept Chloe's sock in my pocket for weeks.* I gave her a smile I hoped would look knowing. I couldn't bring myself to tell her that the sock had simply fallen in.

"I'm not a bad mother," I blurted out now, to Javi.

Javi blinked rapidly. "What? No one's suggesting *that*."

I put my hands to my face. "Don't fire me," I said through them.

I heard Javi come around the desk and settle on its edge in front of me. "Lou, hey." He knocked on the backs of my hands. "Lou, hush. You're not fired."

"I'm not?"

He made a graceful gesture with one hand. "You think I fire everyone who gets a complaint? I'd be working these Rooms all by myself."

"But it was bad, right? What I did?" I snatched a tissue from Javi's desk and wiped at my face.

"Don't take it out on your nose, anyway."

"Was he very upset?"

Javi inclined his head. "He's fine."

"That means he was very upset."

"That means don't worry about it. I made your apologies for you. And I am a beautiful apologizer."

Mr. Pemberton had first come to the Room a week ago. He was wearing the skin of a slight, middle-aged man, with curly hair and an emerald turtleneck sweater. He'd requested a simple hand-holding. We'd sat on either end of the sofa, and I'd taken his hands in mine. His hands had been shaking at first, but I'd held them steady, and after a few minutes they'd stilled. When the half hour was up, Mr. Pemberton had murmured, "Thank you," and slipped his hands from mine. I wasn't sure what he'd gotten out of the session ("We give them not the reason but the room," as Javi might say), but it must've been something, because he'd booked a second appointment.

"Lou," Javi said, and pressed his lips together.

"What?" I said, then, before he could ask me, "It's not that."

"Because we could limit your bookings to women."

"It's not that." I felt my face flush, and I wished I was still in my VR skin so that Javi wouldn't be able to see me pinkening. "My hand slipped."

At his second appointment, Mr. Pemberton had been warmer, friendlier. He'd taken his seat on the other end of the couch and asked me how I was. I was fine, I said. No, I was better than that. I was good. It was a good day. Since I'd come back, it'd felt strong to say that, not some automatic reply, but a promise: that I was good. And so was the day.

I took his hands, and they didn't shake this time, not a single tremor. We chatted through his session, about this and that, about nothing much. And I held his hands, our fingertips and palms warming with the contact. At the sound of the chime to end the appointment, he'd nodded in thanks and begun to slip his hands from mine.

And that's when I'd done it.

I'd grabbed onto his wrists. Hard.

His eyes flashed at me, surprised then confused. He tried to pull away, but I was holding on too tight. He couldn't get free of me. I wouldn't let him get free. We struggled. Then, all at once, he stopped pulling and just looked at me, curious and maybe even sad. No, not sad. Pitying, that's the word.

Here. Here was where I could've let go. But I didn't. In that moment I was doing what I was doing, as simple as that. And the truth was, it felt fantastic. It felt high and mean and singing and free. I had his hands. He could not have them back. Why? Because I would not *let him* have them back.

"Hey," he said.

His voice startled me. I'd nearly forgotten he was there; that's how hard I was holding on to him.

"Hey," he repeated. "Are you okay?"

That did it. I opened my fingers wide. His hands slid from mine. He looked down at himself, free of my grasp. Then he winked out. And I was left in the Room alone with my own surprise and shame.

"The company has sympathy for what you've been through," Javi said to me. "All the sympathy in the world. We understand how things can linger, how trauma can emerge and surprise. We value you here, Lou. *We* the company, and *we* me."

I shifted in my seat. "I appreciate that."

"And *we* appreciate *you*. But"—he raised a finger—"this is a place of business."

"I know," I whispered.

"You're not fired," Javi repeated, "but you are warned."

I kept my face still. Not fired, that was the important thing.

"And," Javi added, "you're going home for the rest of the day."

I rose from the chair slowly, curbing the impulse to turn and run from his office. Javi spun his own chair to the left, to the right. "And that's that," he murmured, as if to himself.

"See you tomorrow, Javi," I said, and I edged out the door, relieved when he didn't correct me, when he didn't say, "On second thought, go. Go and never come back."

THE ROOM

THE ROOM HAD BEEN BUILT TO RESEMBLE A ROOM in the game *Iron Feathers*. It was the one up in the turret in the crumbling seaside castle, circular walls of bleached stone and a table strewn with dried sea creatures pulled from the ocean, which roared and roiled and laid itself still beneath the lone window.

The *Iron Feathers* room was a puzzle chamber with two possible ways to move forward in the game. If you picked up the dried stick of coral from the table and rubbed its edge over the top sheet of paper, the indentations of an old message would appear, instructions on how to unlock the door and find a hidden rowboat on the rocky shore below. Or, if you waited until the sunlight slanted through the window just so, the beam would shine on a loose stone in the wall, behind which you'd find the key to the door. The loose stone itself, if you put it in your pocket, would lead you to an outcropping of matching stones on the shore, behind which the rowboat was hidden.

I'd played *Iron Feathers* as a teenager. Of course I had. Everyone had. The game had been a sensation, people trading clues and spinning theories and setting up online betting pools to see who could get furthest fastest. Even now, someone will bring up the game, say, at a dinner party, and around the table will come soft cries of recognition and delight.

In my early twenties on a trip to San Francisco, driving down the coast with a man I'd been seeing, I'd found myself shouting for him to *stop*, stop the car at the next pullout. He did, and I'd stumbled out and over to the guardrail, near dizzy at the sight of the shore far below me. Something about how the rocks were arranged. Something about how the water spat and curled. He came up beside me.

"Are you okay?" he said. "Are you sick?"

"Yes. No. I've been here before."

"What? Like as a kid?"

"That must be it."

But it wasn't. I'd never been to California before that trip, had never driven down the coast until that very day. I didn't know why the shoreline looked familiar, had only known that I'd needed to stop and see it. I apologized again, and we got back in the car and kept driving. The answer came to me days later, appearing in my mind like a rock when the tide goes out. That exact coastline had been in the game, *Iron Feathers*. I looked it up, and I was right. The designers had used that same stretch of coast as one of their models.

About a year after its release, *Iron Feathers* was recalled follow-ing threats of legal action. People were going into the game and not coming out again. They were abandoning jobs and relation-ships and sometimes even their bodies' basic needs. It turned out that the vast majority of these missing people had been sitting in that room in the seaside castle. They *could* go further in the game—after hours and days, they'd discovered the two ways to open the locked door—but they hadn't left that room. They'd wanted to sit there, they said. They couldn't explain it beyond that. They'd simply wanted to stay.

It was this same room, the sea-castle turret, stripped of its dried sea urchins and hidden key, stripped down to its virtual studs, that corporate had used for their design of the Room, the parlor with two sofas and a fireplace. The idea was not that clients would recognize the room from the *Iron Feathers* game—it looked like a parlor now—but that they'd experience the same sense of famil-iarity I'd had on that drive down the coast. That they'd want to sit and stay.

What can I say? I've felt it myself. That magnetism. That pull. Sometimes I'd stay in my Room after my clients had all gone home. Sometimes I'd come on my day off. Sometimes even still, I sneak in there late at night to be by myself.

6

I ARRIVED HOME IN THE MIDDLE OF THE AFTERNOON, still mutely ashamed at my scolding, still bewildered by what I'd done. Imagine my surprise to find Silas home, too. He was pacing the living room floor with Nova peering over his shoulder. Her face was like the boiled tip of one of her bottles, her curls frizzed like heat waves rising from her head. She had a 102-degree fever. Day care had called Silas, the parent on record.

The parent on record, I repeated dully in my head. And I couldn't help feeling that this, Nova's fever, was somehow also my fault. Because I hadn't purposely tucked her little sock in my purse, because it had only fallen in.

"But why didn't *you* call me?" I asked Silas, pacing alongside him.

"I didn't want to—"

"What? Worry me? But now I'll be worried all the time that something's happened to her and you aren't calling me because you don't want to worry me."

"That . . ." He paused in his pacing. ". . . logic holds."

"You bet your ass that logic holds."

"I'm sorry, Wheeze. I am. I promise. I've just been doing this, walking back and forth with her. Emergency won't see her unless her temp hits one-oh-four."

"We should call Odd. He'll know what to do."

Odd picked up on the fourth ring. He declined video, something he'd started doing only since my murder. I tried not to notice, but of course I noticed. Maybe it was too painful for him to see me now, here again, after he'd already grieved my death. I tried not to think this, but of course I thought it. It was a relief to hear Odd's hello. I tossed the call up onto the live wall so that Silas could hear him, too. Odd's voice echoed around the living room.

"Louise?" he said. "Hold on."

"Nova has a fever, but the doctor won't see her," I burst out.

"Hold on," he said. "I need to go to a different room." It didn't sound loud where he was. I could even hear his steps echo as he walked somewhere else. "Okay," he said. "Say that again."

"Are you at work?"

He'd been refusing to retire from the hospital for years. No one else knew his perfect system, he argued, and his perfect system was unteachable. Besides, what would he do if he retired? Take walks? Read novels? Plant a garden? When I'd said yes and yes and yes, he'd made a sound like he was loosening phlegm in the back of his throat.

But those conversations were from before my murder, when we used to talk for an hour every Saturday, his one day off. We still talked on Saturdays. I can't say that he ever failed to call, but now our calls were ten minutes, tops, before he'd say that he needed to be getting on with his day.

Odd had come to see me only once since they'd brought me back. It was the week after they woke me up. He seemed shy of me. He spent the visit pestering the doctors and hovering in doorways and leaving plates of food by my bed. When he'd left, he'd patted my shoulder, tentatively, like his hand might get stuck there. Silas and I had talked about it, how Odd has his ways, and I tried my best not to be hurt by them. I'd seen how he'd been after Dad's death, back to work the day after the funeral. Odd was who he was; Odd was who he'd always been.

"I'm home," Odd said, but he didn't elaborate. "The fever?"

"We were in just last week for her nine-month checkup," I said, as if that mattered. I didn't mention that I'd recently had my own three-month checkup with the doctors assigned by the replication commission. "Dr. Voss said she was fine. Great. All the milestones. All the percentiles."

"How high?" Odd interrupted me.

"The percentile?"

"No. How high is her temp?"

"Oh. One-oh-two."

"And Emergency says to wait until?"

"A hundred four."

"Okay, that's standard. Put a cold cloth on her forehead. And if you're worried, you can start driving when she hits a hundred three."

"I'm worried."

"I know you are. But don't be. One time you had a fever, and your dad sat in the car with you in the parking lot across from the hospital all night long."

"He did? No one ever told me that."

"Because it was a silly thing to do. Sit all night in a car with a sick baby? Why does a silly man cross the road? That's what I asked your dad back then. And do you know what he said to me? To get to the other side twenty minutes quicker than driving from home."

"And *did* I have to go to the hospital?"

"You did not. You had a fever. Babies get fevers. He was a silly man who loved you very much." This was Odd's perennial description of Dad.

"And you," I added. "He loved you, too."

"Listen, Louise—"

"You have to be getting on with your day."

"Correct."

"But can I call you back if we end up going to the hospital?"

I was suddenly aware of the silence on the other end of the line and, within that silence, my fear that he might say no. I thought about what Fern said in the bar about her parents. *They're not my family.* I thought about Angela's ex-boyfriend, never letting her leave his sight. And then Angela's voice was in my head again. *If I had a baby, I'd love it too much to ever be away from it.*

"Sure," he finally said. "A hundred four. You can start driving at a hundred three."

Then he hung up.

Nova peered at me from Silas's arms; her eyes were a quivering liquid, like if I poked a finger in, there'd be ripples. She stared back at me, then pulled an arm free and swiped the air in my direction. I stopped. I stilled.

"Wait. Si. Did you see that?"

"See what?"

"Can I hold her for a second?"

"You sure? She's just going to . . ." *Cry*, he didn't say. *Because you smell strange, unfamiliar*, he never would say. *Because you're not her mother, not to her, not really*, he never ever would say, but did he think it?

"She reached for me," I said. "Just now."

"Really? I mean, sure," he amended. "Sure you can have her. Here."

And we did the new parents' dance of transferring the baby from one of us to the other. I leaned her back in my arms so that she and I were face-to-face.

"Whew. I can feel the heat coming off of her."

She still stared at me, her skin mottled, her eyes going back and forth, trying and failing to focus. I waited for her face to screw up, like it always did, for her to begin to wail. Instead, she did it again, what she'd done a moment ago. She cast out a hand, swiping the air near my ear.

"There! Did you see?"

"She's feverish. She's going for your earring," Silas said.

"You think?"

It could be true; my earrings were large and sparkly. I unclipped one and offered it to the baby, but she looked past it, swinging her arm out again for the same ear, closing her fingers next to my head.

"No," I marveled, "she's going for my hair."

"Your hair?"

"Where my hair *used* to be. Before I cut it. She remembers when it was long."

"She's too young for memories. The literature says—"

But then she did it again.

"Hey. Look at that," Silas said softly, smiling.

"Do you remember me, Pudge?" I put my forehead to hers, the fever beaming between us. "You remember me?"

Nova let me hold her, sweaty hour after sweaty hour. More than that, she held on to me. And I glowed with my own type of fever. When I tried to pass her off to Silas, she clutched at me, her sharp nails making tiny painful crescent moons in my skin. I didn't begrudge Silas her love, her favoritism, but after all the times she'd rejected me, I couldn't help feeling a quiet satisfaction that now, when she was sick, it was me she wanted. After all, the two of us—our sweat, our spit, our skin—were already mixed together in the deep. That's the thing about having a baby: they are a part of you that is outside of you, so you can love them in the way you can't stand to love yourself.

When Nova's fever hit 103, Silas got ready to call the auto. But just then, the baby's fever broke and plummeted. The day broke with it, plummeting into the night. Sweat beaded up on Nova's brow, and her skin felt like skin again instead of a radiance of heat. I laid her down in her crib. Silas and I stood together and watched her sleep. Every so often we'd dip a hand in to check her forehead. "One last time," we promised each time. At whatever o'clock, Silas pressed a temperature patch on the baby's foot and said to me, "Let's get some sleep."

IN BED, BOTH OF US DRIFTING, I thought again of the green bag, there even now across the room, behind the closet doors, in the dark. I hadn't unpacked it yet. What if I did it now? What if I rose out of bed in the dark of the room and began pulling items from the bag, one after another, floating them before Silas's stricken eyes? What if I cried out, *Look! Will you look at what your first wife put in here?*

"Silas," I blurted, his name a ball of breath in my mouth.

His reply came from the other side of the mattress. "I was almost asleep."

But I didn't tell him. What would it accomplish? He'd only be hurt. And for what? The woman who'd packed that bag wasn't me. She didn't know what I knew, what it was like to almost lose everything. She was a poor thing, down in the dirt. While here I was, up in the air.

"Lou?" Silas murmured. "What?"

I made another confession instead: "I did something bad. At work."

I told him about grabbing Mr. Pemberton's wrists, about Javi's warning, my probation. I braced myself for Silas to say what I knew he was going to say: That this was proof I shouldn't have gone back to work. That I should come home now. That he'd told me so.

I was surprised when instead he said, "That makes sense."

"Does it? Not to me."

"Sure. You needed something to hold on to."

I rolled onto my side to face him. "I'm sorry to be the one to tell you this, but that sounds like a lyric from a bad pop song."

"Everyone needs something to hold on to."

"That sounds like a lyric from a *worse* pop song."

"*Everyone needs something to hold on to,*" he sang, twanging and out of key. "*Even an old man's wrist.*"

"Si?"

"What?"

"Can you be serious for a minute?"

"I can be serious for *ten* minutes."

"Really? Because you're still talking in the pop singer voice."

"Sorry. I'm serious now. See? Regular voice."

"Look at this." I pulled up the leg of my pajama pants. "My scar is gone."

I pointed to my calf, where I'd had a ropy scar from childhood. Now the skin was smooth and unmarked.

"I only noticed it the other day," I said. "It's funny, you know? I can remember how I got it. I was nine. I took a turn too sharp and tipped off my swiftboard, caught my leg on the corner of a bench. It bled like hell. All these strangers stopped to help me. I almost fainted. I know it happened. I know it happened to me. But it didn't happen to *this* leg. Which is *my* leg."

"Hmmm," he said.

I slid my hand under my T-shirt, ran my fingers over the skin of my belly, smooth from belly button to pubis, no ridge of scar tissue, no divots from the sutures, the other scar that wasn't, no C-section. Before, I had traced my fingers over it, pressed on it. The doctor said the scar would look like a smile. I'd pressed on it again to feel the dull ache. It was gone now—no scar, no smile.

Silas reached over and stilled my hand.

"Am I different?" I asked him.

"Different?"

"Don't pretend."

"I'm not pretending. Different from what?"

"From before. From . . . me."

I wasn't sure what I wanted him to say—*Yes, you're an entirely different woman, new and improved. No, you're the same old Wheeze you've always been.*

"Of course you are," is what he said.

"I thought you'd say no." I pressed at the place on my leg where the scar used to be, tracing the line of it, the best I could remember the line of it. "Because I'm trying to . . ." But I didn't know *what* I was trying to do.

"Hey. Wait," Silas said. "Let me amend that."

"Amend away."

"You're still *you*." He took my hand from my leg and squeezed it to stop its fussing. "Of course you're you. I only meant experiences change a person. And you've been through, well, some shit. Right?"

"I guess so."

"I'm different, too, aren't I?"

"I don't know. You still leave your dishes all over the place."

He snorted. "Wheeze, when I say you're different, I guess I mean *we're* different. The three of us." I finally let myself look at him. He was looking down at our hands, the fingers intertwined. "After Nova was born, you were . . . well, I thought the doctor might—"

"What?" I interrupted, but in a tone that didn't welcome an answer. I knew the diagnosis the doctor would've given if I'd told her how I'd been feeling. A new mother who felt dead inside; I knew what that was. But I didn't want to think it; I didn't want Silas to say it, as if naming it might draw its attention, might swing its terrible, foggy eye back to me.

"Might prescribe something," he said instead. "Things were, well—"

"Bad," I said.

"I was going to say tense. And you seemed—"

"Desperate," I said.

"I was going to say sad. And now you seem—"

"Better," I said.

"I was going to say better." I could hear the smile in his voice.

"I am," I said. "That."

"Good," he said. "I am that, too."

He looked up from our hands, and I saw that he was crying.

"I'm glad you're back," he said.

"Si—" I began.

He shook his head. "Let me amend that. I'm glad you're here."

SILAS

"THROUGH FRIENDS," SILAS AND I DECIDED TO SAY
when people asked us how we met. Give them enough time, people will always ask that.

The truth was that Silas and I met because he was dating my roommate. My roommate and I weren't friends, at least not to start with. We'd met through an app. It was something she and I both agreed upon, that it was easier to share an apartment with a stranger, everyone more likely to rinse their dishes and clean out the cat box and all that. Jessup was my roommate's name, not short for Jessica, and don't call her Jess, either. *Jessup*, that's what her name was. I must've heard her explain that to people at least a dozen times.

We got along, Jessup and I, our goodwill built up through our consistently hung-up jackets and evenly split utility bills. Also, I liked her. Her eyebrows raised and drew together with her mood like two punctuation marks. She sang 1970s rock lyrics off-key, doodled cartoon birds on our shopping lists, and brought home pistachio-dusted mabrooma from her aunt's bakery. She held many opinions and would explain them without hesitation. "I have a theory on that," she said so often that I began to repeat the phrase to her teasingly. "I have a theory on that!" I exclaimed when she told me she'd bought more dish soap. "I have a theory on that!" when she said the rent was due. She laughed when I made fun of her, another sign of her good character.

Deep down, I didn't know how Jessup could have all those opinions on all those many topics. It wasn't that I hadn't been taught to think; it was that I'd been taught to see a thing from this way and that way and another way still, until I had an entire crowd's worth of perspectives in my head. To hold one position, I'd been taught, was unsubtle, lazy, even crude. But secretly, it seemed like it might feel glorious, like smacking people on their bottoms as they ran past you.

I was quieter than Jessup, much quieter. My quietness allowed men to ascribe romantic notions to me. They could make up what I liked and what I was like. And mostly I let them do that. What was I really like? Even though I was quiet, I was thinking all the time about how people were and about what they did and, much too often, about how they saw me. What was I then? Twenty-three? Twenty-four? The toddlerhood of adulthood.

I also had a number of wicked thoughts, and sometimes these came out of my mouth without my meaning for them to. I pictured a venomous caterpillar curled up inside me, one of those with all the colors and segments and bristles, and every now and then it would slink from between my lips. When this happened in front of a man I'd been seeing, he'd react with delight, like this meanness was something *he'd* discovered about me, like I didn't already know it about myself.

I don't remember the first time Silas and I met. It was probably in my bedroom, which was meant to be the apartment's living room. Jessup's and my apartment was laid out in shotgun style, so when you walked through the front door, you were in my bedroom, and you had to walk through my bedroom to get to Jessup's, and then Jessup's to get to the kitchen, and then the kitchen to get to bathroom at the very back.

Jessup took long showers and was always running late, so Silas and I must have met one of the times when he was passing through the rooms, waiting for her to get ready. I can't remember the exact date. But I can remember any number of times when he and I would be talking and Jessup would fly past us in a towel, shouting apologies, her eyebrows rising like exclamation points.

"She's a bullet train," I said once after she tore through.

"She's a comet," he replied.

"She's a cheetah," I said.

He frowned. "She's a cheater?"

"No! A *cheetah.* Like the animal."

"Oh, phew. For a second, I thought you were trying to warn me off."

"I meant because she's fast."

"It's not very nice to call your roommate fast, you know." Silas grinned.

He had long hair back then, long for a man, down to his shoulders and curling slightly under, all the way around. His *Prince Valiant look*, I called it, though I didn't really know who Prince Valiant was then, and to be honest, I still don't now. He's a prince with hair that curls under; I think that's probably about right. Silas wasn't tall, only an inch taller than me, but he liked to insist that we were the same height. We measured ourselves once, marking our heights in pencil on Jessup's doorjamb, like little kids. I remember talking to someone, maybe even Jessup, about the sexiness of his forearms. Back then, I'd liked to pick a body part of men that I would say I was attracted to, not their abs or their ass, something obscure. For a while, it was earlobes; I preferred the attached ones, I told people. When I met Silas, forearms were my thing. Mostly this was a joke I had with myself. I don't think anyone ever got it but me.

I noticed when Silas started arriving earlier to meet Jessup, a few minutes earlier each time, while Jessup was always the same amount of late. And it wasn't like I had to seek out him or he had to seek out me. The layout of the apartment put us together, beads on a string. I was around the apartment a lot those days, playing out the last vague gestures of a breakup where my ex and I would meet up in a VR room to fight and fuck, never mind that we were entirely unable to get along in the real world.

At first, I considered myself dutiful, keeping Silas company while Jessup got ready for their dates. In the movies, there was always the roommate who takes on this task, her hair clipped back in barrettes, her sole purpose to give sensible advice to the mixed-up lovers. It was innocent. It was nothing. Silas and I would joke around until Jessup appeared finally fully dressed. "Bye, Lou!" they'd call as they went out the door. Silas would always duck his head as he said it, like the doorway was low, which it wasn't, or like he was tall, which he wasn't.

Silas didn't flirt with me. And I didn't flirt with him, either. I didn't flirt first. It was a principle, I told myself, but really I was afraid of being rejected. I figured Silas wasn't attracted to me anyway because one time I was in my shortest running shorts, and he didn't look at my legs even once. My legs were the only thing I was sure of. They were long and tapered and good, and when they were bare even I admired them. One time I caught Silas staring at my ankle, specifically the little bone that bumps up on the side, but then he snapped to, and I realized he was just staring off into space and my anklebone happened to be where his eyes had landed.

I knew I might be interested in Silas when I didn't tell him about my VR meetups with my ex, and then when I *did* tell him about the meetups so that I could gauge his reaction, which was the appropriate amount of concern for my emotional well-being.

"You're so *appropriate*," I said to him once, not about the thing with my ex, about something else, I can't remember what. I said it as a joke, but he got this funny look. The next day, Jessup announced that she and Silas had called things off. When I asked her why, I was careful about how my voice sounded so that she wouldn't hear the honeycomb that had suddenly appeared at the base of my throat, golden-coated and buzzing. She responded by blowing a raspberry at me, and I didn't dare ask her what that meant.

It must've meant nothing, I decided, because after that Silas didn't contact me in any of the many ways he could have contacted me. And he didn't come over early for his dates with Jessup, because there were no dates with Jessup anymore. *It was your imagination*, I told myself. *You were flattering yourself*, I told myself. And I redoubled my efforts in the bubble VR I was playing at the time to keep my depression manageable and my ex at bay. I floated and expanded and multiplied and glowed. I didn't cry, and I didn't pine. I became many bubbles. And mostly I forgot about Silas. He was a possibility that didn't end up being an actuality. Oh, well.

Three months to the day after Jessup had told me they'd called things off—*to the day*, I went back and checked—Silas messaged me. He'd gotten my number from Jessup. Could we go out on a date?

"He asked *you* for my number?" I said to Jessup later, and I knew enough to wince when I said it, even though inside I was buzzing again, all pollen and honey.

"No. I gave it to him. I mean, I offered it. After he told me his intentions with you." She was leaning on the doorway between our rooms, the one where Silas and I had measured our heights. In fact, her hand was just above her head, right on the pencil marks we'd made, though she didn't know it.

"His *intentions*? Did he say that? I mean, in those words?"

She made a face. "Yep."

"Yuck. I should say no to him just for that." But I wouldn't. I liked that he'd said that, his intentions. Besides, I'd already told him yes.

"I'm sorry," I told Jessup. "I feel like a jerk."

"Don't." Her lively eyebrows drew together, then relaxed. "You didn't do anything. And he did things the right way."

"Yeah, he's really appropriate."

"Appropriate." She put a hand to her chest and fell back against the doorjamb. "Be still, my beating heart."

Jessup moved out less than a month later. Silas and I were officially together by then, though he never came to the apartment to wait for me to get ready, and I always went to his place to spend the night. This was the type of drama she was trying to avoid by rooming with a stranger, Jessup explained to me when she left. She stood in the doorway again, but the other one now, the one leading outside. I was cross-legged in a bundle of sheets on my bed, having just woken up to find her already packed and moving out. It was obvious she'd practiced what she was going to say and obvious that I was meant to feel shamed by it.

This wasn't about Silas and me, she clarified, she didn't care about that. But really it would've been better if we'd fallen into each other's arms, she said, if we'd snuck around, if we'd cheated. The way it all went down, she said, she felt like she'd been dealt with rather coldly.

7

I ARRIVED EARLY AT THE NEXT SURVIVORS' MEET-
ing, hoping to catch Fern before we started up, a silly plan, in
retrospect, since she was perpetually late. I went to the restroom,
half to pee and half to kill time, and came out of the stall to find
Lacey at the sinks applying layer after layer of her dark lipstick,
making her mouth into a negative space. She capped the tube,
checked her teeth, and then came over to lean against the sink
next to mine.

"I have an invitation," she said.

For the past couple of weeks, I'd noticed Lacey watching me
across the circle during group. It was impossible not to feel her
sharp, assessing gaze—needle, needle. And when I looked over at
her, she wouldn't look away, like any normal person would. She'd

keep watching me, blinking one or two slow blinks before finally moving her eyes somewhere else.

"For what?" I replied.

"For you." She smiled. "Don't worry. It's not bad."

"Not bad? That's good."

She went on to explain that she'd joined a group of amateur detectives who investigated cold cases, the serious ones, the unsolved assaults and murders and rapes. The Luminols, they called themselves. Luminol, Lacey informed me, was a powder that detectives used to sprinkle over crime scenes to show where the blood had been cleaned up. There were seven Luminols who met regularly to float their theories and discuss their evidence. Their sleuthing was done entirely online, combing through auto receipts and screen bills, comparing witness statements, and so on. "It's not like we're running around with trench coats and magnifying glasses," Lacey said.

"So . . . ?" she said.

"So what?" I replied.

"So I'm inviting you."

"To come to your group thing?"

"Think about it, Lou. Early was caught. He confessed. I know who murdered me." She put a thumb to her sternum. "But imagine not knowing who hurt you. Not knowing who killed someone you loved. Or thinking you know and being wrong." She wanted me to try out a meeting, more, to consider joining them permanently. "It's not just me," she said, "We all want you to join."

"All you Luminols?"

She pressed her lips together. "It's easy to make fun."

"I wasn't making fun," I told her. But honestly, I might've been, just a little. "Are you asking the others? Fern and them?"

"Only you."

"Why me?"

She thought I would take to the work, she explained, that I'd find it illuminating. She glared at me when she said that, *illuminating,* like she was daring me to make fun of their name again. Really, I didn't think it was funny that Lacey had joined these Luminols. In fact, I was glad she had people who understood her, in whatever way she felt these people understood her. Whenever I talked to her, I couldn't help picturing that circle in the sand, the one made by her toe dragging off the merry-go-round, the one that meant Early had put her body on it and spun her around. And whenever I thought about that, I felt a flush of gratitude that I'd run, crawled, gotten away from him however I'd gotten away from him. Even if I hadn't really gotten away from him in the end.

I told Lacey I'd think about coming to a meeting, but I knew it was a lie when I said it. I'd never been one of those women who read murder mysteries or played true-crime VRs. I didn't need to make sense of violence done to strangers by strangers. People were inscrutable and life was chaos; if I knew anything, I knew that.

Besides, I didn't need the Luminols. I had plans of my own.

FERN ARRIVED halfway through group. She glided in and took her seat like she'd only gotten up for a drink of water.

"We're very sorry for the interruption, Angela," Gert said, looking meaningfully at Fern, who did not appear the least bit sorry. "Please continue."

Fern caught my eye and stuck out the tip of her tongue. I was keenly aware of the letter I'd stolen from her apartment, the one I'd fished back out of the green canvas bag, the one folded in my pocket even now.

Angela had been telling us about her new job. She was quite pleased with herself, a pleased goose, neck curved, feathers fluffed. It's not nice to say this, but some people's pleasure is annoying to behold, and for me, Angela was one of those. I couldn't tell if the fault was mine, because what did I care where Angela spent her days? Or if the fault belonged to Angela because she spoke about this new job smugly, chin tipped up, as if we'd all interviewed for the thing, and she'd won it over the rest of us.

Angela's previous job had been at AutoGoGo, where she'd logged small damages done to the autos as they came back in: a blub of chewed gum in the cup holder, a whisper of shoe scuffs on the dash, and so on. It was up to Angela to get the forms in order, to send out the necessary cleaning requests, and to levy the regrettable fines. I knew all these many details about Angela's work because she complained about it on a weekly basis. The job was no good. Rather, people were no good, so messy and inconsiderate and unable to follow simple rules. Unspoken: Angela was good by comparison, setting to rights what others had upended.

But now Angela had found a new gig, something better. She described the work in gauzy clichés. It was "a thrilling venture" that would "push boundaries" and use her "complete skill set," taking her to "the next level." She would even be going to Detroit sometimes for meetings and, she emphasized this word, *sessions*. She peered around at us as she talked, her eyes flinty and her nostrils pricked. *I dare you*, those nostrils said. *I told you so*, they said that, too. I was relieved when her gaze skipped past me. I had no idea what my own face might look like in reply.

Lacey finally asked what the rest of us were thinking: "What *is it* exactly that you're doing?"

It was obvious Angela had been waiting for one of us to ask precisely this. She shook her head slowly, her smile spreading like a spill.

"I'm so sorry," she said. "I can't tell you. Not just you. Anyone. I signed an NDA. That means—"

"Nondisclosure agreement," Lacey said. "Everyone knows that."

Angela's smile twitched. "I can't break it. It's very strict. But don't worry. We're launching soon. And then you'll see."

"AND THEN YOU'LL SEE," I repeated after group when Fern and I were alone in a downtown bakery, working our way through the giddy tower of pastries she had ordered, our fingers sticky with glaze. "Angela makes it sound like a threat."

"Obviously she's joined a cult," Fern said.

"Either that or she's becoming a pharmaceutical rep," I said.

"I think she's becoming a tiger."

"I think she's becoming a ball of pure energy."

"I think she's becoming a panty liner."

"A panty liner?" I asked.

"With wings." Fern flapped and draped herself across the table.

It was easy to make fun of Angela. And if it was unkind, which of course it was, it was also a way to ask without asking, *Am I like her? No, you're not like her. Okay, phew, you're not like her, either.* I don't need to tell you how many women's friendships are built upon this firm foundation.

"Hey, listen," I said to Fern.

She popped some pastry in her mouth. "Listening."

But my rehearsed words dissolved on my tongue like so much sugar. I'd slid the letter out of my pocket when we'd first sat down and had been holding it in my lap since, the edge of the envelope now crimped by my nervous fingers.

"You stole my mail," Fern said. "Is that what you're going to say?"

I stared at her. "You knew?"

She inspected the caramel on her fingertips, sucking the edge of one.

"I didn't think you'd notice," I said. "The envelope was still sealed."

"I don't open them because I already know what they say."

"I guess I *did* open it?" I held up the evidence. "I'm sorry. I was curious."

"You think I don't understand curiosity? Lady, I am *made* of curiosity. I am a hundred dead cats."

"Can I ask—?"

"What? Why I want to visit him?" she said.

She looked hard at me, as if sizing me up, then equally hard at the tower of pastries, snatching one off the heap and taking an enormous bite. She spoke while chewing openmouthed, her words muffled by the doughy bite.

"It's not because I want an apology. I'll tell you that. That's what his lawyers think. *Sorry I murdered you?* What good would that do me? And I don't want to yell at him. Or watch him cry. Or ask him why he did it. I don't think even *he* could answer that. I just have the one question."

She swallowed the pastry in an audible lump, holding up a finger.

"Why me?" she said. "There are all these people in the world, all these women, whoever, who he could've . . . and so, yeah: Why *me*? Is that such a crazy thing to want to ask the man who killed you?"

"Not crazy."

"Well, they make you *feel* like you're crazy. Even when there's an *actual* crazy person sitting right there across the table from you." She sat back in her seat with such force that the chair squeaked. "Or *not* sitting across the table from you, as it were."

"I wasn't going to ask you why you wanted to see him," I said.

"Oh? No? What were you going to ask, then?"

"I was going to ask if I could come with you."

There. I'd said it.

She raised her eyebrows and popped more pastry into her mouth. I waited while she chewed. "Sure," she finally said.

"Really?"

"What? You want me to say no? I can say no."

"I thought you'd give me a hard time first, make me enumerate my reasons, make me promise if we actually get to see him that I won't run screaming from the room."

She shrugged. "Running screaming from the room seems like a perfectly reasonable thing to do, given the circumstances."

"But I won't do it."

"Lou. Look. For months, I've had these people—my parents, the doctors, the replication commission, Gert, these damn lawyers— telling me what I can and can't do. You think I'm going to do the same thing to you? No way. Not me." She nudged a pastry toward me. "You do what you want."

"You're not going to ask why *I* want to see him?"

"Nope." Fern crossed her arms.

The bakery warmed around me in waves of cinnamon and yeast; the shop bell dinged; someone laughed in a bright, bold burst; these pastries in front of me, they tasted so sweet. Truly, it was a terrible world.

"We almost died," I said.

"'Almost'?" she asked with a laugh.

"You know what I mean."

"Okay. Sure. But we're here."

"That's the thing. I don't want to see him." I curled my hand into a fist, the sugar a grit in my palm. "I want *him* to see *me*. And this time, I won't be afraid."

HAWK

I BEGAN TO PLAY THE HAWK VR AFTER NOVA WAS born, in that time when it felt like I could touch nothing, but everything was always touching me. Nova's mouth, Silas's palms, the bedsheets, my clothes, the air, the minutes of the afternoon, all of them were rubbing up against me, pressing down the little hairs on my arms, smudging the outline that delineated me from the world around me.

When Nova would drop off to sleep, I'd stare at her dumbly. I could see the lavender veins threaded through her closed eyelids. I knew I was supposed to have a feeling about those gossamer threads, but my child's loveliness, this seemed to be the one thing that would not touch me, no matter how hard I tried to feel it. What was wrong with me? What was wrong?

While Nova slept, I lowered my helm and pulled on my gloves, and I became the hawk. I soared high. The desert below me looked like old bones. I'd catch a quiver in the sand and dive, my own shriek filling my ears. Then, suddenly, a rabbit clutched in my talons. I could feel its heart hum through the soles of my feet. After that, it was only a matter of finding a rock on which to perch so that I could slice the rabbit with my sharp mouth, bend my face into the steam of its innards, and pick a string of flesh, stretching until it snapped free from the bone.

I'd clear the live wall logs before Silas got home so that he wouldn't see how many hours I'd spent playing VR when I was meant to be tending to the baby. At the sound of the front door, I'd arrange myself in the chair, a blanket over my shoulder, the baby over the blanket, and the feel of flesh still strung between my teeth.

8

FERN WAS RIGHT WHEN SHE TOLD ME NOT TO BOTHER writing Smyth, Pineda, and Associates to ask if I could visit Edward Early. Their reply came within the week, identical to the one they'd sent her, only our names changed. This was infuriating. But I suppose I was just another woman to them, Victim Five instead of Victim Two. Or maybe they simply felt that they had nothing more to say to us.

Edward Early's benightment was only two months away. Once the doctors put him under, he'd be in stasis, essentially a coma, for the forty years of his sentence. He would dream the dreams the psychologists had designed to increase his empathy, his head stuck with a nimbus of needles arranged to light up the empty spots in his brain.

After that, Fern and I would be old women before we had the

chance to talk to him. The joke of it all was that we *would* talk to him then. If we consented, we would. The rehabilitation process required that offenders speak to all surviving victims and kin. Edward Early would come to see us then, all those years after he'd refused to let us come to see him. I'd be seventy-two. Nova would be older than Fern and I were now. Imagine that! I pictured Edward Early on my porch, my gray head rising at his knock on the door.

I didn't tell Silas what Fern and I were doing. A lie of omission, that's what people call it, the things you don't say. But really, aren't there so many of those—the things you should've said but didn't? Aren't there really, truly thousands?

When Silas asked if I was okay, I assured him that I was, which seemed somehow like the worst lie of all, even if it was the smallest of them. I did other things to make up for it, tiny kindnesses, pebbles placed on the other side of the scale. I tapped on the fingernail he'd split as a kid; the nerves were damaged underneath, and he liked the way it felt when they sparked. I folded all his socks around their mates in tiny rosettes and snugged them in the drawer arranged by color, navies and smokes to burnished reds and umbers. I took the worse slice of cake, the slice that had dried out on the side left open to the air.

If Silas noticed me doing any of these nothings, if he thanked me for one, then it didn't count, and I had to think of a new thing to do instead. Unfortunately for me, Silas was both observant and polite. The only way I could get ahead on my guilty tally was at night while he slept, when I could put my arms around him. His ribs expanded and contracted. I thought about how they caged all manner of things inside them, the webs of vein, sponges of tissues, and faceted jewels of his organs. He was precious when he slept, and by that, I mean his face. I could see Nova in it, the part of her that wasn't me. Silently, I asked him to forgive me.

AH, FORGIVENESS: Mr. Pemberton showed up at my next shift at the Room. Imagine my surprise when I saw his name on the schedule. He'd booked an open slot at the last minute, so I didn't even have time to worry over it. First, the ding of an approaching client, then his name on my schedule, and finally there he was on the couch across from me, his turtleneck sweater gold this time, his face sprouting from it, his eyes heavily lidded, his mouth in a cautious smile.

"You came back," I said, a stupid thing to say.

I folded my hands on my lap, which was plump and covered in a corduroy skirt. I was wearing my default work skin, a composite of the physical features our clients identified as most comforting: old, wide, plush, and female. Essentially, I was an overstuffed armchair of a woman.

"I . . . did," he agreed.

"What I meant is I'm sorry. About before. I acted impulsively. That sounds like an excuse. It's not an excuse. It's just I don't know how to explain it."

He tilted his head. "You did explain: it was an impulse."

"Yes."

"I've acted impulsively before."

"That's kind of you to say."

"I don't know about kind. It's true." He looked past me, out the window that wasn't a window. "I understand how it is. You come up with your reasons after the fact, for why you did what you did, but it feels like you're telling yourself a story. A story about yourself."

"That's it exactly," I murmured. It was. He understood.

He lifted his chin and one shoulder, a genteel demi-shrug. "Maybe it's best for us just to say, *I had my reasons. Even if I don't know what they are, they must exist, because I did what I did.*"

"We're mysteries even to ourselves. Is that what you mean?"

"Maybe we're also the solution."

"That's very philosophical."

"Well, I'm lofty."

I didn't expect a joke from him. I laughed, and he seemed pleased.

"Can I ask *you* something?" he said.

It was an unspoken rule that we not discuss ourselves with the clients, small talk was okay, but avoid the personal, avoid the intimate. Given the circumstances, though, how could I say anything except "Sure"?

And what he asked was, "Are you all right?"

"No." I didn't mean to say it. My hand flew to my mouth. It was true. I knew it was true. And now I'd said it out loud. I puffed a breath into the hand covering my mouth. It was a relief to say it out loud. Slowly, I lowered my hand.

"Something happened to me," I said. "And sometimes it comes up."

"Like with—?" He indicated my hands, still folded innocently in my lap.

"Like with that. But," I said, "I'm dealing with it."

"You are?"

"I am."

"You're sure?" he asked, and it was fair for him to be skeptical after how I'd acted the last time he was here.

"I am," I repeated. And I was, I told myself. In my own way I was.

"Hey, we're using up all your time," I said to him. "Did you want your session? I promise I won't, um, grab."

He looked at me for a moment, then he offered me his hands.

THAT SAME AFTERNOON, Fern and I met at a coffee shop to figure out how to convince Edward Early to agree to see us. I probably wouldn't have noticed the woman a few tables over if she hadn't kept peering at us. She was oldish and plumpish, her hair a lush oceanic blue that practically frothed off her head. Fern seemed oblivious of the woman's staring. But then, it was hard to know what Fern noticed and what she didn't. Besides, by now we were all used to the feeling of eyes upon us.

When Fern and I got up to leave, the woman did, too, angling her path through the tables so that it'd intersect with ours. I held the door for her in that way that's not really holding the door for someone, but only leaving your hand pressed to it an extra moment so that the person behind you has a better chance of catching it. I didn't look back to see if she'd caught it, either.

"Miss?" I heard her call behind us, out on the sidewalk. "Miss?" she said again, more urgently. "Please, Miss!"

Fern was the one who stopped, even though I had been the one anticipating the woman's cry. I stopped only because Fern had. When I turned, the woman was right behind us, inches away. I saw then that what I'd mistaken at a distance for plumpness was, in fact, the sag of rapidly dropped weight.

"Thank you!" she said to us. "Oh, thank you, thank you for stopping."

We hadn't done anything except pause, and her thanking us so profusely made me second-guess doing even that. I glanced at Fern, but she didn't look back at me. She was watching the woman in that beguiling way she had, like you were small and she held you in her palm, turning you this way and that to see all of your facets.

"Can I show you something?" the woman said.

She held up her screen, and on it was a teenage girl draped in a graduation robe. The girl's hair had been dyed and curled in the same bright blue waves as the woman's. The woman tapped, and suddenly a projection of the girl stood among the three of us, flickering in the sun.

"But I don't have anything to say!" the girl protested. "Here. I'll do this." She doffed her graduation cap, made to throw it, but at the last minute she didn't let it go, pressing it to her chest. The image stuttered to start, and the cap leaped back upon the girl's head.

"But I don't have anything to say!" the girl said again. "Here. I'll do this." Cap off, pretend throw, chest, head.

"But I don't have anything to say!" the girl said once more, said forever. "Here. I'll do—"

The woman thumbed her screen, muting the projection; the girl continued in her silent loop.

"That's Laurel," the woman said. "My youngest."

"Congratulations," Fern said.

The woman blinked rapidly. "What?"

"Congratulations?" Fern gestured at the projection. "She graduated?"

"No. Or yes. She did. But that's not . . ." The woman looked at the girl and then back at us. "What I mean is, she's like you. She's only exactly like the two of you."

Fern was silent, waiting for the woman to elaborate. Me, I didn't want to hear another word. I really and truly didn't want to hear how this woman believed her daughter was only exactly like us.

"What I mean is, she's dead," the woman said, like I knew she would say.

"I'm so sorry," I murmured and took Fern's arm to go.

"For my loss?" she asked me. "Is that what you're sorry for?"

I stopped. The words sounded like they should be sarcastic, but her tone wasn't biting. She fingered one of her blue curls, examining its split ends. She'd dyed her hair to match her dead daughter's, I realized.

"Well, she wouldn't leave him," the woman said. "It's hard for some people to understand that. *Why didn't she just leave him?* They don't *say* that to me. People know better than to *say* that." She wetted her lips. Her tongue looked unhealthy, filmy. "He didn't hit her. That's another thing people don't understand. They *do* ask me about that. *Did he hit her?* I try to explain about how it was, how he had her on all these diets. Wouldn't let her eat meat. Because of how it made her smell, she told me.

"And how he picked out her clothes for her. I don't mean that he bought her clothes, though he did tell her what to buy and what not to. I mean he laid out her outfits each morning on the foot of their bed.

"Like on her last birthday, I gave her this coat. I stopped my car in the middle of the road when I saw it in the shop window, turned right around and drove back to get it. That's how much it reminded me of her, of something she would like, of something she would look beautiful . . . well. She opened up the box and handed it back to me, right there, still in the tissue paper. Thank you, she said. It was such a nice coat, she said. But she was so sorry, she couldn't wear green, he didn't like her in it. I told her she looked beautiful in green. She said it wasn't the way she *looked* in it, it was what the color *brought out* in her. *How it makes me act*, she said. And I asked her how was that? And she said, *Mom, you know better than anyone what a bitch I can be.*

"So you can see how even if he didn't hit her, he—" The woman tapped her head and tapped her heart, her motions mirroring the girl's, cap to head, cap to chest.

"But it's true he didn't touch her," she went on. "Until he did what he did to her. And to himself. And then I guess it was the bullet that touched her. Technically. *At least he's gone*, people say. *He must've been so sick*, they say."

The woman's lip curled, revealing the white point of a tooth. I understood what she meant. This man had not only killed her daughter, he'd tethered his death to hers. *Edward Early's victims*, that was what the newsfeeds called Fern and me and the rest of us women. *Edward Early's victims*, with the possessive.

"I don't mean to diminish your experience," the woman went on. "I don't mean to say you haven't been through what you've been through. I know *you* didn't have the chance to leave. But wouldn't you say, when he pointed the gun at her, my Laurel was scared, too? Wouldn't you say it hurt her when the bullet . . . when it went . . . went . . . went . . ."

It was horrible watching the woman stutter on the word, like the hologram of her daughter caught in its loop. I was already on the backs of my heels looking for a way to escape, but Fern held my arm firmly in place.

"Went in," Fern said.

"Went in," the woman sighed. "Yes. Thank you. Went in."

"I'm going to put her away now," she said of the projection. She slid her finger along the edge of her screen. "Just for now," she murmured to her daughter, not us. And the girl disappeared.

"You're good girls," she said. "I can see it."

Fern laughed. "We're not."

"No, no, no, no, no." The woman waved a hand. "People will tell you you're not. But you are. Laurel was a good girl, too." She frowned. "I was going to say *despite everything*. But I won't say that. She *was* a good girl. She was just . . . good. So maybe, if you girls felt like it, if you thought it was the right thing to do, maybe you could tell your people about her? About Laurel?"

Our people? My first thought was that she meant the other women in the survivors' group. I definitely wasn't going to tell them this sad story, because for one thing, it wasn't anything they hadn't heard before, and for another thing, there was nothing to be done about it now. I thought of Angela's ex following her, *stalking* her, I amended. She hadn't mentioned him in a while. Maybe he'd stopped. I hoped he'd stopped.

"Your people," the woman repeated, gesturing past us, down the street, and I realized she meant the replication commission. "I think maybe if they knew what Laurel had been through, maybe they'd consider her for—" She gestured at Fern and me. "I know it's not as exciting as what happened to the two of you."

Fern's hand tensed around my arm at the word *exciting.*

"I know there might not be the same sympathy," the woman went on. "Because Laurel could've left him. She could have. It's true. Except, you know, really she couldn't."

"Yes," Fern said, stepping forward. "Yes, we'll tell them."

"You will?" the woman asked, and I could tell by the way she said it that she'd expected us to say no.

"Of course we will," Fern replied. "We'll tell them about your Laurel."

"See?" the woman said to someone invisible, to the sky. "See? Good girls! Good! Should I give you my number? You can tell me what they say. And then they'll know how to find me if . . . well, if they decide to . . ."

Fern said yes, and the woman did that. She thanked us many more times, all in a tumble, until it was impossible to keep accepting that amount of thanks, so we simply nodded until she sputtered out.

"You're going to talk to Gert about her?" I asked Fern once we were on the next block over and the woman was no longer in sight.

Fern scoffed. "What's Gert going to do?"

"Then who? The replication commission?"

"Lou," Fern said. "Come on."

"What? Who?"

"There's no one *to* tell. They're not going to clone that woman's daughter."

I must have flinched at that word, *clone*, which people rarely use for politeness' sake, because Fern laughed in my face. What Fern said was true anyway. The replication commission wouldn't bring back some random girl killed by her boyfriend. How many of those were there? As a matter of fact, I knew the number: three per day, every day.

The country already had too many people to begin with. We couldn't clone everyone who died or even everyone who'd been murdered, or so the reasoning went. The process was saved for special circumstances. A significant and ongoing contribution to society was supposed to be the criterion, with government oversight to ensure this was so. That's why it'd been a scandal when, about a year ago, it had come out that some of the people brought back had made sizable donations to the replication commission. For research, the commission claimed. But it looked how it looked, and how it looked was bad, especially after a politician the commission brought back turned out to have raped two of his interns. There were protests and inquests and censures, and it looked like the replication commission might be shut down, until Edward Early started murdering women, and the one story eclipsed the other.

The truth was, the commission wouldn't have cloned the five of us if it hadn't been for the news stories, the manhunt, the multiple murders, if it hadn't been for the actresses and pop stars who'd called for our return, the women who'd drawn lipstick lines across their throats.

"But you told her you'd tell someone," I said to Fern there on the sidewalk. "And now she's hoping."

"She was hoping before."

"You don't get it." I stopped so that Fern had to stop, too. "She's not going to forget your promise so easily. It's her *daughter*." Even as I said this, the thought of someone killing Nova came into my mind and took my breath from me. To even think it felt like I'd committed violence.

"I may not be a mother, but I *have* one, don't I?" Fern tilted her head and said slowly, "And the thing is, so does Edward Early."

DADS

I HAVE NEVER DOUBTED THAT MY DADS LOVE ME. I know it was a piece of luck and no small piece either, that there are many people who can't say the same of their parents. I don't know what it's like to be uncertain of your parents' love or, maybe worse, certain that you *don't* have it. I can only imagine that the absence lives deep in the center of you and is impossible to extract, not like the stone of a fruit, but like an oil that has seeped into you, like you've been marbleized.

Odd is all rectangles and no nonsense. Odd because when I was a little girl, he'd called himself "other Dad," but I could only say "Odd," so that is who he became. He works as a nurse for a large hospital and is senior there, in charge of the other nurses. He's probably part of why I ended up working for the Room, if one can logic out such things.

Dad was a fixer for businesses. "Efficiency consultant" was his actual title, but he always called himself *a fixer*. Unlike Odd, Dad was soft and perpetually pleased. In general, I think it's lazy to assume that when two people are together, one is hard and the other is soft, but in my dads' case, that is how it was.

Odd could make braids in my hair, all different kinds. Like a fish's scales, he'd say. Like a rope, he'd say. Like a crown. I let him braid my hair all the way until high school, which was embarrassing at the time but is dear to me now. There were days when I felt like those braids kept me together, a basket woven to hold all the sloshy teenage feelings that would otherwise splash out of my skull and spatter everyone around me.

Dad liked to sneak me things, small presents and skip days and treats. To be accurate, Dad *acted* like he was sneaking me things. Then one time I heard him whisper to Odd, "Pretend you don't see that bracelet she's hiding under her sleeve." I felt alarmed, then betrayed. *He'd told?* But in an instant, the betrayal folded in upon itself, and I saw how I could be part of this game of secrets: Odd would pretend he didn't know that Dad spoiled me, and I would pretend I didn't know that Odd did know, and it was all love in the end, wasn't it?

They told me from the start that their friend Talia had carried me for them, but that she was not my mother, biological or otherwise. I saw Talia only a few times when I was growing up. She traveled a lot, mostly out of the States. When she came through—and this is how they described it, Talia was *coming through*—she wore clashing colors and ate with her fingers (the only meal I ever saw her use a utensil for was soup), and patted her belly when she laughed, like a contented old man. I didn't think of Talia quite as a person, but more like a bird that had accidentally flown through an open window and was now batting around the room. She treated me with the same distant good humor with which she treated everyone except for Odd, who was her obvious favorite.

One time, I couldn't have been older than seven, Talia had pointed at me and said, "You! You over there! You gave me varicose veins!"

"Sorry?" I replied, startled, and everyone laughed.

I didn't feel any special connection to Talia; I didn't think of her as my mother, but I felt proud that I'd grown inside her.

I didn't think about my biological mother either, except that sometimes I wondered what she looked like, and I made a game of peering at women who passed by on the street to see if I might spy my own features in one of their faces. But I looked so much like Dad that the shape of a stranger's face seemed beside the point. In the months after he died, I'd stare at my face in the mirror because I could still see him there in my bones.

None of that is the point. The point is that my dads loved me with parents' love, which is both just enough and too much all at once. And I knew they wouldn't ever stop. Even after Dad died, I felt like his love got added onto Odd's, that it was something Odd and I held webbed between our fingers, like the yarn in a game of cat's cradle.

And that's why I knew that when I needed him, Odd would take me in.

9

EDWARD EARLY'S MOTHER'S NAME WAS CELIA. AND
her last name was no longer Early, but Baum. She'd gone back to
her maiden name after her son's arrest for and confession to the
murders of five women. Celia Baum was fifty-nine years old. She
worked as a coordinator for the Haslett School District superintendent's office. She'd been married and divorced twice. Edward was
her only child.

Fern and I found this information easily enough, standing there
on the sidewalk with our screens. It was the blue-haired woman,
Laurel's mother, who'd given Fern the idea: we would appeal to
Celia Baum and get *her* to persuade her son to see us.

"Look at this one," Fern said, showing me her screen, a video
playing.

At first, I didn't recognize Celia Baum, who was only fourteen in the video, a girl, all earnest cadence and shiny forehead. The video had that odd, thin quality of pre-holo recordings, a person pressed flat and moving rapidly beneath a sheet of glass. Teenage Celia was reviewing a favorite show whose finale had disappointed her. She spoke at an urgent pace, her fingers fluttering up into the frame, as if there were a director off-screen about to call *cut*.

I looked at the girl, and I found that I hated her. I rejected the thought as soon as I had it, but that didn't stop it from being true. I hated her because Edward Early was there, or a part of him at least, a little balled-up thread in one of her ovaries, and she was only a girl who had no idea what was going to happen to her, and it wasn't her fault, and I couldn't help blaming her for it anyway.

I didn't think to blame Edward Early's father, but then he had left when Edward was a baby, had gone on his own way, as men can and do.

"It's perfect," Fern said, "a mother's love."

You don't even talk to your mother, I didn't say to Fern.

"I have to go," I told her instead, turning away from her screen.

"What? Now?"

"I have to get Nova." I was already walking away, the hatred gusting in my chest.

"This is good," she called after me.

"Good!" I said over my shoulder.

"This is a plan!" she cried.

I lifted a hand to show that I'd heard her, but I didn't look back.

I did have to get Nova; that much was true. It was my first

time at the day care in weeks. Silas always handled the drop-offs and pick-ups because the day care was on the same block as his office. But today he'd messaged that something had come up at work and could I get the baby on my way home? And sure I could.

The building was a yellow stucco cube in the center of a large patchy lawn, like a dropped slice of cake. Inside, the lights were low and the floor bumpy with sleeping mats. I'd arrived in the middle of nap time. In the dark, the folds of the children's sleeping faces appeared strangely old, ancient even. I tried to pick out Nova from among the sleepers, thought I had her, then realized it was another child, a stranger.

One of the day care workers crossed to me, her finger pressed to her lips. She navigated the sleeping mats without even glancing at where her feet came down. I watched, fretful, as she stepped around the tiny bodies, but magically her feet fell in the strips of carpet between the mats. Her hair was a soft white frizz, like dryer lint. The day care was full of social work and education students, earning their practical hours under the eye of one beleaguered supervisor who, Silas joked, seemed to be perpetually in the kitchen slicing apples.

The lint-haired young woman whispered, "I'll get her for you."

"It's Nova," I called after her, trying to pitch it as a whisper, "Nova's mine."

And she nodded, like *yes, yes, yes.*

But how did she know? I was sure I'd never met her before. Gossip, I realized with a sinking feeling, that must be how. I pictured the other day care workers jerking their chins at Nova, saying out of the sides of their mouths, *That one, with the murdered mother. Never seen her in here, always the dad. But then she's not her mother, not really, is she? More like a stepmother, if you think about it.*

The day care worker stood with Nova in her arms. When Nova caught sight of me, she reached out, and I felt a corresponding thrum deep in my center like a string being plucked. And the imaginary voices were banished. When I had her in my arms, she immediately buried her sleepy face into my shoulder, pressing it hard, her eyes squinched and her mouth damp.

"Napus interruptus," the woman said, and I forced a smile at the joke and told myself there wasn't any recrimination in it.

"Can you grab her mat?" I asked.

"Oh." The woman glanced back at the abandoned mat, still in the middle of the floor of sleeping children. "You're not leaving her here?"

"I'm her mother," I said automatically, and the woman's eyes widened. I tumbled on. "I'm taking her home, I mean."

"I . . . sorry . . . I thought you were taking her out for a walk."

She waded back and retrieved the mat. When she handed it over to me, she peered around my shoulder and said to Nova, "Lucky you! You get to go home with Mom today!"

She was trying to brighten things up, smooth them over, I knew, I know, but even so I felt I was being judged, the absent mother, and I found myself explaining, "Her dad works just down the street. That's why he does pick-ups. But I'm the one today. Mom!" I said to Nova, inanely, bouncing her in my arms. "Mom!"

. . .

I KNEW something was wrong the moment Silas stepped into the kitchen. Nova was in her high chair, me feeding her a packet of mashed vegetables. *Poise* the packet promised, though watching Nova smear half of the mash onto her face rather belied the claim. Silas kissed the top of Nova's head and then my cheek; his lips were laced with outside air. When he drew away, there was something frozen in his posture and at the edges of his mouth.

"Why are you weird?" I asked him.

"Well, hello to you, too," he said.

"No. Sorry. I mean, what's wrong with you?"

"Mmmm. Let's see. Shellfish allergy. Hammertoes." He sat heavily at the table. "Existential dread."

"You forgot *evasive tendencies*."

He smiled, but a beat too late, and handed me the spit-up cloth.

"Seriously, Si. Is something wrong?"

"I don't know. No? Yes? Maybe?"

"Are you going to tell me?" I said as I blotted the mash from Nova's face. "Or should I start guessing?"

"I'm trying to decide if it's better to just show you."

"*Show* me?"

"One of the guys at work showed me something."

"Ooo! Do I get to see weird work porn?"

When Silas didn't reply, I said, "Wait. Is it actually weird work porn?"

At his face, I decided to stop teasing him. He looked miserable.

"It's not . . . porn," he said, like it was not *not* porn. "It's a game. Kind of."

"Kind of?"

"It's a game of you," he said woodenly.

"A game of *me*?" I repeated, and Nova squawked. I'd paused with the spoon halfway to her mouth. I gave her the bite, more spillage, more blotting. "I don't get it."

"Of your murder, Lou." He put his hands to his face. "I'm so sorry. Someone made a game out of your murder."

A game out of my murder. I repeated the phrase in my head. I tried not to feel the knife across my throat.

"You've played it?" I said.

"We'll sue them," he said.

"We're not going to *sue* anyone."

"Well we'll *something* them."

"Yes, sure, let's *something* them. That'll show 'em."

"Damn it!" He raked a hand through his hair, and the baby stared at the rare sound of Silas's raised voice.

"Hey," I said. "I know you're angry—"

"I *am* angry. I'm angry for you. Why can't they leave us alone?"

"I need you to not be angry right now," I told him.

"I don't know if—"

"Si, *I* need you to not be angry right now. Okay? It doesn't help me."

He dropped his hands, his hair now wild. "Yeah, okay. Can I be sorry instead?"

"Sure. You can be sorry."

"Then I'm so sorry they did this. A game." He shook his head. "A fucking game."

"I want to play it."

"Lou."

"I need to play it." I stood. "I need to see."

"I . . . okay. I'll call Preeti. We can go in together."

"No. Si. I want to play it by myself."

IT WAS WARM in the pantry, and warmer still with the VR helm and gloves on. The air was dry and dusty with cooking spices. I turned in a slow circle and swung my arms to make sure I wouldn't hit the shelves of canned goods. We were nearly out of pasta, I noted. I turned in a circle again. I felt calm somehow, still, like I was floating a few inches above my own head, like I was the avatar in the game, moving my self around. *In you go*, I told her. I lifted my hand and pulled down the VR menu; the pantry disappeared. I found the icon for the game Silas had loaded. I jabbed the air, jabbed the icon. In I went.

I arrived at a door. The door was set with a brass knocker and a row of windows that cast rectangles of warm light across the dark porch. It was the door to a family home lit up at night. How bad could the game be when it opened with a door like this? But then I looked closer at the knocker and saw that it had been molded into the shape of a woman's face, her brass eyes wide with fear, her lips pulled back, her teeth biting the ring. Etched into the plate above her, where the family's name would be, were the words *Early Evening*.

Early. I felt it in my wrists and my neck. Those were the places in my body where I felt his name, like someone had dug their thumbs into my pulse points and was waiting for my next heartbeat.

I suppose I could've pulled the helm off right then and there, could've shucked the gloves, could've abandoned the pantry and gone back to Silas and Nova and kitchen and baby mash. Instead, I reached for the nameplate above the knocker, Early, a reflex. My avatar's hand appeared before me, slender and white-blue in the moonlight, its nails painted a bright red. A woman's hand. A woman with a bright red manicure. I pulled the hand back. I wasn't going to knock with the horrible knocker, wasn't going to touch the ring held in the woman's mouth. That left only the doorknob, which turned readily. I stepped through.

I found myself not inside a house at all, but on a city street bright in midday light: laundry, bakery, corner mart, and party store. In the distance, the capitol dome rose like a blister. I knew this place; it was a block in downtown Lansing. I recognized it by its shop signs; even though the names had been blurred out, the colors and shapes were all the same. I'd lived in this neighborhood. Jessup's and my apartment had been only a few streets over.

I yanked up my wrist, which gave me a bird's-eye view of the game, looking down at the top of my head. I saw that I was Angela. I wasn't entirely surprised, something about those red nails. The coders had spent more time on her than they had on her surroundings. She was recognizably Angela, albeit Angela in a white tank and cargo pants, classic gamer girl clothes. They'd tweaked her in all the typical ways they do: bigger eyes, tits, and ass; smaller waist, arms, and feet.

The Angela avatar tilted her chin and pursed her lips, a programmed movement to show that the game was waiting for the player to make a move. It was also, uncannily, the same gesture Angela made in survivors' group, her little goose face peering out at the rest of us. But then, it wasn't uncanny at all, was it? The game designers would've observed the movement from Angela herself because this was obviously her new job she'd been bragging about. I flicked my wrist again, sinking back into Angela's body, and headed off down the street.

He killed me before I made it to the next block. He stepped around the side of a building and gutted me. There was no pain, only the in-game sensation of a hit, like a fingernail drawing a line from my belly to my chest. Then I was falling, the sidewalk blowing out into pixels as my face rushed toward it.

I regenerated back where I'd begun, went back through the door onto the street. This time, I walked in a different direction. I peeked around corners and raced through intersections, but he didn't jump out at me. I hadn't really seen the killer before, only a blur of motion and a flash of the knife. But I knew who he must be. I wondered how closely he'd resemble the real Edward Early. Then a thought occurred to me with a lurch: Had the game makers hired *him* the way they had Angela? But no, surely that wouldn't be allowed.

The city streets were nearly empty. I saw only a few other Angelas wandering around. Other players. One waved. Another skirted around a corner as if frightened of me. Then something clicked

somewhere in the programming, and night fell over the city rapidly, like a shade being drawn, the moon and stars appearing above
like eyelids opening. I walked on. I came to a park where no actual
park existed. Up beyond the green was a stand of trees, a tamped-
down path bending through them. I recognized this place, too. I
knew those trees; I knew that path. I wouldn't be going in there.
No way.

But when I turned and walked in the opposite direction, the
same splotch of green appeared before me. I turned again and went
a third way, and once more the park set itself down in my path.
There was nothing to do but head into it. I had just stepped onto
the grass when I heard the footsteps behind me, coming at a run.
When I turned, the knife was already above me, arcing down.

I regenerated a third time in front of the same park. Only then
did it occur to me that I was meant to be scared, that this game
was a horror VR and had been designed to make its players afraid.
But somehow I wasn't.

I don't know. There had been other times over the past three
months when my breath had come in thunderclaps, when my
breath had become the breath of the world around me, when I'd
felt like I was a moth caught in the fibers of some great creature's
lung. I'd been afraid when I'd read the letter I'd stolen from Fern's
apartment. I'd been afraid when Nova had bawled in my arms like
she didn't know me. I'd been afraid when I'd woken gasping in
the middle of the night, Silas asleep on the mattress beside me.
But I didn't feel that way now. Maybe because the game was just
so obvious, the most obvious way to frighten a woman that anyone
could ever think of.

My third time in, I walked straight to the park, and then I went and sat on the bench, Angela's bench, and waited for him to arrive. It didn't take even a minute for him to appear between the buildings and then stalk across the lawn, his knife brandished. I sat very still with my hands folded atop my knees and waited for him to kill me. Which of course he came and did.

WHEN I STEPPED out of the pantry, the kitchen was empty. I found Silas and Nova in the living room, Silas reading her a picture book about a bear who gets in trouble baking a cake. Silas looked up at me where I was in the doorway, his expression a question. I padded across the room and tucked in next to them.

"Can you just keep reading?" I said before Silas could say anything.

He didn't even say yes, my husband, my love. He simply turned to the next page and continued in his warm, deep voice, about the bear and her cake and her troubles and her icing. I pressed my cheek to Silas's shirt, the fuzz of the flannel, the solidity of his arm beneath it, beneath that his muscle, bone, marrow. Nova cawed and tapped my head, which was now within her reach. They were real. This was real. The woman with the ring in her mouth, she was only pixels.

SEARCHERS

SOMETIMES I WATCH THE COVERAGE OF MY OWN DIS-
appearance. I watch the footage of the place in the leaves where
they found my screen and a few yards over where they found my
running shoes lined up in the middle of the trail. I watch the row
of strangers who tilled their way across the park like a giant thresh-
ing machine, searching for me among the trees.

The weather turned cold the day after I disappeared. The searchers wear bright jackets, corals and cobalts and marigolds, as if they
want to make sure that, if they, too, were to disappear, their own
limp bodies could be spotted on the ground. Every so often I recognize one of them, the stylist who gave me a bad haircut, a couple from my birthing class, one of Silas's coworkers. I wonder if they
actually remembered me, or if they'd seen my face scroll by on their

newsfeed and had cried out to someone in another room, "This woman—where do I know her from?"

Sometimes Silas appears on these news reports, Silas in triplicate, one outlet capturing him and the others repeating him. On the screen, Silas wavers. His voice, his eyes, his very outline, all of him wavers, as if he is being patched in from a different location, though the people behind him—the reporters, detectives, and volunteers—are all crisp and clear. When he rubs the bump in the bridge of his nose, he looks more insubstantial than ever, as if he is merely a smudge on the screen, as if I could reach out with the edge of my sleeve and wipe him away.

"I'm sorry, Si," I say to him. And I am. Really I am.

Sometimes I click on the VR option and hunt along with the search party, shoulder to shoulder, hip to hip. And even though I know the searchers aren't going to find me—the report of my corpse will come two days later and miles in the opposite direction—still my toes in my boots are ten fizzing sparks, like any minute they might bump up against a body in the grass, might bump up against myself.

10

"YOU'VE PLAYED IT?" LACEY ASKED US. WE ALL
nodded. We all had.

Her sharp eyes were fixed on Angela, who sat next to me, half
hidden behind her long auburn hair. Angela wore a thin red neck-
lace tight around her neck, *a choker*, though I can't stand that name
anymore. It was an impossibly stupid piece of jewelry for Angela
to be wearing on this particular day, the stupidest thing to pull
out of the jewelry box, but as was typical with Angela, I couldn't
tell if she was being provocative or only obtuse.

The women who'd called for our cloning, those thousands of
women, and sure some men too, had drawn red lipstick lines across
their throats. They'd started with the lipstick lines after the third
murder, Jasmine's murder, two before mine. I'd seen them around
town back when I'd been my other me—at the grocery, waiting

for an auto, making my coffee, at the Room, on their necks a waxy crimson stripe, a protest, a point. It had grown after my murder, I knew, had become a movement.

"You've *all* played it?" Lacey said.

We nodded again.

We'd all played it.

Lacey crossed her arms. "Well, *I'm* not setting foot in there. The second you port in, you're giving them user numbers. It's the same as giving them money. And you're giving *her* attention." She jerked her chin at Angela. "Or whatever the fuck it is she's getting out of this."

"Lacey," Gert said, "personal attacks."

"Fine. Sure. You're right, Gert. This isn't personal *at all*. So on a completely *impersonal* note, do you have any idea what this is going to do to our lives, Angela?"

"It's a game," Angela murmured.

"What was that?" Lacey leaned forward.

"She said it's a game," I repeated. I'd heard only because I was sitting right next to her, and her face was turned toward me.

I hadn't planned on talking at all. My plan had been to sit perfectly still and wait for this argument to pass over me, to drift off to wherever arguments go once they're had, leaving behind its pall of bad feelings. But I found myself both annoyed with Angela and protective over Angela, both taken aback by Lacey's anger and sympathetic to Lacey's anger. Impossible, impossible.

"A game?" Lacey shook her head. "A game!"

"I mean," Fern said, "technically . . ."

"Do you know how many rape threats we're going to get because of this *game*?"

No one responded. We'd all gotten our share of those when we'd first been brought back. They were from men who felt we'd gotten some kind of special treatment, who felt we should get back in our place. Which I guess was the ground? There were women who sent death threats, too, mostly religious types who believed our existence was a violation of God's will. You'd be surprised by the number of women. Or probably you wouldn't.

"Has that happened?" Gert asked. "Have you been receiving threats?"

I hadn't gotten any threats lately, not since those first few weeks. The newsfeeds had made a victory story out of our return, with the replication commission cast as the hero, us the damsels who'd been saved, a familiar story, a safe story. The threats had dried up after that.

"You will," Lacey promised. "Give the rapists a minute."

"Lacey," Jazz said.

"What?"

"Take it easy."

Lacey made a sour face, but she sat back in her chair.

"Because you know I'll reports threats, *any* threats, to the commission," Gert said, "and they'll take the appropriate steps to ensure your safety."

"After they're done cloning their latest rapist," Lacey said under her breath, quietly enough that Gert could ignore it.

None of us had much faith in the replication commission. Save for the occasional checkup, which seemed mostly about gathering our medical data, the commission had moved on, leaving Gert to handle our recovery. Last I'd heard, the commission was replicating a professional soccer player who had died of a drug overdose; he'd been known for his unusual kicking style.

Lacey turned to me. "What did you think?"

"Me?"

"You, Lou. You said you played it."

I glanced at Angela. "Nothing much."

"Come on," she said. "You *have* to have an opinion."

"I don't think that's how opinions work," Fern said.

"Lacey—" Gert began.

But then Angela spoke up: "You can kill him, you know."

And with that she had our attention.

"You can kill him before he kills you," she said.

"It's true," Jasmine chimed in. "I've done it."

And then we were all looking at Jazz. She blinked back at us, her eyes blurry behind her glasses, her forehead creased.

"I'm not saying it's easy," she said. "Maybe one time out of fifty you can do it. But if you can get his knife away, you can kill him."

"You've played that horrible thing *fifty* times?" Lacey asked.

"I've played it a hundred times. I can't stop playing it. Every night, after dinner, before bed, I go to the place where I died, the place in the game, I mean. I stand under the traffic light and wait for him to find me there. Most times, sure, he kills me. But *twice* I've killed him." She shrugged. "And I can sleep now." She glanced at Angela. "Before I couldn't sleep."

Just then a second Angela appeared in the center of the circle.

This Angela was propped on a park bench, her arms bare, her head tipped back, and her long hair hanging down dramatically. She was the Angela from the game. Her throat was, of course, slit.

I looked between the real Angela in her chair and the murdered Angela. The real Angela sat very still, her face shadowed by her hair. Across the circle Lacey was projecting the image of the other Angela from her screen, her eyes steely. The game Angela had been shot in noir light, velvet shadows and bare skin tinged blue. Her opened-up throat was a darker blue, like her blood was ink, like her wound was the drip of a pen, like all of this was supposed to be beautiful somehow. And Angela *was* beautiful in the projection, her skin, her hair, the lights, the angle of her arched back. I figured they would know all the angles.

"Lacey," Gert said, a note of warning in her voice.

"What?" Lacey said.

"No screens during group."

"But it's relevant. It's an ad. For her game."

"How do you have that?" Angela asked. "It's not out yet."

"A friend."

"A hacker."

"Yes, a hacker," Lacey replied almost pleasantly.

"I don't know that we need to watch this right now," Gert said.

"We do, though, Gert. Just thirty seconds. We do. They're entitled to see it, don't you think? How their deaths are being portrayed? Being *advertised*?"

The real Angela was staring at the projection of herself, her posture tense. Her fingers were curled around the edge of her seat, nails digging into the chair's fabric, as if she might jump up and run from the room.

From the projection came the uneven footfall of a heartbeat. Not from inside Angela's chest, I realized, but from the park around her. A beat. And another. With each beat Angela's throat began to knit itself back up, the blood drawing back into her body, tendon and trachea smoothing over with skin. Finally her chest lifted with a breath. She sat up. Alive. Her hair was tousled and her eyes smudged with dark makeup, making the whites so wide and bright that I had the impulse to tell her to close them, to close them quick or he'd see their glow. As soon as I'd thought this, she was up like a shot and running across the park. The beating was no longer a heartbeat but had become his footsteps, coming up fast behind her.

And now the footsteps were with the camera, running. At the edge of the screen glimmered a knife and a man's hand holding it. The camera moved to the left and to the right and then fastened on Angela fleeing across the lawn. It was a POV cam, like when you're playing the game, except the perspective wasn't Angela's anymore. It was his.

The words *Early Evening* floated up.

Then *On April 8.*

Then *You are him.*

The image blinked out. We all stared at Lacey, who sat back in her chair in smug elegance, folding her hands in her lap and crossing her ankles delicately.

"You can play as him?" Fern asked. She turned to Angela. "You're going to be able to play as *him*?"

Lacey was the one who answered. "Like it said in the ad. They're launching the update next week. Right, Angela?"

After a moment, Angela nodded once.

"I think it'd be good for us to take a break now," Gert said.

None of us moved.

"No one will do it," Jazz said. "No one will want to play as a serial killer."

"Umm, Jazz?" Fern said. "Have you *met* humanity?"

"It's a *game*," Angela repeated.

"Yeah," Lacey said, "I think that's kind of the problem."

THE MOMENT Gert called it a day, Fern jumped up and crossed the circle, grabbing my hands in hers.

"Come on!" she said.

The other women glanced at us as they gathered their coats from the backs of their chairs, and I felt a flush of embarrassment and affection, twined together, not so different from Fern's fingers in mine.

We ended up walking the block around the clinic, scarves wound around our chins, like schoolgirls with nowhere good to go. Or like the players in the murder game, I suppose.

"Take a look," Fern said.

She tossed something from her screen to mine. I laughed when I saw it, but then I realized it wasn't a joke, and the laugh rattled there in my mouth until I swallowed it back down. Fern had purchased a gift certificate for a session with me in the Room. The certificate said it was courtesy of Edward Early's law firm, Smyth, Pineda, and Associates. And it was made out to one Celia Baum.

"You bought this?" I asked.

"I did."

"You made it look like it's from his lawyers." I tapped a finger against their names.

"It was easy. I already had their letterhead. You know, from when they told us to fuck off."

"What *is* this?"

"It's our plan! Celia will get the gift certificate from her son's lawyers. She'll come see you. And *you'll* convince her to talk to Early."

"Wouldn't it be a lot easier for us to knock on her door?"

Fern shook her head emphatically, her nose pink and wet in the cold. "She changed her name."

"So?"

"So she's ashamed. Or hiding out. If we get threats, can you imagine how many threats *she* must get? Her son murdered people. And people always blame the mother."

I couldn't refute that.

"If we show up at her door," Fern went on, "she'll slam it in our faces. But if she comes to see you"—Fern took one end of my scarf and tickled my nose with it—"she won't know it's you at first. You'll already be in the room with her."

And it was true that since I'd returned to the Room, I'd begun using an alias. I'd had to—too many weirdos, too many true-crime fans. On top of that, I always wore my work skin, the comforting composite, the well-loved armchair of a woman. If Celia came to see me, I'd be in disguise.

"This is silly," I told her. "You're crazy."

"It's perfect," Fern said. "I'm brilliant. You'll talk to her for a while. You'll hug or whatever you do."

"It's called therapeutic touch."

"Okay. You'll therapeutically touch her. And then when she's comfortable, when she feels like she can trust you, you'll ask her."

"No way. I'm already in trouble at work."

Fern's eyes widened in delight. "What'd you do?"

"Something stupid. Something a lot like this."

We had come all the way around the block and were back outside the clinic again. It was quiet. The others had all gone home by now. The glass doors rippled our reflection, two women facing each other, one woman holding the end of the other's scarf. I thought of spinning away, unwinding the scarf from my neck, until Fern was left with nothing but a long red ribbon in her hand. I thought of spinning closer, spinning in, until the fabric yanked tight and her breath was on my face.

"Trouble," Fern repeated. "Don't you get it?" she asked me softly. "We're already in trouble. We've been in trouble this whole time."

She tucked the end of my scarf back in, right next to my cheek. The thing was, she was right. She was right, and I knew she was. I had been in trouble for a while now. Since I'd come back. Since well before that.

"She's never going to use it," I said.

Fern began to dance in place. "Thank you!" she cried. "Thank you, Lou!"

"You're welcome," I sighed. Of course Fern would recognize a *yes* in all of its various guises.

. . .

THE NEXT DAY, I called Preeti to babysit. I thanked her for coming over on short notice. "I won't be long," I told her. "Just running some errands. You know, picking up something for dinner, shopping for shoes."

The girl's eyes dropped to my feet, just where I didn't want them to go. I was talking too much.

I hadn't dressed in my running clothes, the type of clothes I'd been murdered in, because I didn't want Preeti, or anyone, to see me in those. I had put on my running shoes, though, an old pair, my feet settling into their soft divots, their soles smooth and translucent as pulled taffy. I'd spent a good ten minutes looking for my newer pair until it had occurred to me, with a jolt, that those shoes were in an evidence locker somewhere.

"Nova went down for her nap about an hour ago," I said. "You can wake her up soon. I set out some snacks."

Preeti nodded absently. She was sliding her finger along the edge of her gold-tipped glasses. Specs, I realized. She'd been lobbying her parents to buy her a pair for months.

"Hey, you got them!" I said, gesturing at her eyes.

"Only finally," she agreed. "After I was only the very last one of my friends still on a screen."

"I still use a screen," I said, holding mine up.

This inspired no response. Preeti touched the stem of her specs again. I wondered if she was snapping a picture of my smelly old sneakers to send to her friends.

The girl had a feed devoted to me, where she and her friends would assess my appearance and behavior. She didn't know I knew about it. At first, I hadn't wanted to look (god save us from the fashion judgments of teenagers), but I had looked after all, and I'd been touched to see that the kids' comments were tender. For example, a liquid-eyed girl with the handle PandaforPrez had said of a lumpy old sweater of Silas's that I'd been wearing one day, *It looks cozy. I want her to always feel cozy.* They had tracked my favorite snacks from Preeti's photos of the kitchen. One of them had laid out my tarot spread. These teenagers had, I realized, made a pet of me.

"If I'm not back in an hour or two, send out the search party," I said.

Preeti's eyes snapped back to me. I heard what I'd said, and winced. I was still talking too much. But the girl's expression remained unchanged.

"Have fun shoe shopping," she said.

AT THE TRAILHEAD, I shifted my weight from one foot to another. I was here to do what I hadn't been able to do in the game, what I hadn't been able to do in the past three months. I was going to visit the location of my murder. To prove that I could? Because I needed to see it? Because it was calling to me? I could name some reasons, but it felt like aimlessly flipping through a deck of cards, the red diamonds, the kings' eyes, all flashing by without meaning. I started out on the trail.

The park was new, part of the city's Reclaim Green initiative, a campaign against VR catatonia and malaise. The city had bought the tract of land off of a housing development that had just broken ground when their funding fell through. Someone was stealing money from somewhere, I think. The city had cut a crisscross of paths on the acreage, scattered some gravel to keep the mud in the ground, and called it a day. The result was the least scenic, and therefore least popular, of the city's parks, which was exactly why I chose to run there.

Before that, I'd run in more populous places, along the sidewalks, through the neighborhoods, and on campus. The trouble was how strangers liked to wave and shout at you when you passed by, when you were red-faced and pouring with sweat and could barely catch your breath. *Looking good!* they'd call out. *Not much farther now!* Or, strangely, *You're making me look bad!* The comments were friendly, I knew, I know; they were no *Hey, baby*s. Still, they made me want to disappear, to be nothing but a breeze slipping past people, nothing but a whiff of my own sweat.

Once when I was running downtown, I came upon two men in suits who'd paused on the sidewalk to talk. As I approached, the men glanced at me and then turned back to their conversation. They were blocking the entire sidewalk, so I had to weave around them, stepping out into the street. As soon as I'd passed them, I heard something drop to the ground (one of their briefcases, in retrospect) and the footfalls of someone running after me. A bewildered moment later, I realized that it was one of the men, running full tilt, in his suit. He came up just behind me and stayed there at my neck. Out of the corner of my eye, I could see his elbows pumping, could hear him huffing and puffing. He was making a satire of me running. I was terrified and then embarrassed, followed swiftly by a twist of anger at myself for allowing these feelings. Eventually, the man dropped off laughing and, I suppose, made his way back to his friend who was probably laughing, too. I wouldn't know about that, who was laughing, who wasn't. I kept going and never looked back.

I took the park path at a slow jog. It was the first time I'd been running since my murder, and I was out of practice, my calves and arches tight. Also I was in street clothes, except for my shoes. I was running even so. I'd been scared I wouldn't be able to run. I'd been worried that I would panic or sob or fold into a ball on the ground. Instead, it felt good to stretch my limbs, to pace out my breath and fall into my rhythm.

It was the middle of a weekday afternoon. Only a few other people were in the park: a pair of girls walking a wolfish dog; another jogger or two; a group of teenagers sprawled in a loose circle on the grass. As I passed the teenagers, there rose a shout and a squeal. I tensed, but they were only teasing one another. I lowered my head and picked up my pace. I passed the bench where Angela's body had been found. No one was sitting on it.

Two witnesses had seen me in the park on the day of my murder. One was a college kid, also out for a run. The other was an older woman walking with her neighbor and her neighbor's dog. (The neighbor didn't remember seeing me. The dog—who knew?) I'd been running, both witnesses confirmed, at around four in the afternoon. The woman could identify my jacket; the college kid described my running cap. Each witness had seen me at a different point on the path, which was a three-mile loop. The college kid described my demeanor as normal. The old woman said I'd looked pensive.

The third "witness" was my screen. The detectives had found it in the grass about a yard from my shoes. The mileage tracker showed that it was my second time around the loop when the screen had dropped. This was when he'd grabbed me, they surmised. Likewise, my shoes had been located just past the two-mile mark, where the path rises up a small hill and winds through some trees. My shoes had been lined up in the middle of the path, toes pointed forward.

They'd found the shoes first. And for a couple of days, everyone had held out hope that he had taken me alive and was keeping me captive somewhere. Or, better yet, that I'd escaped him and was in the bracken, hiding and hurt, maybe concussed. The park abutted a larger stretch of uncleared forest and fields. A search party had been put together, volunteers walking in lines, bending back branches and kicking through tall grass. They'd searched for three days, finding nothing. In the end, it was a police dog that found my body in a rain ditch, approximately two miles from my shoes. I was unburied and unmolested, aside from my slashed throat. I'd run, they surmised. I'd nearly made it to the road when I'd bled out.

Here, now, I stopped running. I was quickly winded. I had to slow to a walk to reach the top of the hill. My new body felt so tired sometimes, but I guess it was probably me, inside my body, that was the weary one.

I couldn't remember my death, couldn't remember lacing up

my shoes and going running in the park on that day. Gert and the doctors had explained it to me, how this was an effect of the replication; short-term memories don't stick. My murder, and in fact the days before my murder, were a blank, a bone whiteness, like my memories had hit up against the back of my skull. *A mercy*, they said. I didn't disagree.

I gained the top of the hill. There was no one else in sight now. It was just me. I turned in a slow circle. I began to feel strange, as if someone was standing directly behind me and turning at the exact same rate I turned so that I couldn't catch even a glimpse of them, not a wisp of their hair, not a tip of their shoulder, not a puff of their breath.

Edward Early had told the detectives that he'd hidden behind a tree and waited for me. Which tree had it been? I looked for likely candidates and picked out one of the wider trunks a few feet from the path. I went over and stood behind it myself. Yes, you could see the crest of the hill from here. You'd be able to step onto the path quickly. I tried to commit the tree to memory, its place on the hill, the look of its leaves and bark. *I'll ask him*, I thought. *When Fern and I talk to him, I'll ask Early if this was the tree.*

And then, for some reason, I stepped behind it. I stood very still, and it didn't feel like I was waiting for anything. It felt like I was a part of the forest, like I was a moth and my wings were becoming the color of tree bark, like I was a tree and my blood was slowing and thickening into sap. I don't know how long I waited. It felt like a long time, but it was probably only minutes. What I was waiting for, I didn't know that, either. Until the girls arrived.

They were the two girls I'd seen earlier, the ones walking the wolfish dog. I could tell it was them even before I saw them, by the rhythm and scrape of their footsteps. I know that sounds impossible, but it's true. I pressed closer to the tree and shifted so that I could peek around the trunk. The tops of the girls' heads appeared at the crest of the hill—one sandy and straight, the other dark with curls—and then their faces, and then the rest of them, and finally the dog.

"I'm going to spit in her food sometime," the sandy one was saying, "and she won't even know I did it."

Curls made a noise, sympathetic and noncommittal. The dog's ears rotated, and it occurred to me that the dog might sense me and tug the girls over and bark. The girls would discover a grown woman hiding behind a tree. What would I do then?

I had the urge to pull my head back behind the trunk, but I thought the movement might catch the dog's eye, so I stayed very still and tried to hold my breath. I imagined myself a tree again, or a woman turned into a tree, my lips papered over with bark. And maybe it worked, because the girls passed me by and continued around the bend in the path, the sandy one still enumerating the things she would like to spit on or otherwise defile, the curly one making sympathetic noises. And none of them, not even the dog, ever knew I was there.

Once they were out of sight, I stepped back onto the path. It was clear to me now why I'd come. I'd thought, without knowing I'd thought it, that if I stood here, in the same place where he'd cut through me, I'd know something, feel something. I'd thought I might remember my death. But I didn't. That particular constellation of folds and firings was not a part of this brain, this body. The body it belonged to was in a graveyard, slowly softening into dirt. It wasn't a terrible thought. Really it wasn't so bad. Because here I was, thinking it. There were the girls ahead of me. And here I was, turning on the path, turning back the way I'd come. Here I was, heading home.

"WILL YOU TELL ME about that day?" I asked Silas.

"Again?" It was night; we were in bed.

"Please."

"Why do you always ask me these things when the lights are out?"

"Cover of darkness?"

When he didn't respond, I said, "Si?"

I knew he didn't like to remember that day, but he'd do it when I asked. And sometimes I asked. I went through phases. Sometimes I asked nightly, sometimes not for weeks. He was patient with me. He was good, Silas was.

"The day you went missing," he began, as if he were reading from a book, "I came home from work, like I usually do. Picked up Nova from day care."

"Nova," I sighed.

"Nova," he agreed. "She was fine. *Is* fine."

And she was. She is. But part of me hurt from it, that she'd been fine without me. That she'd be fine if I wasn't here now. I tried not to think of the bag on the closet floor, which I still hadn't unpacked.

"We came through the door," he said. "You weren't there. I mean here."

I had meant to unpack it, but I kept putting it off. The bag felt like it was proof of something, who I'd been, who I wasn't now.

"When did you know that I was missing?" I asked.

"An hour?" he said. "Two. We'd talked that afternoon. You said you were going out for a run. But you weren't answering your phone. I made some calls. Your friends, Javi, your dad. No one had seen you. I called Emergency. They said it was too soon to make a report."

I pictured him moving through the house, his eyes hooded, his eyes wide, his steps focused, his steps frantic. I pictured him searching through my things, searching for some clue. He hadn't found the bag, though, hadn't found the items tucked at its bottom.

"I was headed out to look for you myself when Emergency called back. People were reporting a pair of shoes in the same park where the first woman was killed."

"Angela," I said.

"And the operator remembered my call. Probably just a prank, they said. But they wanted me to come look. In case the shoes were yours."

A prank. At the time of the murders, someone had begun leaving women's shoes around town as a kind of grim joke. Kids had been the assumption. But one night I'd come around the corner of a grocery store aisle to find a woman lining up a pair of gold heels, right there in front of the legumes. The woman was my age, nicely dressed, hair twisted up, crisp blouse and slacks. When she'd seen me, she'd pretended that she'd just happened upon the shoes. *Some people!* she'd said, straightening up, and then she'd trotted off, leaving the shoes there on the floor. I never told anyone about seeing her. Our secret. Hers and mine.

"I went to the park," Silas said. "I saw them. The shoes."

"And?"

"And they were yours."

"Do you know where they are now?"

"What?"

"Those shoes. My shoes."

"Lou."

"I only wondered."

"I guess the police would have them." He exhaled. "Can we—?"

"We can stop now. We can stop."

I wouldn't make him tell me the rest, about the searchers wending through the bracken, about the dog following the thread of my scent, about that second identification he'd had to make, not shoes. The body. My body. I wouldn't make him recount Early's arrest, his confession, the replication commission's announcement that they'd bring us back. I wouldn't make him say all that, not tonight.

I rolled over and kissed the upper curl of his ear, the fringe of his hairline, the places I could find in the dark.

"I love you, you know," I said.

"I love you, too."

"I love you monstrously."

"You love me like a monster would?"

"Yep. Fangs and claws."

I found the corner of his mouth. He caught me in his arms, tight, so I could no longer kiss him or even speak, could barely breathe. He pressed his face to the top of my head and growled into my hair. The growl didn't come out quite right, though; it sounded almost like a sob. We stayed there for a moment, for a minute, completely still, the bridge of his nose pressed against the top of my skull, and I couldn't tell if he was crying, and I wouldn't ask him that. When my screen chimed, he opened his arms and let me go. I rolled over to my nightstand and lifted the tiny blue square of light. Celia Baum had made an appointment for the next day.

RUNNING

I'D BEGUN RUNNING WHEN I WAS A GIRL. I'D BE-
come ugly with puberty, parts of me growing at different rates,
parts of me not growing at all. Painful buds of breasts appeared
over a round childish tummy. My little breasts had hard disks at
their centers, like the stone in a fruit. Sometimes I worried that two
tumors were swelling upon my chest. My hair slithered everywhere,
oily and snaky, in my mouth and into my eyes. Odd kept suggesting I cut it short or at least pull it back, but I knew that would be
a mistake for such a thing would only expose my face, where my
nose and jaw outgrew my cheeks and forehead. In the middle of it
all blinked my eyes, small and dark and bewildered at what had
become of me. I screwed them up at my reflection in the mirror. To
be pretty was to have a chance at being loved. And I was not, and
therefore I would not be. That was what I believed back then.

My legs were the one good thing I had. They were still one of the child parts of me, short and sturdy and dimpled at the knees. I could count on my legs. They would carry me. They were of use.

One afternoon, I was with my friends outside the train station, the one that ran commuters to Detroit. We were on our swiftboards, spinning them up the concrete walls and off the benches, annoying the adults. The station was farther than we were supposed to go at age eleven. In fact, our parents believed we were at each other's houses, but one of the girls, Gemma, knew how to fool the tracking app, so we went where we pleased, which was, of course, far beyond where our parents told us we could go.

I had to pee, so I went in to use the station bathroom. When I came out, my friends were gone, and my board was gone, too. It would've been Gemma's idea to leave me there. We were hard on each other. We weren't unkind, never unkind. We girls had been taught kindness from a young age; kindness had been stressed. But there was another lesson in that, one the adults hadn't known they were teaching, how kindness could be expected of a girl, demanded of her really, and then levied against her. We girls didn't talk about this, but we knew it was true—of course we knew it was true—and so we would dare each other to venture into the forbidden area past kindness, where, we hoped, toughness might exist.

I haven't spoken to them in years, those girls. I have a sense of them out there in the world, as I imagine they do of me. The last I knew, Gemma had become a lawyer, Peyton a teacher, and Daisy had followed a husband to France. Peyton and Daisy have kids now, too. I assume they all know what happened to me by now. I know

Peyton does; she sent Odd a note after my murder. But then, Peyton always knew her manners. The others haven't gotten in touch. I understand. It's hard to know what to say.

The day they left me at the train station, my friends knew full well that it was six miles back to my house, which was nothing on our swiftboards, but nearly impossible on foot. They also knew that if I didn't make it in time for dinner, my dads would come looking for me and discover I'd gone all the way to the city center, and I would be grounded.

It was October coming up on November, the light already waning, seeming to come from the ground not the sky. I had an hour and a half to cover six miles. I could make it if I ran. So I ran.

I hadn't run like this before—sprints in the schoolyard, yes, or for games in gym class, but not for distance. I discovered that I liked it. I liked how running both sat me into and removed me from my body. I liked how I could push past the hurt to exhilaration. My legs were short. I wasn't fast, but I found I could keep going if I tricked myself. Someone was chasing me, I told myself. I could stay just ahead of him, but only if I kept putting one foot in front of the other. He was stronger and faster; he had something to gain. But I had the edge; I was more determined; I had something to lose.

The next year, in middle school, I joined the track team, and I told myself this same story every time I raced. He was chasing me; I'd better stay ahead. I was the slowest short- and mid-distance runner on the team, but the coach put me in long-distance events, and I ran as fast as I could the entire time. And I always placed.

11

CELIA BAUM'S APPOINTMENT WAS THE LAST OF THE day. Of course it was. Of course. I kept picturing her from the courtroom footage, her hands over her eyes, skinny hands, old lady hands, so you could see where the veins ran beneath, where the bones forked. I imagined putting my arms around a woman in this posture, how her arms would be bound to her body by my arms, how she wouldn't be able to see me. But then, you can't ever really see the person embracing you, even when your eyes are uncovered. You're looking over their shoulder, and they over yours. You're too close.

I waited until I was in the auto on my way to work before I called to tell Fern. I couldn't talk in front of Silas; he still didn't know about any of this. My call woke her. I told her that she'd been right; Celia had used the gift certificate; her plan had worked.

"That was fast," was all she said.

I'd expected her to be smug. But she didn't waste even a moment on gloating. She was down to business, practical about this impractical situation she had devised. It was something I'd noticed about her since that first time at Bar None, how she seemed to treat chaos as a form of common sense.

"It'll go like this," Fern said, and somehow I knew she was on her back on her bed, her feet stretched in the air above her, flexing one foot and then the other, wiggling her toes in anticipation.

"She'll come into your Room. You'll be sitting there waiting for her. She won't know who you are. You'll be wearing your suit."

"My skin, you mean."

"Your plump old lady suit. You'll say, 'Come here.' And you'll hold her."

Here was the flaw in the plan. Could I hold her? I wasn't so sure. I'd been so angry at that video, the one when she was only a girl. I didn't feel that way anymore. Still. My murderer's mother. Could I lift my arms around her? Could I comfort her?

"You'll hold her," Fern repeated, as if she could hear my thoughts. "And when she relaxes in your arms, you'll say something like, 'You're carrying a lot of sadness, aren't you? I can feel it inside you.'"

"We don't say things like that."

The sky outside the auto was a wash, was a smear, was the cloudy water left behind in the kitchen sink. And this appointment with Celia Baum, I was beginning to realize, was a terrible idea.

"'Talking can help,' you'll tell her," Fern continued.

"Like I said, it's not talk therapy."

"But you *could* say that, couldn't you? There's no rule that you can't."

"I don't think I can do this."

"Sure you can. It's only talking. It's only a few words."

"I wouldn't know the first thing to say to her."

"That's easy."

"Is it? What then? What do I say?"

"You tell her you're a mother, too."

MY FIRST APPOINTMENT of the day was a one-off, someone in a shimmering pixelated skin with the Room dressed as the sky, as if we were floating among the clouds. I had to keep my eyes closed while I held them or else I'd get dizzy at the pixels and the height. After that was an elderly man who wanted me to hold his face in my hands, look into his eyes, and smile. *Kindly*, he said. *Kindly, please.* Just before lunch, Mr. Pemberton came in; his turtle-neck was plum today, his movements light. He sat at the edge of the couch cushion and offered me his hands.

"How are you?" I asked. I found I was glad to see him.

"Today? I'm okay. And you? How are you?"

"Nervous." It slipped out.

He frowned.

"No. Sorry. I'm good."

"Why are you nervous?"

"Please. This is your appointment."

"Yes, it is," he agreed. "And I want to know why you're nervous."

"It's nothing. A new client."

He raised his eyebrows. "Are you worried you're going to grab them and not let them go?"

"Why did you even come back after I did that?" I asked him.

"Oh, I don't know." He looked down at our hands. "Second chances? I guess I believe in them."

"Yeah, okay. I do too."

He looked back up at me, brows drawn. "Do you?"

"Sure. Who doesn't?" I didn't tell him I pretty much was a second chance, my very existence, I mean.

"It's still a nice thing to hear someone say," he said. "Once you become a parent, your days seem to be composed entirely of mistakes. And what's at risk? Only your child's health and happiness."

I paused, looked at him anew. "You have kids?"

"Mmm." He nodded.

"I have a daughter."

"How old?"

"Nine months."

"Nine months. Wow. Been outside as long as she's been inside."

"That's what I said! And you? Yours?"

"Two sons. Thirteen and seventeen."

"Teenagers!"

"And how! But a baby. I remember those days. And nights. My youngest had colic. My wife couldn't take it, said she hadn't known how it would feel, that maybe she wasn't made to do this after all. She even threatened to leave."

"Yes," I said slowly. "Yes, that's hard."

I didn't tell him that I'd had those thoughts, too. I could've told him. Should've. After all, he'd told me about his wife. But the shame of it was too deep. I didn't tell him about the bag in the closet, either. Of course I didn't tell him about that.

"I didn't know what to do," he said, "how to bring her out of it."

After they'd brought me back, after I'd been murdered and cloned, I could feel the life I'd almost lost. Had lost really. Now that I'd been given a second chance, I could feel every last inch of my life, every detail: the snick of the tape on Nova's diaper as I peeled the tab of paper away, the roughed chap of Silas's lips as he kissed my temple, the lace of morning light from the kitchen window, the smooth tiles under my bare feet, my body as it moved through these rooms, held these people, lived this life, which was my life.

"But she found her own way," he said.

"I'm glad your wife got through it," I told Mr. Pemberton.

"She did," he said. "She got through."

ON HER ENTRY FORM, Celia Baum had ticked the box for a standard embrace. For all the other options, she'd marked "no preference." I went ahead and put the Room into its default mode, with the fireplace and the two couches facing each other.

When I ported in, Celia was already sitting on one of the couches, right at the edge of it, her whole body twisted toward the fireplace, which was unlit. She was wearing one of the Room's generic skins, the pretty brunette from our ads, with tiny freckles dusted from chin to forehead. Her head was bent down, and she worked at the nap of the couch with a fingernail. I lit the fire-place, and she startled, turned, snatching her hand from the fabric guiltily.

"You can't damage it," I told her. "If you managed to unpick a thread, I'll be impressed."

"If I unpick a pixel you mean?" she said.

Her voice was raspy, a smoker's voice, older than the young skin she wore. I took a seat at the far end of the couch.

"I like puns," Celia went on nervously. "They're terrible, I know. The lowest form of humor. But if it makes things any better, I hate limericks. Can you imagine what it must be like to actually *be* from Nantucket? Those poor people. They must all say they're from the next town over."

"You're funny," I told her, and like a small chime, I realized I meant it.

Her shoulders relaxed a notch. "And you're nice."

I decided right then and there: I wasn't going to manipulate this woman, wasn't going to upset her, no matter who her son was, no matter what he'd done to me. I'd give her a regular session and send her on her way. Fern would simply have to come up with an-other plan.

"The form said you wanted a simple holding pattern?" I asked.

"Holding pattern. Yeah. I seem to be in one of those."

"Sorry, that's company lingo for a sustained embrace. Should I . . . ?" I gestured. "We could try it?"

She glanced at the empty cushion next to her, and after a mo-ment, she nodded. I came and sat beside her. I folded my hands in my lap so that she could see where they were. Her nervousness had made my own pick up and fly away. She was a client, after all, and I'd given this spiel a hundred times over.

"We can do this however you want," I told her. "You can stay just like you are now, and I'll put my arms around you. Or, if you'd like, you can turn to face me. We'll hold the embrace until the session is over. Unless you want to change positions, in which case you can tell me so. Or if you want to stop, tell me that. It's not a problem. Okay?"

She made a face. "This is a little awkward, huh?"

"It might help to think of it like getting a haircut or a teeth cleaning. Or a massage?"

"A massage, okay. Like this is fine." She was still seated forward on the couch, her body angled slightly toward mine. "From the side."

"Okay," I said. I lifted my arms.

The moment before they enclosed around her, she cried out, "Wait!"

I dropped them and shifted back. "Whenever you're ready."

"No, it's not . . ." She glanced at me, then away. She was working her hands in her lap, pulling on each of the fingers, as if removing stubborn rings. "It's not that. It's just . . ." She sighed. "It's just that I don't really look like this."

"Oh, that's okay. I don't look like this, either." I indicated my ample cardiganed torso. "The skins make things easier, that's all."

"What I mean is, *could* I look like myself? If I wanted to?"

The courtroom came into my head, the woman covering her eyes.

"What?" she said at my silence. "Is that against the rules?"

"No, no," I replied. "Not at all. At the upper right side of your helm, there's an icon, a tiny person. If you have an avatar you usually use, you can import it. Do you see it there?"

"I see it. Like this?"

A second later the freckled model flickered out and Celia Baum appeared in her place. Her hair was a wing of brownish-gray, like a bird whose feathers are designed to blend in with the underbrush; her face ran narrow with prominent cheek and chin bones, and startlingly light eyes, the kind of eyes where the blue is not so different from the white. She looked at me, assessing my reaction.

"Do you know me?" she asked, sudden and sharp. "Do you know who I am?"

I didn't make the decision to lie. The lie just happened to get there quicker than the truth did. "*Should* I know you?"

She watched me for a moment. "No," she said finally. "No, you shouldn't. I'm just some woman. Some woman from Nantucket."

"What a coincidence," I managed. "I'm from the next town over."

She barked a laugh.

"We can . . ." she began. "We can go ahead now?"

I lifted my arms around her. At first she stayed still, her cheek resting on my shoulder, but eventually I felt her arms rise and her fingertips press into my back. A few minutes in, she began to cry softly into my shoulder, which is something many of our clients do, and I felt something deep inside me unlatch. I rubbed her back in slow circles until she quieted, the same as I'd do for them, the same as I'd do for anyone.

"I have one more question," she said, into my shoulder.

And at that, I felt a chill go through me. I could hear it beneath her words somehow, the snap of the twig underfoot, the suck of a held breath.

"Yes?" I said.

She pulled out of the embrace. "You said that this," she gestured at me, "isn't what you look like."

"It's not."

"So you can look like anyone?"

"Not *anyone*."

"But you could look a certain way? You could look like a young man? A man in his mid-thirties, say? You see, I have a son—"

I should have ported out; that's what I should have done. I could've told her that I'd gotten sick or that the system had glitched or, oh, whatever other excuse I might have come up with later. But that's not what I did. What I did was to click the option on my helm, the little icon of a person, stripping off my company skin and revealing my default avatar, the one who looked exactly like me.

Celia Baum blinked. Then she put a hand over her mouth. For a long moment, we stared at each other: her as her; me as me.

"So you do know me," she said through her fingers.

"Yes."

"That's not funny. You think that's funny?"

"I'm not trying to be funny."

"You're trying to hurt me, then."

"What?"

"To make yourself look like one of them? Like her, the last one?"

"Her? No. This is me."

"That's not—"

"This is *me*."

She began to shake her head, her hands still covering her mouth.

"I'm Louise," I said. "I'm her. I'm me. My friend and I, we tricked you into coming here, into seeing me."

She stopped shaking her head and lowered her hands. "Why would you do a thing like that?"

"Because he won't talk to us. Edward Early. Your son. We thought *you* could get him to talk to us. We have questions," I said, but she'd already ported out, and I was talking to an empty couch.

"We have questions," I said again, said louder, said to no one.

"ODD?" I WAS RELIEVED he'd answered my call.

I'd left work before anyone could stop me, before Sarai could ask why I looked upset, before Celia could lodge her complaint, before Javier could call me into his office and finally fire me. There was a park across the street, but I couldn't sit in parks anymore. And the coffee shop at the end of the strip mall would only earn me stares. I was left with the sidewalk out front, where I paced back and forth.

"What's wrong?" Odd said, bypassing hello entirely.

"How did you know something was wrong?"

"Your voice."

And for some reason, that made me start to cry.

"Are you hurt?" he said sharply. "Louise? Are you safe? Is Silas there?"

"I'm—no, it's nothing like that. I'm okay. I just had a bad day. At work."

"Is that all?" he said. "Worse things in the world." But his voice was kind.

"I wanted to call you."

"You did that," he said, then, "No, she's okay," to someone not me.

"Who's there with you?"

"No one," he said. "What are you doing now?"

"I'm walking."

"Walking is good. Are you breathing in? Are you breathing out?"

I did what he said, as he said it. I breathed in. I breathed out.

"I'm better," I said. And I was. "I know you have to go now."

"I . . . do," he said, "But not just yet. I can stay on for a minute."

"You can?" I asked in a small voice.

"I'll walk with you," he said. "I'll walk while you walk."

MYSTERY WOMAN

I WATCHED A MYSTERY MOVIE ONCE WHERE THE killer cuts up his victim and scatters her body parts so that the detectives have to find each one and puzzle them back together into a whole corpse. There's this one scene where they find the woman's dismembered leg. The detectives can't tell who she is without a head to go by or at least a hand. As one detective observes, even a finger would do.

12

"I'M OUT," I TOLD FERN.

It was the day after Celia Baum's appointment, and I was talking to Fern from an auto again. I was ill-tempered and ill-slept. The night before I'd turned and turned and turned in my sheets.

You making a cocoon over there? Silas had asked.

Yes. I've become a caterpillar, I had replied.

What's wrong?

Nothing, I'd lied again. *Butterfly things.*

And he'd laughed and hadn't pushed it.

"Why have you been ignoring my calls?" Fern said. "I've been dying over here. And by dying, I mean *dying.* Blood, guts, the works."

"Didn't you hear me? I'm done. I'm out. I'm sorry."

"Lou," she said sweetly, as if I was in a bad temper and just needed soothing, which only put me in a worse temper. "Come on. We agreed."

"Yesterday didn't go well. She's not going to do it."

"You can try again."

"No. I'm going to apologize to her."

"You're what? Lou!"

My auto slowed to a stop.

"I'm apologizing. I'm here."

I'D PICTURED CELIA BAUM working in a school building with crumbly red bricks, hall passes, and cafeteria smells, but the superintendent's office was, in fact, a generic suite among the orthodontists and mortgage brokers in one of those labyrinthine office parks. I'd pictured Celia seated behind a curving front desk, *may I help you?* and a bowl of hard candy like chips of glass. But the woman who sat at the front desk was not Celia at all. She had big eyes and a bigger puff of bangs and merely nodded when I told her that I was a concerned parent. She gestured to the row of chairs flanking the desk.

I sat where she indicated and tried to figure out what I would say when someone showed up to hear my parental concerns. Lucky for me, not a minute later, Celia herself emerged from the hall on the far side of the desk. She paused to tell the receptionist that she was going out to "the good place," and could she bring anything back?

"Coffee? Chocolate? Bourbon?" she asked.

"How about the lost hours of my life?" the receptionist said.

"Strychnine it is."

She offered the receptionist a quick cut of a smile and was out the door without even a glance in my direction. I followed after, calling over my shoulder to the receptionist that I'd be right back, though of course I wouldn't.

The office park was an origami of manicured walkways and reflective glass doors. If Celia had turned the corner, I surely would've lost her. But she was standing right there on the sidewalk out front, reading something off her screen, like she was waiting for me to catch up to her. I said her name, and she looked up. We stared at each other for a moment. Then she made a decision—I could see it in her face, the making of the decision—and she walked to me.

"Did he not do it?" she said. "Because he told me he would. But he has been known to . . ." She crossed her arms. "Well, he's not supposed to lie to me anymore."

"I'm sorry?" I said. I had no idea what she was talking about.

Her mouth quirked. "*You're* sorry?"

"Sorry, I don't—"

"If you could stop—" She closed her mouth, opened it again. "If you could stop *apologizing*. I don't know what to say to that. So can you stop? Please?"

"I can stop."

"Thank you," she breathed.

"You're . . . welcome?"

She looked down at her feet and spat out a laugh.

"Can I apologize just once more?" I asked.

She didn't say no.

"We shouldn't have tricked you," I said. "I'm sorry we did that. And if I made you feel upset or made you feel—"

"Made me feel *what?* No," she cut in. "No. I was *glad* to do something to help you. You didn't need to trick me, honey," she said, and I winced at the endearment, and she winced at my wince. "All you ever needed to do was ask."

She stepped toward me and reached for my hands, but then stopped with an "Oh!" and clasped her hands in front of her chest.

I'd stepped back when she'd stepped forward; I hadn't meant to, I hadn't even realized I'd done it, but I could feel it now in my feet, how they'd scuffed back. I made myself step forward again, and I thought to reach for her hands, but I found I couldn't do that, either. So I clasped my hands like hers, in front of my chest. And we stood there, mirrors of each other.

"He's my son," she said quietly. "He'll always be my son."

"I have a daughter."

"I know," she said. And of course she knew. *The young mother*, that's what they always called me in the news reports. It was how the prosecution had referred to me at the sentencing when they'd described what her son had done to me. It was what the replication commission had trumpeted when they announced they were bringing us back.

"He's my son," she repeated. She brought her clasped hands to her lips and touched them there, as if kissing a charm. "I've asked myself: Can I not love him? I want you to know, I've asked myself that question. And the answer is always no. Just—no. It's like when people say, 'It isn't a question.' It isn't. A question. It's only some words I've said that mean nothing.

"I have twenty-seven days left with him. Then they'll put him in stasis. He won't be dead. But I will be, eventually. So that will be it. For us. I do find comfort in the thought of him waking up in a future world, of him waking and being . . . healed. I don't know. Maybe I shouldn't feel that way. But like I said, he's my son."

She opened her eyes wide and didn't blink. I knew she was trying to keep the tears off of her cheeks. I'd employed the same trick myself a time or two.

"I talked with him. And he's agreed to see you," she said. "If you want to visit him now, you can."

She tilted her head up, and when she lowered it again, her face was dry.

WHAT DID I DO in the week before Fern and I went to visit Edward Early? I had more shifts at the Room. I held more clients. A little girl who locked herself so still that her muscles began to vibrate with tension, and I could hear her teeth sliding against each other. An enormous man who quaked with sobs the moment my arms encircled him. An elderly woman who whispered *now, now, now* as if she was working herself up to do something; with each *now* I braced myself for her to spring into action, but whatever it was, she never did it.

After every appointment ended, I sat on the couch for an extra minute, five, twenty. It was calming there in that room. It was. I could feel where my body had pressed against my clients' bodies, even though we'd never actually touched. My breasts, my stomach, my arms felt good. Which is to say they felt of use.

The last person I held before going to see Edward Early was not a client, but my very own girl, my Nova. It was Saturday morning, and she snuffled against the side of my breast. I thought about how her little face had grown inside me, right there among my guts. She was the only person in the world who had nestled against the inside of my ribs.

These ribs.

Not these ribs.

I kissed the top of the baby's head and settled her back in her crib. And then I went to meet the man who'd killed her mother.

FERN DROVE US THERE. She'd borrowed a car from a friend, the distance to the stasis center enough to merit the trouble. I couldn't remember the last time I'd been in a car instead of an auto. This car smelled of large dog and was littered with candy wrappers all turned inside out to expose their silver linings. The steering wheel looked outsized, ostentatious, an ornament not a tool. Fern wrapped her fingers around it lightly, her nails painted silver like the candy wrappers.

The stasis center was in Kalamazoo, a little over an hour away. We didn't talk much. Fern played some music that I'd heard vague snatches of somewhere. I'd lost track of what was popular at some point I couldn't locate, somewhere between motherhood and murder. Fern hummed a little of one of the songs, then mouthed a word or two, and finally burst out with the chorus at the top of her lungs. She was thrilled, I realized; she was in a high-octane state of being. I, on the other hand, was a curdled puddle of dread. Fern yodeled another lyric and spun the wheel with a sure, unbroken movement, catching it as it spun back around.

"You like driving," I observed.

"Of course I do."

"What do you like about it?"

She glanced at me. "The same thing everyone does."

"And what's that?"

She looked almost offended, like how dare I not know? "That you can go anywhere. You can just decide, and in a minute you'll be gone."

"I don't know how to drive," I admitted. It was true. I'd lived in a planned community growing up, and after that, there were always autos and buses and trains.

"I could teach you," she said, eyes still on the road.

"I wasn't hinting."

"But it's easy. It's basically two buttons and lever. And then you keep this thing pointed in a reasonable direction." She patted the wheel. As soon as she released her grip, the car drifted into the other lane. The autos around us adjusted to the incursion, speeding or slowing so that we were safely in a pocket of empty road. Fern righted the car. "Don't pay attention to that," she said. "Alignment needs adjusting. Driving is easy. You should learn how. You'll like it."

"Somehow I can't seem to forget the fact that I'm responsible for a ton of metal hurtling through space."

"There are brakes, you know. That's one of the two buttons I mentioned."

"Yes, but which button?"

She grinned. "You'll drive us back."

I scratched a fingernail against the window. "Back," I repeated.

We were silent for a moment, two women inside a ton of metal, hurtling through space. We were out of the city now and driving through the farmlands. The sky hung low and flat, a foggy tablet. It was barely spring; the plants were all still underground.

"Are you nervous?" Fern asked. "Don't be nervous."

"I'm . . . in a car. I'm in a car and someone else is driving me," I said, and then, "Are you? Nervous?"

She gave me that faintly offended look again, like I was being purposely and relentlessly ridiculous. "Me? No way."

The road curved just then, and the sun broke through the haze, making everything warm and glowing and impossible to see. As the glow retreated, the sign for the stasis center appeared, four more miles.

One time at support group, one of us had asked what dreams Edward Early would be given when he was put into stasis. Gert had said that we couldn't know precisely, but that usually in a case like this, the person would be shown kindness, would be petted and soothed and held in giant arms for a decade or so. Then they would be given opportunities to show kindness back, to offer fruit to a hungry rabbit or to bandage a child's skinned knee.

"I thought maybe they'd scare him," someone had said.

Actually it was me. I was the one who'd said that.

The stasis center was surrounded by a tall fence with a motorized gate, a small parking lot at the foot of the gate. The lot was almost full; Fern nabbed the last spot near the highway. We waited. There were other people waiting in their cars, too. The sun was still coming in at a slice, so we could only see movement and shadows behind the windows, the suggestion of things. When the gate rolled back and the bus came through to get us, everyone emerged from their cars, and we saw we were all women. We kept our eyes on our feet as we shuffled onto the bus, maybe for privacy, maybe out of shame, I don't know. What I do know is that I saw many shoes and no faces.

Fern and I took seats in the stasis center waiting room. Everything was covered in tile or vinyl. A room you could wipe clean. After about an hour, our names were called, and Fern muttered, "I've waited longer for less."

She sprang up from her seat with a big breath and then grabbed my arm and looked me up and down, as if checking for injuries. "You ready?"

"Yes," I said, "I mean, no."

My breath was thin, like my lungs couldn't fill properly. I hadn't known this until I'd spoken and been barely able to scare up a whisper.

"But I don't know if I'll ever be ready," I went on. "That's how it is, right? Things just happen and then they're happening."

"Yeah, that's it," Fern said. "Things just happen and then they're happening."

She took my hand, and we walked through the door together.

. . .

SOME SERIAL KILLERS are handsome. Ted Bundy had those warm eyes and that slick of a smile, his arm bound up in its fake sling like he was taking a pledge. Theodore Harp was supposed to be even more beautiful in person than he was on the newsfeeds. One reporter talked about how she had to keep herself from reaching out and cradling his cheek, even knowing how he'd dissolved all those people in acid, turned them into sizzle and vapor. Then there are the hulking uglies, the mountains and the moles. And finally, the nondescript ones, the driver's-ed-looking fellows like BTK Killer or the cubicle mates like Arlo Lowell, the weak-chinned and bespectacled and who would've ever suspected?

Edward Early was too gangly and long-faced to be considered handsome, but he had beautiful eyes, large and limpid as a silent movie star's, and he moved with the lank-limbed grace tall thin men can have, like they're dancing an oiled waltz through the world. The news stories all liked to talk about Early's blushing, which he did frequently and furiously, his pink face racing to red at the slightest provocation, except when conversation turned to his murders; then his complexion became waxen.

He was blushing even as Fern and I stepped into the visiting room. They'd given us a private room, a small replica of the waiting area, vinyl couch and chair set and the tang of cleaning solution in the air. Behind us, the door swung closed; the lock clicked. Before entering, we'd been given a brief orientation on safety practices. Edward Early was no longer at risk for committing violence, we were assured. Also, we'd be monitored the entire time by the center's cameras. Still, we were given a word to shout if we needed help, a code word that wasn't *help*.

What did it feel like to meet my murderer? It's a perfectly reasonable question to ask. Somehow, it felt like nothing much at all. I felt like I was far away. I felt like I was someone else. I felt like I was watching a tiny me walk into the room toward the man sitting on the vinyl couch.

Edward Early had chosen the couch's center cushion, its vinyl crinkling as he shifted in his seat. He didn't look smaller in person, like they say famous people do. He didn't look bigger, either. He was bigger than Fern and me, though. I'd expected a lawyer or two alongside him, but the three of us were alone in the room. I learned later that he hadn't told his lawyers we were coming. He was blushing, like the reporters said he did, his face entirely red from hairline to collar. His eyes, I noticed with a start, were glossed with tears.

I stopped just past the doorway when it occurred to me that he might stand up to greet us. What would I do if he extended a hand? Deny it? Spit at it? Shake it? Simply shake? All seemed like equal possibilities. Fern strode right past me. And while Early shifted again, the vinyl whispering beneath him, he stayed seated. Under the blush and the tears, his face bore an expression of polite expectation as Fern approached, like he was about to be asked for the time.

Fern made a gruff noise of greeting, something like "hey" or "huh."

"Morning," Edward Early replied, and I noticed he'd left the *good* off of it.

Fern took one of the matching chairs across from him. I was still stuck in the doorway, but I couldn't leave her alone in there, so I made myself go into the room and take the other chair.

Early was looking at Fern, his large dark eyes fixed upon her. His gaze wasn't threatening. (On the other hand, how could it *not* be threatening when a man like that looks at you?) It was neutral, steady, his eyebrows lifted, like he was waiting for her to speak first. His politeness infuriated me. I thought about killing him back. That's the phrase that came into my head: *I'll kill him back.*

Fern, for her part, held herself so tall and still in her chair that at first I thought she was staring him down, waiting him out. It wasn't until she spoke, her voice as small and untethered as a ventriloquist's act, that I realized what was happening. Somewhere between the waiting room and the visiting room, somewhere between the doorway and the chair, Fern had lost her nerve. She was trembling. She was frozen. She was afraid.

"Fern?" I said.

Now she glanced at me, her eyes as glassy as a rabbit's. She swallowed audibly. Her hair had fallen into her face, and she tried to toss it back in a way that I think was meant to look uncaring but ended up looking like a shiver. I wanted to go over and comfort her, but I couldn't do that in front of him. So I said her name again.

That's when Early decided to speak. His tone was pleasant, which was terrible. "How are you?" he asked her.

"How are *you?*" I shot back.

I meant it to sound rude, but Early only smiled. The tears quivered in his eyes, and his blush spread like a rash across his forehead and chin.

"Thank you," he said, "for asking after me. I ate oatmeal this morning, with sliced fruit on top of it. Apples. Banana. The apple slices had oxidized a little. I ate them anyway. It's only a chemical that reacts to the air. It doesn't mean there's anything wrong with them. They're not rotten." He looked down at his hands, which lay limp in his lap. He looked back up, still at Fern not at me, as if she had been the one to ask the question. "I'm all right, I suppose, as far as things go. Yes, I'm all right. But, Fern, how are *you?*"

"I'm . . ." Fern said, and her voice petered out.

"That's a much better answer than mine!" Early replied with a laugh, which crinkled his face and made the tears spill down from his eyes to his cheeks. "Can I change my answer to that?"

"She's *fine,*" I said. "She's great is what she is."

Finally he looked at me and something flitted across his features. Anger? Suspicion? The expression came and went before I could put a name to it.

He rubbed his eyes and showed me his wet fingertips. "Look. Here. I'm sorry about these."

"What?" I said.

"My tears. They're offensive to you."

"They're not," I said, even though they were.

"Well, they'd offend *me,* if I were you. The doctors have me on a drug therapy to increase my capacity for empathy. A preparation for the stasis. It works a little too well, if you ask me." He knuckled away a new wave of tears. "That's how I can tell you're offended by my tears. I can feel it on you."

"You don't know me."

Fern made a noise. I got out of my chair and went over to hers and took her hand. It was a cold, tight ball of bone.

"Do you want to go?" I said. "We can go."

"This is difficult for you," Early said.

And I turned to spit something at him again, but Fern spoke before I could.

"Was I like this?" she asked. "Was I like . . . *this*?"

I didn't understand what she meant, but he did.

"You weren't," he told her. "You fought me."

"Don't," I warned.

"That's right. You don't remember," he said, as if he'd just re-membered that we didn't, though surely he knew it all along. Now that we were talking about our murders, the blush had retreated from his face. The blood had run backward, back to wherever it went, down into the dark well of him.

"She doesn't," I told him. "None of us do. So it's like we never met you. Like you never touched us." I grinned at him meanly; my mouth felt like it'd peeled all the way back to my ears. Maybe it shouldn't have surprised me, how much I wanted him harmed. "It's like you're no one. Like you're nothing."

"You're angry," he said wonderingly.

He was wearing that expression again, the one I couldn't place. Then suddenly it came to me: He was looking at Fern, but he was *watching* me. He was studying me, like he was waiting to see what I would do next.

"You don't know me," I said again.

"No," he said simply, "I don't."

It was an innocuous comment, but there was something in the way he said it. Suddenly I had that feeling like when you're in *Early Evening* and you know the killer is coming for you, winding through the streets behind you, turning the same corners you have seconds before, making his way to you. Even if you can't yet hear his footsteps, you know they're following you. It's only a matter of time.

Early inclined his head toward Fern. "*Her* I know. *Her* I killed." He paused to wipe his eyes, which had filled again with tears. "I'm sorry," he said. "That was indelicate."

"Do you want to go?" I said again to Fern. "Come on. Let's go."

"You, however," he said, "*you* I never met before today."

And there were the footsteps. And here was the knife.

"I don't know who murdered you," Early said. "I only know it wasn't me."

GULP

I WAS A NERVOUS KID. WHEN DAD PAINTED THE LIV-
ing room a toasty cinnamon, I pressed my cheek to the walls,
walked my fingers down it, and worried about how the previous
color, the pale blue it used to be, must feel trapped underneath.
The night before class field trips, I would lie flat on my back,
work up handfuls of bedsheet, and say to myself, *Tomorrow night, I
will be back here in my bed.*

That gulping feeling, I began to call it, that belly-hollowing mix
of anxiety and despair. It felt better to name it, the way a diagnosis feels better. That gulping feeling. I told the name to my parents, and over the years, it shrunk down to only "the gulp," which
they'd say to me: *Is that the gulp, Louise? What do you think, Lou?*

Gulp? Their words were tatted with an unlaughed laughter that infuriated and isolated me.

Why was I like this? And why were others *not* like this? Why didn't they understand—and why could I not explain—that the gulping feeling wasn't me swallowing something too big? It was something too big swallowing me.

13

"YOU'RE LYING," SOMEONE SAID. IT WAS FERN WHO said it.

She'd sat forward in her chair, her hand coming to life under my own. And me, I was still here in this room hearing this. *I am here in this room hearing this*, I repeated to myself. I felt further away than ever. I felt like I was an old woman looking back on my life. *I am here in this room hearing this.*

"We don't believe you," Fern said.

Early sighed. "I understand. I have no credibility."

"Stop it!" Fern told him. "You can't make yourself thoughtful. You can't make yourself nice. You *sawed* through my throat and stuffed me in a shopping cart. That's what you did. And I may not remember it, but it happened. And *you* remember it." She jabbed a finger at him. "So you can say whatever you want, but you did what you did."

"I did . . . do that . . . to you. But not to her." He was crying again, tears running down his cheeks in rivulets. "Excuse me," he said, and dabbed the tears up. "It's this *treatment* they have me on. These!" He brandished his damp sleeve. "They just happen!"

And with that, I was back in my body. I sat back into it hard. I could feel all the way to the very edges of me, the parts of me that wouldn't hurt even if you cut them away, my hair, my eyelashes, and the dead, dirty moons of my fingernails.

"You confessed," I said to him. "You told the detectives. You followed me, you said. You had a notebook. You hid behind a tree and waited for me to run up the path. Why would you say all of that if you didn't kill me?"

"I can't say it . . . nicely." He glanced at Fern.

"Say it anyway."

He paused, swallowed.

"They already thought it was me," he said. "And I *had* killed the others. So I figured: Four? Five? What's the difference? More seemed better."

"Better," Fern said from somewhere deep in her throat.

"I know how that sounds. I see it *now*. . . . This *treatment* they have me on, I can see how flawed, no, I can *feel* . . ." He glanced between us and put a hand to his chest. "No, no, I won't do that. I won't make you listen to how I feel."

"Why tell me now?" I said. "Why tell me at all?"

The tears ran freely down his cheeks. "Is this what people feel like? *Bad*? Guilty? And when they do the right thing, the virtuous thing, is it only to keep themselves from feeling like *this*? Is that what *good* is? What it means to *be* good?"

"Why tell me now?" I repeated, louder.

He looked at me as if he'd just heard me, the tears meeting at his chin and dripping off the end of it.

"Because I started to feel bad," he said, "the way people do."

And I couldn't. I couldn't hear any more. I had gotten up and gone to the door. I was knocking on it and shouting for them to open it. I was calling out the word that wasn't "help."

FERN AND I sat in the borrowed car in the parking lot outside the stasis center gate. Every so often, the gate clanked open and the bus eased its way out, depositing visitors who hurried to their cars and away. No one lingered. No one gazed wistfully back at the center. They wanted to be somewhere else, away. Me, I could stay for a while in this parking lot; I didn't know where to go from here.

I'd collected a few of the candy wrappers from the car's floor and was making a project out of turning them inside to out, outside to in, red to silver, silver to red. Next to me, Fern was fiddling with the car controls. She blipped the radio on and then back off again, turned the heat up and down.

"I don't believe him," she finally said.

I looked over at her. "You don't?"

"He's a murderer."

"Why would he lie about just me? Just my murder?"

"Why would he slit women's throats? Why would he take off

their shoes?" She made an expansive gesture. "Are we really trying to apply logic to this man's behavior?"

"Oh, no." I'd just remembered. "You didn't get to ask him."

Why me? she'd wanted to ask. Instead, she'd frozen. And I'd fled.

"It's okay," she said.

"It's not."

"I got my answer: There's no why. It was silly of me to want a why."

I focused on my candy wrappers, while Fern watched me. They had cheerfully rude names like ChuckleBar, Fazbo, and Mister Winks. I wondered who'd named them. I pictured a group of executives at a long table lobbing nonsense words at each other. Fern reached out and touched the very end of my shoulder delicately with her fingertips. Her pretty face was full of concern. If I were that pretty, whenever I was upset, I'd gaze in the mirror and soothe myself.

"Are you hungry?" she said. "Should we get something to eat?"

I shook my head.

"A drink then maybe? Something strong?"

"No."

"We could go back to my place? Or drive around?"

"I don't know."

"One more question—" Fern began.

"None of these questions are the question," I told her.

She bit her lower lip.

"You know the question."

And I could tell by her face that she did.

The question was this: *If Edward Early didn't murder me, then who did?*

"I need to talk to Lacey," I said.

"NOW," LACEY SAID, when I'd asked when Fern and I could come over.

I gave Silas an excuse. Brunch had gone long, shopping, something. Did he mind? He didn't. He didn't at all. I could tell he did, a bit, in the way he said he didn't. I knew he wanted me to have this time, a normal time, he thought, like times before out with a friend. I would've laughed if I could've laughed. Nova was fussing in the background; she had a tooth coming in. They're already there when the baby is born, a full set of teeth buried in the gums, waiting to cut through. *Nova*, I wanted to cry out in reply to her wails, *Nova! Someone murdered your mother!* But I didn't cry and I didn't laugh, and I told Silas I'd be home soon.

When Fern and I arrived at Lacey's address, a two-story in Okemos, gabled and shaggy with ivy, it was her mother who answered the door. Lacey's mother, it turned out, also belonged to the Luminols.

"Lace probably didn't tell you, but *I* was the one who got her into all of this," she said with a dab of pride as she took our coats. "What happened was this man contacted me after Lace was . . . and before she was . . . well, we call it *the in-between* around here, that time when you girls were gone and before we got you back. Anyhow, this man contacted me and said he and his friends were looking into Lacey's murder and would I be willing to answer a couple of questions? And I thought, *Why not?* They seem like nice people. Their hearts are in the places you'd want hearts to be. That's here." She indicated her chest. "Not here." She tapped her head. "Or, often as not, here." She swatted her own ass.

"So we met up. And that man turned out to be Brad. Brad!" She repeated, like we would know who this was. "And well, I just *took* to it. To the work, I mean. It's what I should've been doing my whole entire life. Isn't it funny? Life is what I mean. What one does and what one doesn't do is what I mean.

"Then when Brad got evicted and Thistle couldn't afford the dorms, it only made sense that the two of them move in here with Lace and me. And with the four of us all living here, well, that pretty much made this Luminol HQ.

"HQ stands for *headquarters*. Maybe you already knew that. I never know what people know and what they don't know. Me? I like to know everything, so I don't mind if people explain things to me. But Lace tells me some people find it presumptuous. I hope you don't find me presumptuous."

She fitted Fern's and my coats onto hangers. She was a tiny woman, blowsy and breezy, with snub features and huge eyes, like a cartoon doll or a little dog you can carry in your purse. I would never in a million years have guessed her as the mother of sharp, tart Lacey, though that's what she said we should call her, Lacey's Mom.

"Tatum is my other name," she said. "What they call me at the bank."

"You work at a bank?" I asked.

She smiled pertly and said, "No. Should I?"

"Mom, what are you saying to them?" Lacey appeared in the foyer, carmine lips turned down like a misshapen valentine.

"Who? Me? Just making conversation. Look who it is! It's Fern and Louise!"

"Yeah, I know. I'm the one who invited them here."

"But I mean, just *look* at them!" Tatum hugged our coats and beamed at us.

"Yep, there they are. I see them every week. Sorry," she said to us. "She's enthusiastic."

"*She* is," Tatum said, "and she makes no apologies for it. You girls are miracles, each and every one of you."

She turned her smile on Lacey then, and somehow it deepened, widened. It almost hurt my own cheeks, the width of that smile, the love in it. I glanced at Fern, who still wasn't speaking to her family, stuck in a stalemate over her refusal to move back to Arizona. And then there was Odd, who was always too busy to talk, so quick to get off the phone, like he could rush past my voice, my very existence. Odd smiling at me, I realized with a pang, I couldn't picture it.

"You are beautiful, pure souls," Tatum went on, "and we have clawed you back from the abyss. Fuck that Edward Early."

She looked at us expectantly.

"That's right," Fern said gamely, "fuck him."

"Yeah!" Tatum raised a fist in the air, holding our coats aloft.

Lacey rolled her eyes.

Tatum beckoned us deeper into the house, buzzing on ahead.

"I made lemon bars," she said. "Do you like lemon bars? Why am I asking? Who doesn't like lemon bars? You'd have to be a psychopath." She flashed a smile over her shoulder. "That's a joke. Do you like jokes?"

"She'll tone it down in a minute," Lacey said, adding, "maybe."

We emerged into a formal dining room, or what used to be a formal dining room. There were still divots in the carpet where a long table must have been, heavy drapes hung round the windows, and the sideboard on the far wall was stacked, not with dishes, but with VR power packs, helms, and gloves. In the center of the room, six VR hammocks dangled in a circle around a cobwebby chandelier. Two of the hammocks were currently occupied by people with their helms down.

"I know it looks like a crazy coders' den," Lacey said. "It got this way, like, gradually."

Tatum came out of the kitchen with the promised plate of lemon bars. She fell back into one of the empty hammocks and kicked out her feet.

"Thistle! Brad! Company!" she sang. The people in the hammocks lifted their helms, and Tatum swung a presenter's hand at us. "Say hello to Fern and Louise!"

Fern gave a little wave.

"Everyone calls me Lou," I said.

"We know," they replied in unison.

I'd pictured the Luminols as skinny, beaky, sun-starved men; Sherlock Holmes meets Steve Jobs. They didn't look anything like that. Brad was fortyish with a beard curled into ringlets, like some barefooted fantasy-novel friar. Thistle appeared to be barely out of high school, skin scrubbed and ponytail still wet, like a girl fresh from gym class.

"Those ones are free." Thistle pointed a toe in the direction of two hammocks across from hers. "Jae is visiting her sister, and Charlie is at work."

Fern sank easily into one of the hammocks. I went to the other and tugged on its bungees. "You're sure they won't mind?"

"Mind?" Brad said. "Charlie will be honored."

"You're his favorite," Thistle added.

"Favorite what?" I said before I realized: favorite murder victim.

My reaction must have shown on my face because Thistle grimaced miserably. "Sorry. That was—"

"Not at all." I sat gingerly on the edge of the hammock. "Who wouldn't want to be someone's favorite?"

"Yeah, she's right. How come *I'm* no one's favorite?" Lacey dropped back into the last hammock, scuffing her feet against the floor.

"You're *my* favorite, honey," Tatum told her.

"Wow. Thanks, Mom."

And I felt that twinge again, like I was a parentless child. *Nova,* I thought, soothing myself. *Silas.*

Tatum turned to Fern and me. "She was sarcastic before all of this. It's not new."

"You mean I wasn't cloned by a very sarcastic scientist?" Lacey said.

"You see? Like that," Tatum continued. "She's said things like that since she was a little girl."

"Or maybe Edward Early dipped his knife in a vat of sarcasm before stabbing me with it."

"She can go on all day," Tatum said.

"Or, hey, I know, maybe everyone around me is endlessly annoying and this is the only way I can hold on to a sliver of sanity."

Thistle put a finger to her chin. "I'm guessing it's that last one."

"Well?" Lacey said. "Why are you here?"

"Lace!" Tatum cried. "They don't need a reason to visit our home."

"But they have one," Lacey replied. "Because I invited *her* before." Her eyes clicked onto me. "And she only laughed at us."

"I wouldn't say 'laughed,'" I said.

"Would you say 'mocked,' then?"

"Lace," Tatum repeated.

"We saw Edward Early today," Fern announced.

And no one was laughing after that.

In fact, they weren't saying anything, and then they were all talking at once.

"You saw him?" Thistle said in an awed voice. "Like *him* him?"

"His lawyers allowed it?" Brad asked.

"Are you girls all right?" Tatum asked.

"That asshole," Lacey said, "denied our requests to visit."

"Well, you can go now if you want," I told her. My own sentence echoed in my head: *You can go now. You can go.* But I stayed where I was.

Fern was watching me, holding the bungees on either side of her face. She was waiting for me to tell them the rest. It was what we'd come here for, after all. She nodded at me. I had to be the one to say it. So I said it all in one go.

"He didn't kill me."

They all turned and stared at me; of course they did.

"The rest of us, he admits he did it," I went on. "Me, he says he lied. He says someone else murdered me. Not him."

Still they stared, none of them speaking. They were in shock, I thought, the news was shocking, which is why it took me a minute to realize something was wrong with their faces.

"He could be lying to mess with me," I tore on. "I know by visiting him, I gave him the chance to do that. Which is, you know, a risk Fern and I knew we were . . . a risk we knew we were . . ." I couldn't think of the word. "It was risky. But I thought that since you all have been doing, well, what you all have been doing, I thought you might like to know what he said in case it, well, in case it informs, in case—"

"Sweetheart," Lacey's mother said. She said it like she was my own mother. It hurt again. It hurt.

And here was what was wrong with their faces: They weren't surprised. They weren't surprised at all.

I clamped my mouth shut, and then I opened it again, and then I regretted doing that because what came out was, "You *knew?*"

I followed the Luminols' silent negotiation over who would be the one to speak next. Lacey was somehow selected, and her voice, which in group had always delivered words whole and unvarnished, her voice, which had always been rough as the toe of a dead woman scraping in the sand, her voice was suddenly gentle in a way that made me want to sob.

"We *suspected*," she said.

She folded her hands in her lap and adjusted her posture. When she spoke again, it was in her typical unforgiving tone. "There were differences with your murder."

"Differences?"

"That he didn't display the body."

"Because I ran."

"*That* you ran," she emphasized.

"The time of day," Fern put in, and I couldn't help but feel a twinge of betrayal.

"Yeah," Thistle said. "Lou in the afternoon, the others at night."

"You had witnesses," Lacey continued. "Two of them. No witnesses for the rest of us. Also the location. A repeat. The same park as Angela."

"But the shoes," I said.

"Which a copycat killer would leave."

"There's also the fact that—" I stopped myself and shook my head. "I don't know why I'm trying so hard to argue that it was him."

"Because it was an answer," Brad said. He had his hand in his beard like it was a glove, his fingers inserted in the hollows of its ringlets. "Hey, you're in good company. Everyone here is pretty much obsessed with finding answers."

"That's why you invited me before, isn't it?" I said to Lacey, realizing it as I spoke. "To come here? You wanted to tell me your suspicions. About my murder."

"Yes."

"Why not just *tell me*? Why not tell me at group?"

"*No.*" Tatum nearly shouted. "Don't say anything to that group."

"What?" Fern and I both turned to her. "Why not?"

She took a breath, collecting herself, and leaned forward in her hammock. Her hands were clamped on either side of the lemon bars, as if she might crack the plate in two upon her knee.

"You girls weren't here in the in-between," she said. "I know you've been told about it, seen the newsfeeds, all of that, but what you'd understand if you'd *been* here, what was clear and became clearer and clearer, is that *your* death, Louise, was the turning point. Your grieving husband on all the newsfeeds. Your newborn baby. Do you know how hard it is to make the case to bring someone back? *Five* someones?"

"Five someones who are no ones," Lacey put in.

"Well, you won't hear *me* saying that." Tatum smiled at her daughter. "You girls are miracles, each and every one of you."

"Mom," Lacey said, as if embarrassed, but I could hear how underneath she was secretly pleased.

"The replication commission was caught up in that scandal," Tatum continued, "with the bribes and that awful man they cloned. But after Louise's death, the serial killer story went viral, the celebrities took notice, and more and more women started putting lipstick on their throats, calling for them to bring you back." She paused and looked at me softly. "Sweetheart," she said, "*you* were a case they could make—a pretty, young, white woman who holds people for a living. You weren't *out at night.* You were *married.* You were a *mother.* You were blameless."

Fern was shaking her head. "So now you think if people find out it wasn't Edward Early who killed Lou, that it was some other man, they're going to . . . what? Take it back? Kill us all over again?"

"No, dear. Not necessarily that," Tatum said.

"Not *necessarily* that?"

"Here. Have a bar." She thrust the plate of lemon bars at us.

"Mom," Lacey groaned.

"What? I thought maybe something sweet. Who doesn't like something sweet?"

"Personally?" Thistle piped up, looking at me. "If it were me? I wouldn't tell anyone what Edward Early said to you." She kicked off, making her hammock swing. Our faces followed her up and down. "I wouldn't have even told us."

"That's rude," Lacey, the rudest, replied.

"It's sensible," Thistle said. "Think about it: If someone else killed Lou, then that person feels safe right now. They think *Lou* thinks—they think *the world* thinks—that Edward Early did it."

"You're saying I'm not safe?" I said. "I should go to the police."

"The ones who got it wrong the last time around?" Tatum said.

"And may I ask," Brad said, "*why* did they get it wrong when we amateurs could see all the discrepancies?"

"You're saying the police knew it wasn't Early who killed her?" Fern asked.

"I'm *stating* that the police are bunglers whose investigations can't be trusted." He smiled. "It's kind of our credo around here."

"Who murdered me, then?" I said.

"Yes. Who?" Lacey sat forward like she'd been waiting for the conversation to get here to this point. "You'd know better than us, Lou. Who comes to mind?"

"No one."

"You're sure?"

"Yes. No one."

It was true. I didn't have any feuds or grudges or enemies. I had a regular life. It was like Tatum said. I had a husband and a baby. I worked as a touch therapist for a franchise in a strip mall. I was just some woman.

"No one? Then it could be anyone," Lacey said.

"Exactly my point," said Thistle, still swinging. "Whoever murdered you, now you know more than they think you do. That's an advantage. Why give it away?"

I took a long breath and looked around at the circle of faces, worried faces.

"You're right," I told them. "I won't say anything to anyone. Not even Silas."

And the Luminols were back at it again, the four of them glancing around at each other in silent debate.

"I know, I know, he's my husband," I went on, "but he'd only worry, and he's done so much of that already. Worrying. What?" I said because they were still giving each other looks. And when none of them answered, I said it again, "What."

"Statistically, if Edward Early didn't murder you," Lacey began, "*statistically*—"

"No," I said.

Lacey arched a penciled eyebrow. "You can say no all you want. They'll keep on being the statistics."

"No to what you're about to suggest. No to *that*. Silas isn't a statistic," I said. "He's my husband."

"That's what I'm—"

"And I *know* him. Besides, if we're going by statistics, there would've been warning signs. Threats. Abuse. There wasn't anything like that. Not once, not ever."

Lacey lifted her chin. "Even in the days before your murder? You can't remember. You can't say."

"That's only a week at the most. You think he became a completely different person in a week?"

I heard it after I said it. A completely different person. Like us. But even we weren't that.

"You saw him on the news," I went on, "when I was missing, when they found my body. You saw how upset he was."

"He seemed very upset," Tatum replied diplomatically, but I caught the word she'd used. *Seemed.* And honestly, it was as much of a cliché as the pretty young murder victim, wasn't it? The murderous husband, making a quiet, masculine display of his grief.

"He was upset," I said, though I hadn't been there to see it for myself. I'd been nowhere. I'd been not. "He *is* upset. And he's relieved that I'm back. He wouldn't be relieved if he was the one who killed me."

There was a long pause, then Tatum said, "We just want you to be safe."

And the others murmured their agreement.

What she didn't say, what none of them said, what was left for a small traitorous voice inside me to say was: *He'd be relieved if he'd gotten away with it, too.*

SOME THINGS SILAS HAS DONE

GATHERED MY HAIR in his hand and held it at the nape of my neck until I was done chopping the onions or lacing my shoes or whatever else I was doing that had the hair falling in my face.

COLLECTED EYELASHES from my cheeks. Also sleep crust from the corners of my lips or eyes. Also my toenail clippings from the floor.

TOOK THE SIDE of the bed where the air from the vent tickles and the streetlight leaks in.

CALLED ME WHEEZE.

LET ME GO.

14

FERN HAD TO RETURN HER FRIEND'S CAR, SO I TOOK
an auto home, a state of affairs that left me dangerously, disas-
trously alone. The whole ride there, I argued against the Luminols'
implication that Silas was my murderer. My interior monologue
rattled on, a ceaseless psychic chatter that didn't allow for a moment to consider the fact that none of the Luminols were in the
auto with me, so *whom* exactly was I arguing with?

I was still at it as I came through the front door. I found myself
nearly running to find Silas, but he wasn't in the living room, not
in the kitchen, either. Halfway down the hall, I caught myself on
the frame of Nova's bedroom doorway, because there he was. He
had just finished changing the baby and was snapping her pajamas back up. The last light of the day came in through the win-

dow, chalking the domestic scene in a dusky blue: Nova pedaling her feet in the air, Silas catching up one and kissing its sole. I stood in the doorway and watched the two of them.

But then. I don't think I even blinked, but it was like I had. It was as if a filmy lid had lowered itself over my eyes, a second translucent scrim like dogs and lizards have. Or maybe it was the opposite of that, like an invisible lid had finally peeled up, and I was no longer peering through its fog. You know how sometimes, *sometimes*, you can look at your partner and see a stranger? All of their familiarity is suddenly snapped away, and the dear shapes of their face become just that, shapes. Who was this man in my home?

Silas was singing to Nova in that free, fanciful way you sing when you're alone. The song was something he'd made up, rambling and tuneless. He was at the changing table, facing away from the door, his head bent over the baby. My palms were still pressing into either side of the doorframe, but now my fingers had curled, ready to propel me forward into the room or away down the hall, one of the two. If I left now, before he raised his head, he wouldn't know I'd ever even been there in the doorway.

But I waited, attentive and tense, for the moment when he would turn around and see me. I was watching. For what? For the unguarded expression of his face.

When he turned, he startled at the sight of me. But then, what else would he do? I'd surprised him after all. And in the very next moment, his face broke into an easy smile.

"You're back," he said. "How was brunch?"

"You know. Brunchish."

"What did you eat?"

The question caught me off-guard, and I fumbled to remember foods. "Eggs and toast. A coffee."

"Over-easy, raspberry jam, one cream, one sugar." He recited my preferences softly, like an incantation, and I imagined each item on a plate before me, on my tongue.

"That's my order."

He looked out the window at the darkening sky. "Where did the day go?"

Away, I wanted to say. Then I did say it. "The day went away."

And wasn't that just it? That morning, I'd been sitting across from Edward Early. My murderer.

Not my murderer.

Now, only hours later, here I was back in my house, and everything had changed.

"I missed you," Silas said. Then he crossed the room, and my breath knotted itself up under my sternum, right there in that place where the bone curves like a keyhole. I wondered if, when he touched me, I'd flinch.

I found that I wouldn't flinch. More than wouldn't. I found that when he kissed me, I'd press into him, that my lips would part, that my mouth would open. Even if part of me stood in the doorway still watching him. Even if some part of me couldn't be completely sure. Even if there was a chance, the flake of skin of a chance, the stray eyelash of a chance . . . but no. Impossible.

When we pulled back from the kiss, his eyes were lit in that way. You know the way. He hoisted the baby and said, "Let me just . . ."

He settled Nova into her crib. I waited for her to cry, to shake me from whatever spell this was, but for once she went down without a whimper. The whole time, I was aware that I was watching Silas while he was not watching me. I was aware of the blades of his shoulders as he bent over the crib, aware of the column of his spine, aware of his back muscles rolling over his bones, aware of the soft place where his skull met his neck.

Silas straightened and came back to me. Again my mouth opened under his.

And there was a moment when I thought I might stop things. Silas was looking down at me, and I thought about how my body had been destroyed and then remade. I wondered if he thought about that, too, if he was thinking the same thought now. I began to curl in on myself. I had the urge to push him away. But then, somehow, the very same idea rotated and became lustful: To be both old and new, both born and made, both familiar and strange. To be all those things at once under his hands.

After, Silas fell back on the mattress, and the springs sang. He stretched his arms out to either side. He'd been missing that, he said.

"Me too," I replied, both because it's what you say and because it was true.

I could've told him then, in that moment, under the cover of dark, with the sticky sea-smell of us on each other. I could've told him what Early had confessed to me. But then I thought of what

Thistle had said: *You know more than they think you know. That's an advantage. Why give it away?* She was only a girl, but she was right. I had given away so many things, for custom, for love, for nothing in return. Why not keep an advantage? Why not hold it tight and sharp in my hand for when I needed to slice?

"Will you tell me again?" I said instead.

A pause.

"Wheeze. Not now."

"But it's my murder."

"Can you not say—"

"Fine. It's my life."

He was quiet again, then he said, "I came home from work."

I turned onto my stomach. Silas still lay on his back, his arms spread wide. In the scant light from the window, I could see the line of his forehead, nose, and chin, but I couldn't see his eyes. That didn't matter. It didn't matter whether I could see his eyes or not. He wasn't a suspect. He was my husband.

"You picked up Nova on the way," I prompted.

"I picked up Nova."

"I'd called earlier in the day."

"It was nothing. Normal."

"I told you I was going for a run."

"You'd see me later, you said. *See you at home.*"

"But then I wasn't at home."

And then he was silent. The bedroom, the halls, the house, all silent.

"You waited for me," I said.

"Waited, called, looked—"

"Looked?" I half sat up. "Looked for what?"

"Nothing. For your sneakers. To see if you were still out running."

My sneakers. He would've looked in the closet.

"You didn't say that before. You've never said that."

"I . . ." He slapped the mattress lightly. I didn't see the gesture in the dark, only felt the sweep of air, the sound of his palms, the slight ripple of springs and stuffing. "I forgot."

I pictured Silas striding into the bedroom, yanking open the closet doors, pushing back the heavy hangers, the clothes shivering with the force of his hands. And then he would've spotted it, the bag on the floor. He would've knelt and split it open, seen the passport, the dried umbilical cord, and all the rest. Just then, in the very moment of this discovery, the sound of the door behind him, I'd come back from my run, and he would've, could've, stormed down the hall, looking for an argument, for an explanation, for an apology. Instead, we'd begun to fight. And maybe he'd pushed me. Or maybe not that. Maybe he'd only taken a sudden step toward me, and I stepped back too quick. I'd fallen. I'd hit my head on some corner, some surface, some edge. Maybe a corner of my house had entered my skull. My murder.

It could've happened that way. An accident. He wouldn't have meant it. He would've stood over me in shock, in shame, in grief. He would've looked down at me—

But no. Just no.

"Did you find them? The sneakers?"

He looked at me. "They were on your feet."

But they weren't, actually. They were lined up on the trail, empty.

My feet were bare when the police dog found me, leaf pulp and loam and rusty blood.

I kept my gaze trained on the bedroom window, on the evening light and tracery of branches. I kept still even as a cold bead ran down my throat and into my belly, like breaking an old-fashioned thermometer and swallowing one silver droplet of its mercury.

"Did you hope I was alive?" I said.

"What?"

"Before they found my body, when I was only missing, did you hope they'd find me alive?"

"Lou. *Of course* I did."

"No. I asked it wrong. I mean, did you *believe* I was alive?"

He swallowed.

"The truth," I said.

"The truth," he agreed. "I told myself you were lost or confused or hurt. Unconscious even, but alive. I made all the bargains. But did I *believe* it?" He exhaled. "In the end, I'm practical."

That was true. He was a practical man. Everyone says so.

"And when they found me? My body, I mean?"

"What?"

"What was it like?"

He was silent again, then he said, "It's like they say it is. It's like it is in the movies. The detectives knock on your door. You know what they're going to tell you when you see them there on the porch."

"And?"

"And what? What more do you want me to say, Lou?" His voice broke. "It was a nightmare."

I touched his arm.

"But it's okay now." He caught up my hand and pressed it harder into the muscle of his arm. "It's okay. You came back. You're here."

And I imagined one more thing, one more possibility, something else. I imagined a man kneeling on the floor of an empty bedroom, this bedroom. I imagined a man who'd thought he'd lost his wife. This man, this wife.

"JAVI?" I SAID. His office door was unlatched. Knocking would've swung it all the way open, so I called in through the crack.

"Whose dulcet tones?" he called back. "Whose delightful chirp?"

I took that as permission to enter. Javier stood at the far wall, straightening a picture, an abstract print of bright colors and skating lines. He nudged the frame, then took a step back to see, stepped forward and tweaked it an inch in the other direction. The picture ended up exactly the way it had started. He nodded in satisfaction and spun on his heel.

"What do you think?"

"Looks straight to me."

"Of course it is. I just straightened it. What do you think *of the painting*, I mean? Would you eat it up? Would you take bite after delicious bite?"

"Would I *eat* your *painting*?"

"That's how you decide if art is any good. If you want to devour it. If you want to chew it and swallow it and digest it in your belly. That's how you decide the value of anything. For example, you want to eat your baby, don't you?"

"What? *No.*"

"No? You don't want to gobble up her cheeks? Nom her ten little toes?"

"People say that, but they mean it metaphorically."

"Art is metaphor."

"Javi."

"What? You don't want to talk about art?"

"Not really."

I sat in the chair across from his desk, hoping he'd take the hint. Thankfully he did, ambling over and sitting across from me. "So serious." He swirled a finger to indicate my face. "You didn't fuck up again, did you?"

"No, Javi. I didn't fuck up."

"I'll protect you if you did, you know. For you, Lou, I'll fill out all the forms. But please oh please don't make me fill out the forms."

"I'm not even on the schedule today."

"You're here on your day off?" He shuddered. "So serious!"

"I want to ask you about my murder."

He frowned an actual frown, but then covered it over with a mock frown. "So serious. See? I could tell you were. Those are my instincts, finely tuned."

"Impressive."

"You're being sarcastic, but underneath you *are* impressed. I can tell that, too. See? Instincts. So you want me to tell you what I told the detectives, is that it? About seeing you that night?"

I stilled. "What night?"

"Oh? No? I thought you were asking about that."

"I am now. What night?"

"About a week before . . . well."

"A week before my murder."

"Right. I saw on the in/out logs that you were coming in after hours."

"To the office?"

"You did it once. Then twice. The third night I waited for you."

"And you saw me? We talked?"

"You said you needed to get out of the house."

"Because of Silas?"

He paused, frowned.

"Silas? No. You were coming in and sitting in your Room, that's all. You were down. Having a hard time. I think they call it *the baby blues*."

"I don't think they've called it that since the 1950s," I told him.

He steepled his fingers and touched the tips to his mustache. "And you said you were being followed. By the killer."

"I told you Edward Early was following me?" I repeated. "The week before my murder? I told you that?"

"We didn't know his name back then."

I gaped at him. I wanted to shout, *Why did no one tell me this? Why didn't you tell me this?* But I already knew the answer. No one wanted to talk about my murder; they couldn't even say the words.

They wanted to move past it, forget it, make a fresh start. I was a fresh start.

"Why did I think that?" I pressed. "Had I seen him follow me?"

"I don't know. You were quite certain you were being followed by the serial killer who left the women's shoes. You were worried you were going to be his next victim." Javi touched his mustache again. "I'm sorry."

"Yeah, well, no one *wants* to be murdered."

"No, I mean me personally. *I'm* sorry. I should've believed you."

"Why would you? I must've sounded like a crazy lady."

"You certainly did." He tilted his head and studied me like I was the painting he'd just been straightening. "But then you weren't a crazy lady, were you? No, you weren't. You were right."

IT TOOK TWO ROUNDS of knocking before Fern answered her door.

"Lou?" she said forcefully, as if we were long-lost friends, as if we hadn't seen each other for months, for years. She glanced over her shoulder. Did she have someone over? The wedge of apartment behind her was full of her usual mess but, so far as I could see, empty of people.

"I messaged you," I said, feeling suddenly sure that I should've waited for her reply instead of coming straight over. I shrugged. "And now here I am, on your doorstep, interrupting your game of *Early Evening*."

"What?" she said, blinking.

I nodded at her hand; she was wearing a single VR glove.

"Oh. This? No. I was in study group. Guess who has one VR glove and has done none of the assigned reading?" She raised her gloved hand and made a wry face.

"You're studying. I'll go."

"Hey, no. We're done now." She opened the door wider and waved me in. "Quick! The cat."

But Spoon was lounging on top of the fridge, gazing down at me with one lazily discerning amber eye. Fern made room for me on the bed, gathering her VR helm and second glove and a heap of books and clothing and depositing them with a *whomp* on the floor. I perched on the edge of the mattress as she bustled about, moving objects from one place to another in a way that didn't tidy anything, only rearranged the mess.

"I talked with Javi, my boss, about my murder."

Fern stopped, her arms full of sweaters. Her back was to me, so I couldn't see her face, but her voice was tense. "I thought you weren't going to tell anyone. You told the Luminols you weren't going to tell anyone."

"I didn't. Tell him about Early. I only asked him about the days before, the days I can't remember. In case there was anything he noticed."

She put down the sweaters and came and knelt in front of me, resting her hands on my kneecaps. I couldn't help but see how her eyes moved around my face, from temple to nostril to lower lip, from earlobe to eyelid as if making a catalog of me.

"I did a bad thing," she said.

"You?" I scoffed. "Never."

"I should never have brought you with me, to see Early. You were fine. Happy."

"I wasn't."

"But you were *okay*. I should've left you alone."

"No, I'm glad you brought me because—"

"Because now you're—"

I spoke over her. "*Because* I should know what happened to me."

She closed her eyes. Her eyelids were the faintest purple, not from a shadow, but from the blood that ran just beneath her skin. She opened them, and her eyes were the deepest brown and flecked with gold and green, like colors bent through glass.

"But we *do* know what happened to us," she said. "We were murdered. And now we're alive again."

"Javi told me something," I said.

She sucked in her lips.

"The week before my murder," I went on, "someone was following me."

"What?"

"I told him Edward Early was following me."

"Okay." She nodded slowly. "And that matches Early's confession to the police. So then he was lying when he told us it wasn't him. He was only messing with you."

"Maybe. But what if I just *thought* it was Early following me? What if it was really someone else?"

"Who?"

"I don't know."

Fern watched me for a minute. Then she patted my knees, two

quick taps. "I get it," she said. "I wanted an answer, too. A reason for the unreasonable thing. The evil, unfair, horrible thing. But sometimes a horrible thing happens. Sometimes a horrible thing happens to you."

"This isn't about acceptance."

"Isn't it? It's over now."

She kept watching me steadily, intently, as if willing me to agree with her. She was impossible to understand. First she wanted to forget the woman she was before her death, then she wanted to run back and confront her murderer, and now she'd whipped around again and was urging us to march forward, to not look back over our shoulders, not even a glance. She was as mixed-up as I was, and it was no wonder. This entire situation was like some child-hood game where you're spun around and around and then every-one laughs when you stumble and lurch in a zigzag.

"It's over now," Fern repeated. "Let it be over."

"I don't know—"

But before I could say what I didn't know, which was practically everything, really and truly everything, Fern took my hands and pressed them to her mouth, not kissing them, but holding them there against her lips, her breath coming soft on them, in and out. When she lowered them to my lap again, their backs were brushed with her lipstick.

"Lou," she said.

But I was looking down at my hands, the whispers of red from her lips.

"What?" I said.

"They gave us new lives."

"But—"

"Let's live our new lives."

ODD ANSWERED MY CALL with "What's wrong?"

"Is that your new hello?"

"You called me at work."

I knew I had. I couldn't wait for his day off. I was in an auto on my way home from Fern's. I could hear the hum of the hospital behind Odd, a steady pleasant burble; you wouldn't guess that people were sick there, were in pain, dying even.

"Before my murder . . ." I paused, ready for him to interrupt me or rush me past the phrase like Silas would.

But he merely prompted, "Before your murder—yes?"

I let my forehead rest against the auto window for a moment. It was a relief, to hear someone else say the words. "Did we talk?"

"What do you mean?"

"That day. Did I call you?"

"No. No, Silas called me. When he couldn't find you."

"He told me that, too."

"Well, that's what happened."

"What did he say?"

"Who? Silas? Had I seen you? You weren't home. You weren't answering your screen. Had I heard from you?"

"And?"

"And I told him I hadn't."

"How did he sound?"

"How did he *sound*?"

"Yes."

"Worried, Louise. He sounded worried." Odd exhaled, and the hospital noise was, for a moment, subsumed by the sound of his breath. "I imagine your situation must raise certain questions about how you came to be—"

"It's not that. It's not . . . existential."

"Then what?"

And I almost told him right then and there what Edward Early had said to me. Because Odd wasn't Gert. And he wasn't the replication commission. He wasn't Silas. He was my father. He'd known me since I was blinking and blobby, known me when my only words were cries, known me how I knew Nova, from the cells, from the start. If I needed something, he'd give it. I knew that, too. But in the end, I didn't tell him. I didn't want to worry him; that was the lie I told myself. The truth was in the slight pause he made now, every time, before he said my name. The truth was he hadn't come to see me since the hospital. The truth was he was avoiding me. To me, he was my father. But who was I to him?

"I can't remember that day," I said instead, "and some days before it."

"Retrograde amnesia: the loss of memory before the event. It's an effect of the replication process. Your doctors didn't explain that to you?"

"No, they did. I just wondered . . . when was the last time we talked? Before my murder, I mean?"

"The Saturday before," he said automatically. Of course he would remember the last time he spoke with his daughter before her death.

"Did I tell you someone was following me?"

"Following you? You mean *him*?"

"I don't know. I didn't say anything like that?"

"No. Nothing."

"Was I upset, though?"

"About someone following you?"

"About anything. I think I was upset or worried, maybe."

"Are you feeling those things now? Upset? Worried?"

"No, no. Not now."

"Okay," he said. "That's good. That's okay."

"But back then? That last time we talked?"

"You were your regular self."

I felt a pang at that somehow. The way he'd said it maybe.

"What did we talk about?"

"Nothing. The usual things."

"About what? What was one thing I said?"

"Let's see. You told me Nova had learned to open and close her hands."

"Oh!" I bit my lip; I hadn't meant to cry out.

"What is it?"

"I just wish I could remember seeing that."

The tears rose to my eyes. My forehead was still pressed against the auto window. If I were to cry them, these tears would drip directly from my eyes onto the glass and run down it. Do you ever think about how tears undo themselves as they run down your face, how that's what crying is, tears unrolling themselves until they are nothing?

"Well," Odd said slowly, "she can still do it now, can't she? Nova? She can open and close her hands?"

It was what Fern had said but in a different way: Let's live our new lives.

"You're right. I can see her do it now."

"Why don't you go do that, Louise?" my father said to me. "Why don't you go home and see her do it now?"

And I told him I would. I would do just that.

PREGNANCY

I'D LOVED BEING PREGNANT. I'D LOVED RUNNING MY hands over my belly, a sphere, a seedpod, a striated globe. I'd heard women talk about feeling the baby turn or kick inside them. Me? I could feel Nova hiccup inside me. I could feel her every little *hic*.

Okay, I hadn't loved the full forty weeks of pregnancy, not every dang moment. I hadn't loved the acid reflux or the swollen veins or the fatigue. Who loved those things? Well, I'd loved the fatigue a little, when it would feel like I was floating on the surface of something, that I *was* the surface of something. I was the gloss on a glass of milk; I was the liquid quivering at the rim of the glass, about to break over the edge.

Then I did break over the edge. Nova was born, and I was washed out to sea. Days later, I was spat back ashore, the jetsam or the flotsam, one of those, whichever one used to be the ship. I came to myself, days later, lactation net snapped on my head and Nova latched to my chapped tit. I was both on the mattress and of the mattress. I know what that's called. I know there's a name for it. I don't need to say it.

It didn't mean I didn't love her, no matter how I felt, how I didn't feel. There are different ways to love people. There are ways.

15

"I SHOULD BE BACK BY FOUR," I TOLD PREETI, "FIVE at the latest. Or Silas will be here by five-thirty."

When the girl didn't acknowledge any of this—she was on her specs again—I said loudly, "Preeti?"

She jerked to attention. "Sorry."

"You can't ignore Nova like that, you know."

"I would *never*."

And it was true; she wouldn't. Silas and I peeped at her through the live wall sometimes. She was lovely with Nova, really. She carried the baby around for hours singing little nonsense songs in her ear.

"Sorry," she said. "It's just . . ." She held a finger up, like *just a minute*, and then took that same finger to the stem of her specs. "I'm going to ask her," she said, to someone else, not me, "so you can stop arguing about it now, okay?"

"Sorry," she said again.

"I'm assuming I'm the her?" I said.

"Yeah, you're the her." She reached up and tugged on her lower lip, pulling it down so that I could see its wet slug underside and a wedge of her gums. She let go and the lip popped back up. "My friends and I, well, we're wondering, um . . ."

I braced myself for one of the usual questions, the rudely curious ones of the what-was-it-like-to-be-murdered variety.

". . . what's Angela like?"

"Angela?"

"*Angela*," she repeated, with great meaning.

"You and your friends must be *Early Evening* fans, huh?"

I wasn't sure how I felt about Preeti and her teenage friends dodging Edward Early's knife, but then the game probably wasn't so different from the other VRs they must play, probably tamer.

Preeti screwed her mouth to one side. "Um, no. We don't . . . play. Games are . . . you know."

"I don't know."

"They impoverish choice."

"They—sorry?"

"No, no, *I'm* sorry." She put a hand to her cheek, first the palm and then the back of it, as if to test the temperature of her skin. "I'm preparing for exams, you know? So it's like essays and oratories from breakfast until bed. Sometimes a practice word pops out."

She pressed the stem of her specs and said to her friends, "Me again." She paused, her eyes scanning the response. I could see the tiny font reflected in her pupils. It had always reminded me of sparklers, how you could write your name in the air with the tip. "Impoverish," she said. "Add it to my list, will you?"

She dropped her hand and looked back at me. "We're keeping a tally. Whoever says the most exam words in, like, regular conversation has to buy the next pizza. Because, you know, none of us wants to be *that asshole*."

"Sounds fun," I said.

Preeti shrugged with one shoulder, like my wooden adult response didn't merit two shoulders, which really it didn't. She touched her specs again, and said, "Kat says hi."

"To me?"

"Yes to you."

"Hi to Kat."

"She says hi back." Preeti's eyes lost focus. "Janelle wants to say hi, too, now."

"If you don't play *Early Evening*, then how do you girls know Angela?"

At this, Preeti beamed. It was the widest smile I'd ever seen on her face. "*Everyone* knows Angela. She's, like, a role model. I *know*, I know how that sounds, but I really mean it. She's making things over. We're making ourselves over, too."

"Making yourselves over, what does that mean?"

"From the way you all made us."

"Me?" I touched my chest.

"Not *you* you. The big you. You the world."

"You know what teenage girls usually mean when they talk about makeovers?"

"Yes. Lip gloss."

I smiled, hoping she'd smile back.

She replied in a very serious voice, "We don't have anything against lip gloss."

FERN WASN'T AT GROUP. If she was late, she was *very* late. We were over halfway through the hour, and she still hadn't showed. Jazz was in the middle of a long story about how her sister-in-law kept suggesting she write a tell-all bestseller about her murder.

"That's what she calls it," Jazz said, "not a book or a memoir, a 'tell-all bestseller.' The other day, she sent me a list of title ideas."

It'd been three days since I'd shown up at Fern's apartment. I hadn't heard from her, but then she hadn't heard from me, either. Still, I was unsettled. She was probably just late. She was always late. I kept looking at the door, then trying not to look at the door.

"All her title ideas are knife puns," Jazz went on, "*The Deepest Cut* or *The Edge of the Blade.* And each one ends with the subtitle *The Jasmine Jacobs Story.* Like, *Puncture Wound: The Jasmine Jacobs Story.*"

"That's amazing," Lacey said. "Can she be my sister-in-law?"

"Please take her."

When I'd first sat down in the circle, Lacey had given me a cool, assessing look. I'd replied with a tiny nod, and she'd pressed her lips in acknowledgment. We were in agreement. Neither of us would mention my visit with Edward Early here at group.

"And what might you say if your sister-in-law brings this up again?" Gert asked.

"She *will* bring it up again," Jazz said. "That's guaranteed."

"So *when* she does, then?"

"Well, I told her I'm writing the book. The tell-all bestseller, I mean."

Gert raised her eyebrows. "And when no book materializes?"

"Has anyone heard from Fern?" I burst out.

Everyone looked over at me. I'd interrupted.

"Lou," Gert said, "if you wish to share something with the group, you can raise your hand."

I raised my hand and, as it went up in the air, I said, "Has anyone talked to Fern?" I scanned the circle: shrugs and headshakes all around. I turned back to Gert. "Did she tell *you* she wasn't coming today?"

"Is there a reason you're so concerned with Fern's absence?"

"It's just . . . I saw her a few days ago and . . ." I faltered.

"I saw her last night," Angela said.

"What?" I nearly shouted. "Where?"

Angela swept her long hair behind her shoulders, one shoulder at a time. She'd taken to wearing her outfit from the game, not the white tank and cargos exactly, but versions of it. Today she was in a tight white sweater and square-pocketed pants. If this was a little obnoxious, maybe it was also empowering. At the beginning of today's meeting, she'd reported that she'd told her ex to stop following her; when he'd ignored her, she'd turned around on the sidewalk and started walking straight toward him. Baffled, he began to retreat, and she followed after him for two, three blocks until he began to run away from her. I'd made a note to tell Fern later; she would love a story like that, would maybe even love that Angela had been the one to do it.

"I saw her at the park," Angela said of Fern now.

"Which park?"

She teased a strand of hair that had gotten caught in one of her hoop earrings. "You know, *the* park. *Our* park."

Everyone looked at me, and I didn't know where to look. *Our park.* The park where she and I had been murdered was what she meant. What would Fern be doing there? And then I asked myself the question beyond that question: What would Fern be doing there after she'd told me to stop asking questions about my murder?

"What was she doing?"

Angela shrugged. "Standing there."

"Fern was just standing. In the park. At night," Lacey repeated skeptically.

"Wait. Do you mean in the game?" Jazz asked, and everything spun again. "You saw Fern in the park in *Early Evening?*"

"Yeah, in the *park*," Angela said, like this was obvious. "I've seen her there every night this week."

"Every night since when?" I said.

"Since . . . Saturday."

Saturday. The day we'd visited Edward Early.

"Did you talk to her?"

"Talk? No. The people make it hard to stop."

By the people, she meant her fans, the hundreds of players who met at an appointed time and place in *Early Evening* in order to surround Angela as she played the game. They acted as a human shield, Angelas a dozen layers deep, so that the people playing Edward Earlys couldn't hack their way to the real Angela. Apparently, it was considered a great accomplishment to kill the actual Angela in the game.

"Ummmm." Lacey drew out the sound into a hum. "How'd you even know it was Fern? Wouldn't she look like"—she pointed at Angela—"you?"

"Yeah, but it was her."

"If you click on a player it brings up their info," Jazz explained.

I remembered the VR glove on Fern's hand when she'd answered the door. For a study group, she'd said, she hadn't done the reading. But I'd seen her lie before.

"Ladies," Gert said, "I have to ask: Is it fair for us to be discussing Fern in her absence?"

"She kind of looked like she was waiting for someone," Angela continued, ignoring Gert entirely.

"Waiting for Early to come kill her, you mean?" Lacey said with an edge.

"Not that. It's a virtual space so," Angela explained, tugging on a strand of her hair, hard, like she might pull it straight out of her head, "people meet up there."

"And she was in the park?" I said.

"Like I said. On the trail."

The others looked over at me again and then down at their laps. *What trail?* I didn't need to ask, and Angela didn't need to answer. Every night since Edward Early had told us he hadn't killed me, Fern had gone into the game and waited on the trail where I'd been murdered.

FERN WASN'T RESPONDING to my messages, so I went straight from survivors' group to her apartment building, where, in my agitation, I immediately became lost in the hive of identical hallways. Finally, I found her door. Or I thought I had, but then a woman who wasn't Fern answered my knock. She wore pajamas with tiny fluffy clouds stitched all over them, and her hair was tied in two knots, one on either side of her head.

"Yes?" she said brusquely.

"Oh! I'm sorry," I said.

"Sorry—for what?"

"Waking you?"

"I wasn't sleeping." She drew in her chin. "It's the middle of the afternoon."

"Right. I just thought . . ." I glanced at her pajamas.

"It's my day off. I like to be comfortable."

"I knocked on the wrong door," I admitted.

"This building is a maze," she replied.

"But maybe you've seen a neighbor, a woman, long dark hair, pretty?"

The woman frowned and repeated, "I just moved in."

I made myself smile. "Sorry again. For bothering you."

"You did. Bother me. But okay. Good luck finding your . . . whoever." She began closing the door, but before she could get it shut, a yellow cat darted out. "Damn! Can you grab him?"

I already had him. I'd snatched him up on instinct. "Spoon!" I said. "This is her cat," I told the woman. "The person I'm looking for. My friend."

The woman took the squirming cat back from me. "You're at the right door, then. The cat came with the apartment."

"I don't understand."

"I'm subletting. The cat belonged to the original renter. She left in a rush. Management asked if I minded taking care of him. And I didn't. Mind. Much." She swung the door open so that I could see inside. "Is this your friend's place?"

Fern's bed was still in the middle of the room, but now tidily made. The rest of her mess had been cleared to the sides to make space for the woman's half-unpacked boxes. I nodded.

"I guess she didn't tell you she was moving, huh? Like I said, it was a rush. She left all her shit. Left her cat, too. But he's okay." She bumped her forehead against his. "What'd you call him?"

"Spoon."

"Like the utensil?"

"That's his name."

"Weird."

"Yeah, it's kind of an inside joke."

"No. Weird because she left instructions for feeding him and everything." The woman shrugged. "She said his name was Lou."

I MESSAGED FERN again on my way home.

> I went to your apartment. There's someone else there
>
> Where'd you go?
>
> Are you okay?

She didn't respond to any of it. I felt like I was dropping stones into a lake, each one absorbed into the body of water without a ripple.

Why had Fern left? Why had she said her cat's name was mine? I needed to talk to someone, but I had no one to talk to. I could talk to Lacey, except I couldn't because she believed Silas murdered me. I could talk to Silas, except I couldn't because I'd been lying to him. I could talk to Fern, except I couldn't because she'd left. And I couldn't shake the feeling that she'd left because of me.

The auto cut through the afternoon; stripes of shade and sun slid over my face. The mud had finally overtaken the slush, and there was a loamy smell in the air, a mix of rot and growth as winter things turned their bloated bellies to the sky. It was spring; soon it would be summer. You could already see the tiny knots on the trees, the hard green buds whose skulls would explode into clotted blossoms. A sudden calm came over me, a silent, steady, sunshot certainty that everything would be okay. My other me may be gone, but I was here now. I was here.

But then the auto turned onto my street and there were an Emergency van and two police cars in front of my house. Silas stood on the lawn talking to an officer. He was faced away from me, which meant I couldn't see his arms, which meant I couldn't see if he held the baby. I couldn't see the baby at all. I shouted for my auto to stop, even though I was still half a block away. It didn't matter. I was already out of the car and running down the street, my feet, my breath, the blood in my ears, every last bit of me pounding for Nova for Nova for Nova.

LEAVING

I HAD A FRIEND WHOSE LOVER WOULD RECOUNT IN exhaustive detail all the dreams he'd had the night before. Every corridor that turned back on itself, every cake of soap that wouldn't bubble, every stray cat wearing his mother's face, he'd tell her all about it. As soon as her eyes fluttered open, he'd prop himself up on an elbow and start in. It was his version of "Good morning." She thought maybe she could've stood it if he didn't dream so damn much. He had at least four dreams a night, sometimes as many as six. It took forever to hear about each of them, all the way to the bottom of the coffeepot.

My friend started getting her lover drunk at night, hoping he'd fall into a deep, dreamless sleep. But still the dreams came, and the next morning he would describe them under a brow crumpled with hangover. Next she tried crushing cold pills into his bedtime tea. This just made his dreams foggy, the recounting slower and duller. One night while he slept, she, desperate, held a pillow over his face, just for a moment. Just for a moment, she said. But that only made him dream of clouds. In the morning, he told her the shapes they'd made in the sky.

In the end, when there was nothing else to try, she left him. She kissed him goodnight and, once he'd fallen asleep, she tiptoed right out the door. She changed her number, her apartment, her job, and her friends, all so that he wouldn't be able to find her. She wasn't angry with him, she said. She didn't intend to hurt him. It was, she told me, the kindest thing she could think of to do for him, to make herself into a person from one of his dreams, someone who disappeared come morning.

16

AFTER SECONDS THAT WERE YEARS, SILAS TURNED
in my direction, and there like an exhale, there like a heartbeat,
there Nova was in his arms. Her face was animated and her feet
kicked gently against his stomach. At the sight of her, I missed a
step and stumbled, but I didn't fall to my knees like I wanted to
do. It was all right. She was all right. I could slow now and walk
the remaining distance to them and take the baby into my arms.

Everyone on the lawn was staring at me in a way that made me
think I had been shouting as I'd run. I might've been. Even a year
ago, had I seen a woman running pell-mell down the street shriek-
ing for her child, I would've thought something vague about "a
mother's love," but I wouldn't have understood. I wouldn't have
known back then how the baby had fed from me, had fed from the
meat and milk of me, had fed from what I am; how she was of me,

her face was mine in its flashes, it was Silas's in its folds. She was me and she was him and, in a turn of fate, she was herself. And what's more, I'd promised to protect her.

My auto still idled in the middle of the road, its door swung open. One of the Emergency workers went and closed it, sending the auto on its way. Silas stepped in front of me, blocking my view of the others or their view of me. "Okay," he kept saying about something. Something was okay—the baby or me or everything. *Everything*, I decided. *Everything's okay*, as I ran my hands over Nova's skull, her blessedly unbroken skull.

"We've had an intruder," one of the officers explained to me, the way you might say *We've had dinner* or *We've had some rain.* No one was hurt. Nothing was taken. The intruder had gotten in and out through the bedroom window. The officer looked at me mean-ingfully. I'd thought the window was locked; I told him so. Drones were circling the neighborhood, he said, looking for . . . someone. The babysitter hadn't been able to give a description.

The babysitter. Preeti. How had I forgotten about Preeti?

The girl was in the yard, too. I hadn't seen her because she was standing off to the side with another officer in the shade of the neighbor's birch tree. She was turned to face the tree trunk, peel-ing off strips of its bark. Her hair was in her face.

I went over to her, even though the officer was still in the mid-dle of talking to me. Preeti was a child, after all. Someone should check on her. Someone should brush her hair out of her eyes and tell her it was okay. Why was no one brushing her hair out of her eyes? Behind me, I heard Silas say something to the officer and fol-low after me.

Preeti stared at the tree as if it was an object of great interest. Gone was the cattish teenage demeanor, the disaffected drawl and sniff of the air. Her eyes were huge under her bangs, not blinking at all and then blinking many times in rapid succession, as if they were seeing nothing and then many things all at once. Where were her prized new specs? Somewhere not on her face.

"Preeti," I said, "where are your specs?"

"We can't talk to her until a parent or guardian is present," the officer standing near Preeti said.

"Maybe *you* can't," I told him.

The officer made a frustrated noise, but he didn't try to stop me as I passed by him. Preeti was worrying at the strip of birch bark in her hands, shredding it to bits. She must've heard me approach, but she didn't glance up until I was right next to her. She looked like she might run at the sight of me.

"It's you," she said in a small miserable voice.

"It's me," I agreed. "I'm here now. Everything's okay." I hoisted the baby over to one hip so that I had a free hand, which I lifted. "Your bangs. Can I . . . ?"

After a moment's consideration, Preeti nodded, and I brushed her bangs from her eyes. A shiver ran through her, and she dropped her hand from the tree.

"You did good," I told her. "It was scary. You were brave."

It was what I would've wanted someone to say to me if I were a girl in such a situation. Hell, it was what I wanted someone to say to me right now, as a woman in the situation I'm in, what I wanted someone to say to me all the time.

"And you're still being brave now," Silas said.

He nodded at her in that way he had, like he could nod your agreement out of you, convince your chin to bob along with his. I hated when he did this to me. But on Preeti, it worked. She began nodding, too, in small quick dips.

"What happened?" I asked her.

"She heard a noise at the back of the house," Silas said. "Right, Preeti?"

"I heard a noise," Preeti repeated. "I was in the kitchen."

"Folks," the officer called out, "if we could wait until a parent or guardian is present . . ."

But now that Preeti had started talking, it seemed she wasn't going to stop. "I thought it was Nova," the girl said. "Sometimes she doesn't want to go down for her nap? So I called out, 'Who's being naughty?' Not in a mean way. Just joking." She glanced at me. "I wouldn't *really* call her naughty."

"I know you wouldn't," I said.

"That's when I heard the footsteps. Nova she doesn't . . . I mean, she doesn't even walk. That's when I knew someone else was in the house." Her eyes wheeled to Silas. He was still feeding her his nods. "So I said, 'Who's there?' And when no one answered, I called Emergency. The operator said to get out of the house, but—"

"But Nova," I said, my stomach lurching. Nova had been in the back of the house *with the intruder*. The baby squawked as if to emphasize this very fact, but it was just to protest that I was holding her too tightly.

"I couldn't leave her," Preeti said.

"And you didn't," Silas said. "You went and got her. And the intruder ran."

"Down the hall."

The girl was back at the tree again. She pulled another strip from its trunk, this one long and curling. I glanced at the window to see if the neighbors were witnessing her torture of their tree. I waved, feeling ridiculous; they stepped back and drew the curtains.

"You saw him, then?" I asked Preeti. "In the hall? Who was he?"

"Maybe we shouldn't get into this right now," Silas said.

"Yes. Please stop talking to her," the officer stressed.

"I didn't," she said. "See anything. Not really. A shadow. I mean, I couldn't say." Her voice was flat and distant, like someone talking in their sleep. *Shock*, I thought. *This is what shock sounds like.*

"And then she called me," Silas said. "Right, Preeti? I got here just before Emergency did. The intruder was long gone."

The intruder. Something occurred to me then, a possibility that opened up beneath me like the floor falling out, like my bones disappearing within my body, like the monster exhaling its hot blood-breath over my face. *Him.* The intruder could be him. My murderer. And then a second thing occurred to me, worse still.

"He ran down the hall," I repeated. "That's what you said?"

Preeti murmured a barely audible yes.

"That means he was in Nova's room."

"We don't know that," Silas said.

"What would he be doing with her?"

Silas looked momentarily alarmed. "That's . . . no. The baby's fine. Look."

"People steal babies," I said.

"Folks," the officer interjected again.

At the same time Preeti said, "I don't think she was stealing Nova."

It took a beat for me to hear what the girl had said. I turned on her, and she bumped back against the tree.

"*She?*" I repeated.

"Lou." Silas touched my arm.

"She said 'she,'" I told him. "You said 'she,'" I said to Preeti. "Was it a woman you saw? Running down the hall, could it have been a woman?"

"I don't . . . I don't really . . ." Preeti mumbled.

"Let's slow down," Silas said.

"A woman who looks a little bit like me?"

The girl stared at me, her eyes young and naked without the sheen of her specs covering them. Slowly, she began nodding again. "Yes," she finally said. "I think it was a woman." She turned to the officer. "It was a woman."

I would've raised my other hand to my mouth to cover it, but I was still holding the baby, so instead I buried my face in the top of her head.

"Lou?" I felt Silas's hand on my shoulder. "What's going on?"

I raised my head and found that he, that all of them, were watching me intently, worriedly.

"The intruder," I told him. "I know who it is."

THAT EVENING, after everyone had gone, I walked through the rooms of my house, my home. It was Fern who had run through these same rooms hours before: down the hall, into the bedroom, and out the window. The police officers had listened patiently, as I'd explained how I'd had a friend who'd suddenly disappeared, how this same friend had known I'd be out of the house at the support group we both belonged to, and how she had been absent from this meeting herself. I could tell they didn't believe me; it was in the set corners of their mouths, the quick glances they couldn't help but throw to one another. To not be believed was nothing new, nothing new. Maybe they would've believed me if I could've explained *why* Fern had broken into my house, if I could've pointed to some act she was committing, some object she was stealing.

But I couldn't tell them what she'd stolen. I didn't even know how she'd known it was there. After everyone left, I slid open the closet door. The closet floor empty. My green canvas bag gone.

I stood in front of the closet, the bag missing, the baby in my arms. Fern had stood here, too. Right here where I was standing. I gazed down at Nova, and she gazed back up at me. She reached out at the space above my shoulder, where my long hair used to fall.

"Nova," I said, bouncing her. "Nova, Nova."

And there came a small sound from the small person in my arms. My rib cage expanded with surprise and wonder, expanded with love, until I thought it would crack open and could not rightly be called a cage anymore.

I said it again, and again Nova made the sound.

I almost called out to Silas, but then I didn't. I wanted to keep it to myself, for an evening, for now. Tomorrow I would tell him that the baby had learned her own name.

STAYING

I'VE ALWAYS BEEN GOOD AT STAYING. THAT'S WHAT I am good at.

I sit through the movie credits, all the way to the last makeup artist and key grip. I think about how if I were them, I'd want at least one person to have seen my name.

I'm always the last guest at the party. In fact, I'm known among friends and acquaintances for helping out with the dishes, for drying the plates in soft circles, for asking where the glasses go. I sit with the family dog and stroke her ears, until she gets tired of me and crosses the room to her bed.

I've always been like that. When I was a girl, I wanted to stay home. I couldn't go to sleepovers. I'd cry and cry and one of my dads would have to be called to collect me, bleary-eyed and trying not to be cross, his coat over his pajamas.

A child crying to come home from a sleepover, this is not an unusual story. But I wasn't crying because my friend's house smelled funny or because I couldn't fall asleep in someone else's bed. I cried because I was convinced that my parents would forget about me, that after a night away their love would fade and wisp. I pictured myself returning home the next day, and the two of them looking up and saying to each other, "Who is that knocking on our door?"

17

"SOMETIMES I JUST SIT IN HERE AND WATCH," JAS-
mine told me, "if I'm not feeling like, you know, *action*."

Here was the front stoop of an apartment building, somewhere
within the world of *Early Evening*. Stoop, no, it was a culvert really,
a narrow hidey-hole set into a block of apartments, made narrower
still by the stone columns on either side of the door. To me, it
looked like a good place to find oneself trapped, but Jazz said she
used it as a hiding spot. She settled herself easily, cross-legged, on
the ground behind one of the columns. I took a seat across from
her, behind the other column.

She didn't look like Jasmine in here. She looked like Angela,
but then so did I. We were both wearing our Angela skins, cleav-
age rolling out in front of us, ponytails streaming behind. If the

avatar was meant to make me feel tough, it didn't. I felt as thin as a layer of paint on the side of a building, someone else's idea of a girl action hero, a sketch easily erased.

"They've fixed it up around here," I said, tracing the green and gold clover pattern laid into the step upon which we sat.

"Yeah, they've got coders for days now. Just wait until you get stabbed. They've coded all the way down to the bones." Jazz scratched the inside of her spindly Angela arm as if to demonstrate, but her fingernails didn't leave marks. "And look at this." She leaned toward me, tapping an earlobe; it was punched through with a set of tiny holes.

"Oh, hey. Pierced ears."

"Angela's idea. Verisimilitude, she says."

"I'm surprised she knows the word."

Jazz gave me a wry look. "*Monetize* is the word. You can buy hoops for these." She tapped the piercings again. "But no one does that, because the Edwards will just grab you by them and yank them out."

"And let me guess: The blood dries on your neck?"

Jazz snorted. "It does."

"It's easy to make fun of Angela," Jazz said after a moment. "She's different from how she looks."

I fidgeted against the rise of shame and defensiveness. "And now we all look like her," I said lightly.

Out on the street, Angelas passed by our hiding spot with quick steps and nervous glances over their shoulders. Every once in a while an Edward loped past, knife at the ready. How was this entertainment? How was this a game? Who would enter this world to kill or be killed? To stab or to run? I had, though. I'd come in here.

Back in my house, I'd lay on my bed with my eyes closed, until a snore thin as smoke rose from Silas's side of the mattress. Then I'd slid out from under the covers and padded to the kitchen pantry, lifting the helm and gloves off their shelf slowly so as not to make the slightest scrape. I'd put them on. I'd ported in.

Given the late hour, there were a surprising number of players in *Early Evening*. I'd gone to the park first. I'd stood at the edge of the grass, the bench where Angela had been murdered a slatted shadow on the lawn, the running trail behind it disappearing into the trees. This was where Angela had seen Fern. I knew it was where I should go and look, but I couldn't bring myself to step into the park, not one foot. Instead I'd walked the city blocks, evading the Edwards and their knives, following the Angelas, like I was an Edward myself. I'd clicked on every head, every profile, looking for Fern's name. One of my clicks had brought Jasmine's name floating above an Angela's head in a spiky aura.

"Funny finding you here," I said.

"Not so funny," Jasmine replied. "I'm in here a lot."

Jazz was different in the game. It wasn't just that she was wearing the Angela skin—her short plump frame stretched long, her streaky white hair spun auburn, her round bespectacled face recast in Angela's small goosey features. It wasn't just how she looked, though; it was how she carried herself, how she cocked her head like she was sizing things up, how she clipped her sentences instead of letting them collapse, how she rolled her shoulders and cracked her knuckles and kept a steady eye on the road. You can't ask a person if they've changed, though. You can't ask them that. So instead, I said, "Are your nightmares . . . ? I mean, how are they?"

"How are my nightmares?" she repeated. "Huh. They're doing well. The oldest nightmare is applying to colleges. The little one joined a T-ball league."

I flushed. "Sorry. That was stupid."

"No, no," she said. "You can ask. They're . . . fewer."

"Because you play the game?"

She gazed out at the street, shrugged. "The game. Group. Time. Who knows?"

"You like it in here, though."

"Like? I don't know about like. It calms me." She pulled her mouth to one side and shrugged. "It probably shouldn't. But it does. And I've learned not to question the things that help me along."

"Do you ever see any of the others in here?"

Jazz leaned back against the building. "Only Angela. Amid her adoring crowd."

"There are lots of them? Her fans?"

"Dozens."

"My babysitter's one."

"I haven't seen Fern, though. That's what you're asking, right?"

"I . . . yeah. I need to talk to her."

Jazz began to say something more, but then stopped and lifted a finger to her lips. She drew back into the shadows of the entryway and gestured for me to do the same. A second later, an Edward passed by, right by the doorway, knife brandished. If he turned his head, he'd see us there, poorly hidden in the shadows, only a breath away.

Unlike the Angela skin, which was detailed down to the earring holes, the Edward Early skin was not a replica of the actual man. The game's serial killer had the same lanky build and dark-lashed eyes as the real Early did, but the designers had muscled his arms and squared his jaw. I guess he was supposed to look scarier that way. I thought he was scarier the way he really looked, like someone you might meet, like anyone.

From her side of the stoop, Jasmine lifted two more fingers to join the one at her lips. She lowered each of them in turn, counting down. When she was done, Edward Early was gone.

"So you're in here looking for Fern," she prompted.

"She moved out of her apartment. She won't answer my messages. And this afternoon, she broke into my house while we were at group."

Jazz whistled through her front teeth.

"I know. It's . . ." But I didn't know what it was.

"Did you two have a fight?"

"It's not that."

"An affair?"

"Not that, either." I tipped my head up. There was a crack veining through the alcove's ceiling, like one little shake and the whole building might crumble down upon us. "Fern found out something about me. And now she won't talk to me."

"That must hurt," Jazz said.

I was about to protest that I wasn't hurt; I had questions; that was all. But I ended up saying, "I thought she was my friend."

"And Angela saw her in here, so now you're looking for her here. I assume you tried the park."

"I went by it. I . . . couldn't go in."

Before I could explain how I knew it didn't make any sense, how I'd been to the actual park, in real life, how I knew this was only a game, before I could say any of that, an Edward swung around my column. His eyes were gleaming; his knife was raised. When you looked at the blade from this angle, raised above you, it didn't look like a blade at all, but like a line coming to a point. I opened my mouth.

But before I could scream, Jazz pushed herself up off the tile with a sigh. She reached over my head to grab the Edward's wrist, the one with the knife, and twisted it. His arm made a cracking sound. He cried out in surprise and dropped the knife. Jazz reached down with her other hand and caught the blade in midair. She let go of his wrist, and took a handful of his hair instead, yanking up on his head and exposing his neck. She drew the knife across his throat. Blood sprayed the entryway and sheeted down his collar. His eyes flashed with fear and then they emptied of all shine, like coins flipped in the air and fallen. Jazz spread her arms and opened her hands, dropping what she held. The knife bounced out into the street; the Edward collapsed in a heap at her feet. Dead.

She turned to me, brushing her hands on her cargo pants, though her hands were the only clean parts of her. The rest of her was dappled in blood.

"Jazz," I breathed. "Jesus."

"You want me to come to the park with you?"

JAZZ DISPATCHED Early after Early on our way to the park. She killed them efficiently, perfunctorily. As their bodies dropped, I imagined the players within them, boys and men on the other side of reality, cursing and tossing their helms to the floor. After much murder, we finally reached the edge of the park. The running trail curled out ahead of us, pale gray in the moonlight, as if made of crushed shells or bones. I took a breath, set my shoulders, and stepped onto the path.

As we walked, the gravel crunched beneath our feet, another new effect coded in. On our way here, Jazz had kicked one of the Edwards in the face, and a tooth had flown from his mouth and grazed my cheek. I'd found it on the ground and picked it up, examined its divots and prongs. Such detailed violence.

We crossed the lawns of the park, alone. But just as we entered the woods, an Edward stepped out from behind a tree. He began to lift his knife, and Jazz snatched it away, punching it into his belly. He dropped. After a moment, his corpse flickered out. He'd stepped onto the path in front of us; that had been his mistake. He should've waited until we'd gone by and stepped out behind us, like Edward Early had done to me. Or someone had done to me.

When I saw the hill up ahead, the hill where he'd stabbed me, I began to run toward it. I felt prickles in my palms and cheeks. My gloves and helm glitching out, that was my first thought, but no, it was only me, only my fear. I ran up the hill. I wasn't on this hill, wasn't in these woods, I told myself as I ran. I was a woman in her kitchen, in her pantry, lifting her knees high, running in place. I collapsed at the top.

Jazz reached the top, too. She bent over, hands on her knees, to catch her breath.

"She's not here," I said.

"We could wait," Jazz offered.

So we waited. I crouched by a tree and Jazz paced.

"Strangers used to mistake me for her," I said into the silence, "for Fern. After her murder, before mine."

Jazz paused her pacing, shrugged. "I've never noticed a resemblance."

"Back then I thought, what if he murders me next? What if he murders me because I look like her?"

"You think that's what happened?"

I considered it. Even if it wasn't Edward Early who murdered me, that could be how it'd happened—a copycat killer, a copycat victim.

"No," I decided softly. "I think it was just bad luck."

"Bad luck." Jazz snorted. "You know what I used to think? When I first saw those girls in the news, those smiling pictures? I thought, *Thank goodness you're too old for that now. Thank goodness you're not some pretty young thing.*"

"Thank you for coming with me," I said.

"Made my night interesting."

I stood. "We can go now."

"You don't want to wait a little longer?"

"I don't think she's coming. When Angela said she saw Fern here, I thought . . ."

"You thought what?"

"No. Nothing. I was wrong."

"Come on. What did you think?"

"I thought she was waiting here for me."

UNHAPPINESS

IT IS HARD TO DESCRIBE THE WAY I FELT, BUT I'LL TRY.

I felt like the echo instead of the sound. I felt like the chaff instead of the stem, the dirt instead of the root. I felt sodden. I felt mucked. I felt like I was peering over my own shoulder. I felt nothing much.

The sadness was one thing. I could move through it. Sleep, I could do that easily enough, hours and hours of it, my dreams mired, muddy, forgotten. Waking, I could manage that, too. I could rise and stand under the stream of the shower. I could tug the comb through the knots of my wet hair. I could put my arms into the sleeves of a shirt, first one, then the other. I could put food into my mouth, could chew, could swallow. I could lift that same mouth when Silas paused to kiss me goodbye. I could offer up my lips.

And the baby. I could nurse the baby, I could change the baby, I could hold the baby, I could rock the baby. I could not feel the baby.

The sadness was one thing, but the fear was another. I could do nothing with it, and it would not leave me.

The fear was nameless, so I gave it names. I would step on the baby. I would suffocate the baby. I would drop the baby. I would leave the baby.

The fear was shapeless, so I gave it shapes. It was a lake, and I was under its water. It was a floor, and I was under its boards. It was a mouth, and I was under its tongue.

No one likes to hear about unhappiness. Even I don't like to hear about my own unhappiness. I'll just say one last thing: I got out from under it. I took one step, then another, then another.

I'll say one more thing: I want to live.

18

WHEN I WOKE THE NEXT MORNING, GROGGY AFTER my night in the game, Silas was already up and calm, so calm. He had that look like he was determined to affix this same calm to me, whether by sheer will or hot-glue gun. I had barely sat up in bed but he had a coffee in his hand and a smile on his face, a smile as placid as a wading pool, as placid as a sand dune, as placid as a petting zoo. He'd taken the day off from work, he announced. We could take Nova somewhere, the gardens, the playground, the zoo.

I fumbled with my screen. Its buzzing was what had woken me. It buzzed even now, in my hand, a message from Lacey:

Come over

And again.

New evidence

Come now

Silas sat on the edge of the bed. "Who's that?"

I smiled regretfully, making my best guess at the appropriate angle my lips should take. "Javi."

Silas frowned. "No zoo?"

"Everyone's calling out sick. I have to go in and cover. I'm sorry."

He took a breath, forced a smile onto his own face. "Go help Javi. We'll say hi to the monkeys for you."

LACEY ANSWERED THE DOOR WITH "You're not going to like this."

"But you do?" I said. Her crimson mouth was like a candy, half sour, half sweet.

"Me? No. But then I don't like anything."

She stepped aside, and I entered the house, following her into the dining room where Tatum sat across from Brad, who was raking the curls out of his beard.

"Oh, *Louise*! You're *here*!" Tatum cried out.

"Where's Thistle?" I asked.

"She's at *school*!" Tatum said the word as if it were a tragedy.

I took a free hammock, and the Luminols and I stared around at one another for a long, awkward moment, until I said, "Whatever it is, you can tell me. I'm ready."

This was a lie. I'd been following the signs since I'd arrived: Lacey's smug anticipation, Tatum's desperate cheer, and Brad's downcast eyes. Whatever this was, it was going to be bad.

"I'm sorry." Brad bowed his head, revealing the sparse hair on its crown.

He brought his fingers to his screen, gathering up something and tossing it onto the live wall. It was a bank statement, Silas's and my bank statement to be precise, the record of a withdrawal for ten thousand dollars to be preciser. I hadn't looked at the account since my murder.

"So he withdrew some money, so what?" I said. But it was half our money. And I hadn't known. He hadn't told me, not that he'd done it, not what it was for.

"Look at the date," Lacey said.

"That's not the date of my murder," I shot back.

It wasn't. It was three days later, the day my body was found.

"Why do you think he'd need a chunk of money like that?" Lacey asked. She gave me a keen look, waiting for me to arrive at the answer she clearly already had in mind.

"Lots of reasons," I said. "Maybe he hired a private detective to find me. Maybe he offered a reward for my safe return."

"Or maybe he was going to make a run for it," Lacey said.

"Or maybe he paid someone to kill you," Tatum said with chilling simplicity.

"It was for a private detective," I insisted. "Or a reward."

"Did he ever tell you about a detective? About a reward?" Lacey asked.

I looked away. She knew he hadn't.

"Because we've been through all the public documents, all the news stories, and there's nothing about either of those things."

"How'd you even get this?" I said.

"Brad has a friend."

"I'm so sorry," Brad murmured again. He combed his fingers through his beard, shredding the fat curls.

"You're friends with a detective?"

"A file clerk."

"And they gave you this? My private bank statement."

"She could lose her job, it's true." Brad's eyes were wetly frightened. "She risked it because she's worried about you."

"Worried about me? I don't even *know* her," I said.

"You know *me*," Lacey said. "So trust *me*."

"Lace," Tatum murmured.

"What? I don't get why she's being so stubborn."

"You don't get why I'm not immediately agreeing my husband murdered me?"

"Yeah. I don't get it." She swung her hammock toward mine, catching herself on her toes. "Because you could be living with a murderer. You could be murdered all over again."

"Then why am I still alive? Why hasn't he murdered me already?"

"Maybe he's going to."

"I sleep right next to him. He could do it anytime."

"And you find that reassuring?"

"It's not just the money, dear," Tatum said quietly.

"What?" I said. "What else?"

Tatum looked to Lacey who looked to Brad who nodded. Lacey

turned back to me, and she didn't look so smug anymore. "Brad's friend, the file clerk, she said that before the replication commission got involved, before they caught Early, before he confessed, before all of that, the detectives were sure it was Silas who'd killed you."

"Because it's always the husband," I said. "That's who they always suspect."

"No. Because they thought he was lying."

"About what?"

"They don't know," Lacey said.

"Well, that's ironclad."

"But they all had the same feeling after they questioned him. Every last detective was convinced he was lying about your murder."

IF I HAD BEEN A BETTER WIFE, I'd have had faith. I'd have had love, unquestioning, boundless. A better wife would've held firm to the conviction that her husband would never have hurt her, never laid a finger, never harmed a hair. Me? What did I do? I went home and immediately started searching through all of Silas's things.

Silas was still at the zoo with Nova, and I was supposedly still at work. I kept track of his whereabouts through a series of cheery messages that I pretended I was sending between clients. Was this how people covered up their affairs? Step into the other room and slap your face with a waxy smile and a bright bit of bravado?

I checked our bank account first, half hoping the statement Brad had shown me was a mistake. But the ten thousand was really missing, and that was no small amount. Half of our savings, that's what that was. Silas and I both had access to the account. He must've known I'd see the missing money at some point. He would have a story ready. *An explanation*, I corrected myself. *A reasonable explanation.*

That the money hadn't been replaced disproved Lacey's theory at least. It couldn't have been money to flee, because Silas was still here, and the money was still missing. If he'd changed his mind about running, he would've put it back. A killer for hire, that's what Tatum had proposed. And that would square with what Edward Early had told me. If he hadn't killed me, maybe a hit man had and, to cover his tracks, had made it look like I was one of Early's victims.

I kept on searching, feeling like an intruder in my own house. There was nothing hidden among Silas's socks or sweaters, nothing under the mattress, nothing on the top shelf of the pantry. No love letters to another woman. No passport under a false name. No knife. I hadn't really thought there'd be a knife. Still, I'd prodded the stack of folded sweaters with tentative fingers, alert for the cold tooth of a blade.

Silas sent another message. He and Nova had just finished with the zoo. They'd be home in twenty minutes.

I was home now too, I sent back. Could he pick up some takeout on the way? my despicable self asked, buying me a little more time.

Really? Because the baby was fussy.

Please. My shift was long. I was starving. There was nothing in the fridge.

And he agreed because he's good to me, because he feeds me,

because he loves me. And I was terrible for those exact same reasons.

How well can you know someone? Really know someone? That is one of the questions of marriage. *The* question maybe. Some people argue that attraction requires *not* knowing someone, requires the blank spaces, the dark corners, the soft focus on the lens. Mystery is essential, they say. Mystery. Well, I was in one of those right now, and I couldn't say that I liked it very much.

How well do you know yourself? That is the other question of marriage. How do you know you'll stay faithful? Interested? Loving? How do you know you'll stay in love? And even if you stay all of those things, how do you know you won't one day fling out an arm and shatter something irreplaceable? And the truth is, you probably will do that, so then the question becomes, How good are you with a tube of glue?

I tried getting into Silas's mail, but he had his accounts on ocular sign-in, and I did not have his eyes.

I had just about given up when I remembered the live wall. I could dig into its guts. I'd learned how to do this during my bad old days, the months after Nova's birth, when I needed to clear my hours and hours playing the hawk game instead of tending the baby. I scanned the logs and found the usual domestic detritus— bills paid and movies streamed and calls thrown up onto the live wall. There were the hours I'd been playing *Early Evening* the night before. There was the call I'd made to Odd when Nova had a fever.

The call just above it, I at first mistook for one of my own. But then my eye snagged on another similar call taken a few weeks earlier. Once I knew what I was looking for, I spotted more of them. A call on a Wednesday morning, when I had a shift at the Room. Another on the Saturday when Fern and I had visited Edward Early. And more. There were more. *Proof,* I thought as I found another one. And again: *Proof.* But of what, I didn't know.

Just then came the sound I'd been listening for: the decisive snick of an auto door on the street out front. Next would be the turn of the front door bolt, the rustle of takeout bags, and my husband's footsteps down the hall. I had only seconds, but now I knew where to look.

I shouted out the date of my murder.

At first, nothing happened. Then the list of data began to scroll backward through the weeks and months, frustratingly slowly at first, then faster, a blur, finally coming to a halt on that day. On the day of my murder, Silas, frantic, pacing, searching through the house, must have routed all his calls to the live wall, because there they all were, the time stamps amassing as he made more and more calls: to Javi; to my friends, women I'd mostly lost touch with after Nova's birth; and finally, one call to Odd; and then one to Emergency. All of this matched what Silas had told me: he had called around to find me and, when he couldn't, had reported me missing.

Behind me, back through the halls of our house, the bolt turned, the door opened, and Silas called out, "Wheeze?"

That's when I saw it, what I'd been looking for, the name I'd seen elsewhere, time and again, in the list of calls: Gert.

Gert had been calling Silas every week. Every week since my murder.

My first thought was that she'd been reporting on me, on my recovery, and my cheeks had burned with outrage. But the calls went back too far for it to be that. There were calls before the survivors' group had ever met, before I'd arrived home from the hospital, before the replication commission had even brought me back. And here was the time stamp for the first call, the call where Silas and Gert's conversation had begun. It wasn't on the day of my murder; it was on the day after. Two days after that a police dog would find my body curled in a rain ditch by the side of the road.

Gert had called Silas when I was still missing, before my body was even found, which seemed to suggest that she already knew I was dead.

MURDER MYSTERY

THE NEWSFEED FED US. IT FED US THE MURDERED women, the lurid headlines, the wild speculations, the touching profiles.

Angela's murder, the first of the bunch, was a shock, an "in this quiet town," a "How could this happen here?" Reporters loved describing her long hair, her torn throat, against the backdrop of trees. The fairy-tale comparisons wrote themselves. The empty pair of shoes barely got a mention.

When Fern was found in the mall parking lot, the feed ran picture after picture of her. It was the same picture, in fact; they just ran it over and over again. You could practically hear them say it: *So pretty! What a shame!* Less of a shame if she'd been plain, I suppose.

Jasmine's death made three, the number of murders it takes to qualify as a serial killing. The reporters had noticed the shoes by then, a signature, a calling card, a promise for more murders. The articles began to include sidebars with safety tips: *How to find a walking buddy! Beware the ponytail, a.k.a. the attacker's handle! Five everyday purse items you can turn into weapons!*

How does a moment of curiosity become an obsession, the lone seed become a field of weeds, the single germ become a fever? By the time Lacey was discovered, spinning on the merry-go-round, I had become a consumer of these murders, an avid follower, a fan. I scoured the feed every day, multiple times a day, reading all the way down the curling tail of reader comments. My brain was an evidence catalog, a matrix of details and clues and what-ifs. If only Angela hadn't gone to the park at night . . . If only Fern hadn't been so pretty . . . If only Jasmine hadn't worn those shoes . . . I turned the women's decisions around and around in my head, as if I could make different ones, as if my attention, my keen attention, could cause everything to turn out differently, as if I could save them myself.

19

WHAT DID I DO?

What would you have done?

Me? I ran.

Not like that. Not straight past Silas and out the front door. First, I turned off the live wall. Then I turned off the expression on my face. I heard Silas come into the bedroom behind me. He said my name again, now with a note of laughter and frustration because I hadn't responded to his earlier calls. *Turn around*, I told the woman who was me, *turn around and smile.*

I watched myself from deep inside myself. I was surprised by how easy it was to be her. It was like reaching up to the highest shelf, taking down a great glass serving bowl, and turning around with it clasped carefully between your hands. I turned. I smiled. I walked to my husband. And I kissed him. I kissed his mouth.

I took Nova from his arms, but I didn't look at her too closely, because I knew I couldn't while keeping the smile on my face. To the kitchen we went! I set my child in her high chair, lifted the takeout bag from my husband's hand, and busied myself with arranging the many containers on the countertop. The whole time I was talking to Silas; I sang out my half of a bright conversation, asked the thoughtful follow-up question, delivered the inside joke. I remember not a single word of it. I ate some mouthfuls of the food I'd asked him to bring me, the requisite number of mouthfuls. I don't remember the taste. I do, however, remember the chewing because I told myself, *You are chewing. Chew. You must chew now and swallow.* I don't remember the excuse I used to get out of the house. When I came back to myself, I was in an auto a mile away, and that other woman, that smiling wife, was now gone, disappeared, had run away over the hills. I bid her farewell. She'd been there when I needed her, and I was grateful.

I programmed the auto to go to Odd's house. It was nearly four hours to Rockport. When I got there, I'd tell him everything. He was my parent. He felt about me how I felt about Nova.

Nova. I'd left her with Silas, I realized with a lurch. What kind of mother does that? But it was okay, I soothed myself. It was okay. Silas would never hurt Nova; if I knew one thing, I knew that.

I'd keep going. I'd go to Odd. I could trust him, if not to believe me, then to listen. From there, I could figure out what to do next.

And that's what I would have done, I suppose, if my screen

hadn't buzzed once more, buzzed again. I opened the message without a thought, and an embossed invitation floated up from the
screen, the kind you get for a wedding, envelopes unfolding other
envelopes, like a queen in her many wrappers. The outermost envelope had been pressed with a dab of wax that made a little
cracking sound when it opened. The wickedest calligraphy appeared on the paper inside, fecund loops and slashed serifs. The
message read:

You have been formally invited to
The Evening Is Ours
Location: Early Evening
Time: Now

The invitation folded itself back up, reaffixing the wax seal,
which I could now see had been pressed with a woman's face. She
looked familiar, that woman. I peered closer. It took me a minute
to place her now that her face was cast not in metal but in red
wax. She was the knocker on the door into *Early Evening*. She was
the woman biting the ring. She didn't have a ring in her mouth now.
She had nothing in her mouth except her teeth. And she grinned
with all of them, ferociously.

My screen buzzed again, a message from Lacey to Jasmine and
me: Did you get it?

Jazz and I both replied yes.

From Lacey: You know it's from Angela

Is it? Jazz asked.

Who else? What is she up to this time?

Then a reply from Jazz: Not sure. Heading in

A minute later, Jazz again: Get in here now

My heart began to pound. I checked my route. My auto would pass by the Room on my way out of town. I had a helm and gloves there, my cubicle. It was late in the day. Javi would have gone home by now; everyone else would be with clients. I could slip in and out without anyone seeing me. I would look and then I would leave.

I changed the auto's destination to the strip mall, and ten minutes later, I was in the Room. As I'd predicted, the office was quiet, everyone tucked away in their cubicles, helms down, hands twitching gently. That's why I nearly collided with Sarai coming out of the kitchenette. She made a noise and danced back a step. Her eyes were bright, and she said my name in a conspiratorial whisper. I tried to move past her, but she turned eagerly.

"Are you going in?" she asked.

"That's right," I lied, hoping she wouldn't have looked too closely at the day's schedule. "I've got a client waiting."

"No, are you going *in*?"

"Yeah, I'm just—"

She smiled. "You don't have to lie. About a client."

"I'm not lying."

"I got the invitation, too."

She passed a hand over her face, and when she lowered it, she was baring her teeth. It took me a second to understand: she was imitating the door knocker, the woman on the wax seal. She dropped the face, her expression bright and blank again.

"We should get in there," she said. "Don't want to miss it!"

She hurried down the hall in the direction of her cubicle. I watched her go and then headed toward my own, fitted on my gloves, pulled down my helm, and ported in. And I shouted out in surprise.

Mr. Pemberton was sitting on the couch in my Room.

He jerked upright; he'd been lounging, feet up on an armrest. "Shit," he breathed.

"What are you doing in here?"

He stuttered a nonanswer.

Did we have an appointment? I tried to remember the schedule, the furthest thing from my mind. I wasn't even working today. Maybe we'd had an appointment tomorrow, and he'd gotten the days mixed up? Even so, a client shouldn't be able to enter my Room on their own.

"How did you even get in here?" I asked.

He wetted his lips. "I don't know. I just came in."

"You just *came in?*"

"I ported in, and then I was here."

"And you stayed?"

"I'm sorry." He raised his hands and got up from the couch. "I needed somewhere to think and . . . I'm so sorry. I'll leave now. I'll leave."

I took a deep breath, during which I reminded myself that he was a client. I also reminded myself how gracious he'd been after I'd grabbed his wrists, how he'd come back for another appointment, how he'd forgiven me, how we'd talked, how he'd listened to me talk.

"It's fine," I said. "A misunderstanding."

"A misunderstanding, yes. And I *will* go now. Thank you, Lou."

I opened my mouth, but he'd winked out before I could ask how he knew my name.

THE DOOR to *Early Evening* was ajar. The door knocker with the woman's face was no longer affixed to it, as if she'd grown metal arms and legs, pried herself from the wood, and walked off somewhere. I stepped through. The streets of *Early Evening* looked the same as they always did: darkened storefronts; security gates rattled closed; lit windows where a curtain might stir and a face peer out but no one would come to your aid. There up ahead was the intersection with Jazz's traffic light blinking its stop, stop, stop.

A duo of Angelas milled on the other side of the street; they were looking around, the same as I was. I wondered if one of them was Sarai, but when I clicked on their profiles, they were strangers. I waved to them anyway, and one waved back.

"Do you know what's going on?" I called across the road.

They conferred, then the one who'd waved motioned in the direction of the park. "I think it's this way."

"What is?" I began to ask, just as the other one shouted, "Watch out!"

By the time I turned around, it was already too late. The Edward was coming up on me, running full tilt. I raised my hands to cover my face and throat. I waited for the knife to pierce my gut instead, braced myself for the accompanying vibration that would send me back to the porch, back to the beginning of the game.

The pain didn't come.

Slowly, I lowered my hands, expecting to see the Edward standing there, grinning, waiting for me to drop my guard so that he could slash my throat after all. But the sidewalk in front of me was empty. I turned and spotted him farther down the street, still running. He'd blown past me and kept going. He took a sharp turn at the next block, the one with Jazz's traffic light, and disappeared from view. Where was he running? *Why* was he running?

The two Angelas were still across the street, whole and unharmed. They were staring after him, too.

More footsteps came up behind me, and an entire group of Angelas rounded the corner. They slowed when they saw me. One of them asked, "Which way did he go?"

I pointed and they headed in that direction.

"Did you see that?" one of the Angelas across the street called to me.

"See what?" I called back. There had been so much to see.

And the other said, "Those Angelas had knives."

I whipped back around. The group of Angelas was just now turning the corner, but I thought I saw a flash of silver in one of their hands. As soon as the thought crossed my mind—*knife*—my glove buzzed. I looked down at my own hand, or rather Angela's hand with its bright red manicure. A long serrated knife had appeared in my grip. I held the knife up, rotating the blade this way and that, gleaming under the streetlamps. When I turned to show my newfound weapon to the other Angelas, I saw they were now holding their own knives, staring at them in wonder.

"All right!" One of them laughed and the other shouted, "Let's go!"

They ran after the others. Behind me, another Angela ported in, stumbling onto the sidewalk. Her eyes widened at the sight of my knife, and then a knife appeared in her own hand. I beckoned to her, and we both started to run, catching up to the other two Angelas as they turned the corner.

The group chasing the lone Edward was no longer in sight, but it wasn't hard to guess where they'd gone. The park was up ahead. We kept on running. When the narrow city blocks opened up to the expanse of green, there they all were: Angela after Angela, brandishing knife after knife. And they were cutting down Edwards.

The Edwards were outnumbered by Angelas, at least five to one. What's more, the Edwards were now empty-handed, while the Angelas were armed. Most of the Angelas had formed small packs, like the one I'd seen earlier. A pack would surround an Edward, each Angela stepping in to take a turn swiping at him until he fell. When an Edward died, he didn't disappear back to the start of the game like usual. Instead, he lay there for a moment and then his eyes blinked back open, reawakening to this world of Angelas and their glittering knives.

"They can't reset," I said to the Angela who'd followed me here. "Look. They just stay there." The other two Angelas had joined the melee in the park, and I could no longer tell them apart from the rest.

The new Angela grabbed my arm, pointed, and whispered, "It's her."

I followed her finger. More Angelas were coming through the trees, rows and rows of them, dozens, scores. They marched out of the woods where I'd been murdered. An army of Angelas, that's what they were. They were arranged like an army, too, flanked around a single Angela at the front. I clicked on her and brought up her name. She was my Angela, the real Angela. Of course she was.

"Angela!" I called as they passed me. "Angela! Wait! It's Lou!"

But so many of us were calling out to her, she didn't even turn her head. The army of Angelas streamed behind her in hundreds, across the park and out into the city streets, Edwards fleeing before them.

"Lou?" One of the Angelas had broken off from the crowd, a trio behind her, their knives held loose at their sides. I clicked on her profile.

"Preeti?"

"Yeah. Hi."

"But I thought you didn't play these games."

"Oh, this isn't a game," said one of the others reverently. "It's an event."

"These are your friends?" I guessed.

"Say hi," she ordered the Angelas behind her, and they waved sheepish teen girl waves with their knife-free hands.

"Go on," she told them. "I'll catch up in a minute."

The Angela procession was still passing by us, and her friends rejoined the end of it. Preeti stayed with me, fidgeting with the pockets of her cargo pants.

Finally she looked up and burst out with "Are you *okay?*"

"You mean about the break-in?"

She nodded.

Not hardly, I wanted to say, but she was a child, so I said, "I'm okay. Are *you* okay? You were the one in the house."

Someone in the park screamed, louder and longer than the other screams. We both turned at the sound, but it was impossible to see who was screaming or why. When I turned back, Preeti was watching me. She opened her mouth, closed it again.

"What is it?" I said.

She fidgeted with her pockets, chewed the inside of her cheek.

"Preeti. What?"

"He said not to say anything."

"Who said?" I asked, and then it dawned on me, "*Silas* said?"

"He said it would only upset you, because you wouldn't remember." She squinted. "And you *don't* remember, do you?"

"Remember what?"

"Being in the house."

"What house?"

"*Your* house."

"My house?" I repeated. "I don't—"

"You were the one in the house," she said. "You were the intruder."

There it was again, the silver droplet of mercury running down my throat. And this time I'd swallowed it, and it spread across my stomach, my organs, my skin, until all of me had turned to metal, cold and hard and—

"Tell me," I said.

She shuffled her feet and balled her fists. "It was mostly like I said. I heard someone in the house, and I called Emergency. When I went to get Nova, someone ran down the hall. But I lied about not seeing them. I did see them. It was you."

Me, I told myself.

Not me.

Me.

"I didn't recognize you at first," Preeti went on, "because of the wig." She touched the ends of her hair, Angela's long hair. "But then you looked back. I called after you. But you just kept running. And I was scared again. I didn't understand why you'd come back without telling me. Or why you ran away. So I called Silas.

"He said you were confused because of, well, because of everything you've been through. He told me he was on his way. He said to call Emergency back, to tell them I'd made a mistake about the break-in. But it was too late. They were already pulling up to the house. So we decided I'd say I hadn't seen the person, I'd only heard them."

"Oh, Preeti," I breathed. And along with everything else I was feeling, I was so angry at Silas for asking this girl to lie.

"Then later, out on the lawn, when you said the intruder was a woman, a woman who looked like you, I thought you must have remembered after all. So I said, yes, that's who I saw, a woman who looked like you, because, well . . ." She shoved her hands into her pockets, turning them inside out and outside in again. "That *was* who I saw. I saw you."

. . .

AND THEN, SOMEHOW, I was out of the game and back in an auto on the road, Preeti's confession echoing in my head. It would take another two hours before I'd get to Odd's house. Too long. Too slow.

"Odd!" I cried out when he answered my call. "I'm coming to you."

But before he could tell me that I shouldn't come there, that he couldn't see me, which surely was what he was going to say, I heard someone in the background. I didn't even hear what words she said, just a snatch of sound, but that was all it took for me to recognize her voice.

Odd began talking louder and faster. I knew he was hoping to cover up the voice, hoping I hadn't heard it.

But I spoke over him. "Who was that?"

"What?" he said. "No one. The television."

"Odd," I said slowly.

"Louise," he breathed in defeat.

"What is Fern doing at your house?"

ODD

MOSTLY, ODD MAKES MY FAVORITE FOODS FROM when I was a kid. Lots of grilled cheese sandwiches, lots of packet noodles. We eat them together while we watch reruns of instructional shows where people carve furniture or blow glass, nothing with blood, nothing with tears. Breath is okay. Sometimes we watch cooking shows. Eating is okay, too.

Odd doesn't make me talk about what happened. Doesn't make me talk about that day or about all the days after that day. About Silas. About Nova. He doesn't make me talk about you. When you call sometimes, he hurries into the other room so I won't have to hear his side of the conversation.

I confessed to him last night, about how I'd been sneaking out, going back to see the baby, to see you. I explained it to him, how I needed to make sure she was okay, you were okay, that *you both* were okay. Because I was going to leave, I told him. And this time, I needed to make sure I left everything right, not like before. This time I was leaving, not running.

He didn't get angry at me, Odd didn't. He didn't try to talk me out of it, either. He was quiet for a minute, and then he said okay. I'm more grateful for that than for all the grill on all the cheese. He's my dad, and even if he doesn't understand me, he still loves me. He loves me still.

20

MY PLAN WAS TO SIT IN THE AUTO AND NOT THINK. But that didn't work. While the auto hummed the miles between East Lansing and Rockport, I sat and I thought. I thought about the day care worker who knew Nova was mine without my telling her, who'd assumed I was there to take her out for a midday walk. I thought about Gert calling Silas all those times, every week, even before my body was found. I thought about the missing money from our bank account, the $10,000 that had never reappeared. Finally, I thought about Nova reaching into the empty space above my shoulder, reaching for my long hair.

Odd hadn't answered my question: What was Fern doing at his house? Or I suppose he had in his way. "I'll explain when you get here. We'll see you soon," is what he'd said. *We.* He'd admitted he wasn't alone. He hadn't been alone for months; I now understood that.

The highways were empty. It was late and I was traveling in an unpopular direction. Every so often another auto would pass by, its headlights causing my shadow to spike up and then collapse back into me. My screen buzzed with one message from Silas, then another. I couldn't speak to him, not now. I let them go through.

It seemed like I'd never get to Odd's, but then there I was, the auto curling off the highway, through the Punnett squares of Rockport's downtown blocks, past the tufted fields of crops, and onto an unpaved road marked with a number, the road where Odd lived far away from everyone and everything, where no one would think to look.

The trees surrounding Odd's small house had already decided upon spring. They were budding green and singing with bugs. Odd was waiting on the top step of the porch, a bottle of beer resting against his foot. He had a second bottle for me and, always prepared, a bottle opener, which he tapped against his leg. He was alone.

When I stepped out of the auto, my legs nearly gave way. I'd been sitting too long, frozen in one position, and my legs had fallen asleep. I steadied myself on the side of the auto and waited for the blood to come back into my limbs. Around me, the bugs sang with their wings and their feet, and Odd waited for me on the porch.

I tried to peer past him through the screen door for movement inside the house, but the orange mosquito lamps glowed brighter than the dark rooms. There in that moment, I had never felt newer, not even when the doctors had woken me in the hospital and told me I'd just been born.

When I could manage walking, I went and sat on the step next to Odd. Neither of us moved to hug the other. Odd opened the second beer and handed it to me.

"You don't have to tell me," I said.

"No?" he asked.

"No. I already know."

"The babysitter?"

"She doesn't know what she saw. She thinks she saw me."

"Good." He nodded over his bottle. "Simpler."

"Fern's here?" I said, taking a sip of the beer. It tasted as green as the trees, or maybe that was only my tongue.

"She arrived a few days ago."

"Why?"

"The same reason as you, Lou."

I looked over at him. "Do you want to call me something else?" I said softly. "Maybe my middle name? Would that be easier for you?"

The mosquito lamps reflected in his specs, making his eyes look like lanterns, orb-like, golden, oracular. My heart was pounding. I didn't know if I wanted him to say no or to say yes. And then I did know: I wanted him to say no. That I was Lou, his Lou, had always been, would always be, his Lou, how he and Dad had named me together.

"Hey now," he said, "hey."

I was crying.

"She needed somewhere to go. And I took her in." He lifted an arm, and I folded into it. He rubbed my back in small circles, like how he did when I was little. Even though he'd never rubbed my back. Even though I was never little. "I'd take you in, too, if you needed it."

I lifted my face. "You would?"

"Of course I would. You're my daughter. You're both my daughter." He pulled back and smiled down at me. "But you, you're doing okay."

"I'm not."

"You are."

"I'm trying," I said with a sniff.

"You're doing okay, Lou."

"The world is mad," I said.

"Mad angry or mad crazy?"

"Mad both."

"Yep," he said. "Yep, it is. Should we go inside now?"

I looked at the screen door again. Now that my eyes had adjusted, I could make out a faint light all the way at the back of the house, where the kitchen was. "Maybe once I finish my beer?"

We sat in silence while I did that. I took deep pulls of my drink with long breaks in between, wanting to go inside, never wanting to go inside. Finally, I set my bottle down on the porch; its glass bottom made a hollow sound that seemed to encircle us, all of us, the house, the bugs in the trees.

"Wait," I said when he started to get up.

He paused.

"I'm scared."

He looked down at me. "Yep," he said again.

Yep.

"Okay." I stood. "I'm ready."

I followed him through the dark living room with its antique television and pilled couch, down the narrow hallway with the fingerprint smudges, and into the back of the house where there was a tiny kitchen filled with hanging plants, its counters tacky with old cooking grease, and a round red dining table at its center.

At that table sat Fern. She looked up at me with a mischievous smile, like she knew she'd behaved badly, but how could I be anything but pleased to see her?

The woman sitting across from Fern looked up at me, too, and I was staring into my own face. She was me.

She was not me.

She was her, my other me.

THE PLAN

I DIDN'T EXPECT ANYTHING. I DIDN'T WORK IT OUT beforehand, and I didn't think about what would happen after. So there. How's that for a sound plan?

It started that night when Javi found me sneaking into the office. The look on his face, I couldn't stand it. He'd caught me here in this vulnerable spot, caught me in my shame and despair. He had a look in his eye, a look that made me feel like I may have to go home and peel off all of my skin. I opened my mouth to explain how I'd needed to leave my house, and no I didn't know why, I only knew that I needed to leave, which meant I needed somewhere to go, so I'd come here to my Room. I didn't say any of that, though. I don't know why I said what I said instead. Maybe some corner of my brain remembered when Javi had shown up on my doorstep sure I'd been the latest victim. Because I told him I was being stalked by the serial killer. The story sailed from my mouth like a fleck of spit and landed on the floor between us.

Even though it was a lie, it felt like not a lie. It felt like a way to say the truth. For months I'd been stalked by some*thing*, if not by someone. I was perpetually on the edge of panic. I felt certain I was going to die. That's where it started, the lie, the lie that became you.

It ended that afternoon in the park, when I eased my feet out of my running shoes. Like I said, I hadn't planned any of it, hadn't planned to run away, hadn't thought about how it'd look after I did it. But there I was on the trail, toeing my foot out of one shoe and then the other.

It was a joke at first, a joke with myself, just to see what my sneakers would look like there on the path without my feet inside them. People were doing that with shoes during the time of the murders, a prank, a rotten prank. But then I was sliding my screen out of my pocket, too, and dropping it in the grass. And then I was running, running through the trees in my sock feet. And suddenly it wasn't a joke anymore.

I was running, but I wasn't being chased. And I wasn't chasing anything, either. I was running like you do when you're a child, with no purpose except to feel how your legs have been made in order to propel you forward.

The road was before me.

I reached it.

A woman, a stranger, stopped her auto for me. She stopped because she saw another woman shoeless, screenless, on the side of the road. It could've been her, after all. It could've been any of us.

She asked where my shoes were. I said they were back in the trees somewhere, that I'd left them when I ran.

I left them when I ran. I let her fill in the rest.

She told me to get in the auto. We rode in silence. She got out at her stop but left her credit running. She told me to take the auto anywhere, somewhere safe. So I took the auto here, to Odd.

Later on, I waited for the woman to come forward, to call the police, to go to the news, to say how she'd seen me, how she'd given me a ride. She hasn't done it yet. Maybe she never saw the news reports. Maybe she thinks she's protecting me. Or maybe they found her and explained to her how things were now, about what I'd done, and what they'd done to fix it.

Once I was gone, it was too hard to go back. There was the upset, the news stories, all the people volunteering to search for me. There was Silas. How could I begin to explain to Silas? There was Nova. Nova—I couldn't, I can't. Also, the truth was, the truth *is*, I didn't want to go back. I kept waiting to want to go back. The feeling never came.

I didn't know about you when I did what I did. I want you to know that. I didn't know that they'd do that. Make you. I didn't know they'd pretend to find my body. And then they'd make your body instead. Because there was no body. Or rather, my body is here. I'm still inside it. It's me.

21

"HEY, LOU," FERN SAID, EASY AS CAN BE.

"You've been avoiding me," I told her.

She smiled winningly and leaned back in her chair, putting one bare foot on the table and then the other.

"If you think *she's* been avoiding you, I can't imagine what you think *I've* been doing," said the woman with my face. And even though she wasn't me, I have to admit, it was the kind of thing I might say.

On the drive here, I'd prepared myself for meeting her, my other me, but then there was no preparing myself for meeting her. Meeting her was not like gazing at my own reflection in a mirror. It was not like watching a clip of myself on the newsfeed. It was nothing like having an identical twin. What was it like?

It was a little like having a song in my head and then hearing someone else begin to hum it. It was a little like going to a place I'd only seen in a photograph and finding the corner of the room where the camera had snapped the shot. It was a little like listening to Odd tell a story from my childhood and not knowing if I remembered the actual event or only his retelling of it. It was a little like all of these things. It was a lot like nothing else. I was her, and she was me. But I could see at a glance that we were not the same. And I didn't know how to account for that difference.

"Fern," Odd said with a pointed look at her bare feet, his clean tabletop.

"Sorry, Odd." She let her chair rock down and slipped her legs back under the table. She pushed out the chair across from her with a foot. "Take a seat?"

I was still in the doorway staring at my other me. Her mouth twitched and she shrugged one shoulder. I knew what she meant: this was all impossibly awkward.

"Does anyone want coffee?" Odd asked, and when no one answered, he said, "Well, I do," and moved to the counter to start making it.

"Lou," Fern said. "Sit down."

I took a seat at the little red kitchen table. I remembered staring down at this tabletop on the morning of Dad's funeral, at the scuff marks made over the years by our hastily pushed plates, and thinking that some of those scuffs had been made by the force of Dad's hands, thinking how he'd been here, and how he wasn't here now, but I was still here.

From across the table, my other me watched me silently. I wondered if she was remembering that same morning. I felt like I should be able to guess her thoughts, but honestly, I had no idea. Her hair was still long. The hair Nova had reached for. I touched my bare neck. I'd cut mine. She was dressed in some old clothes I kept at Odd's, a sweatshirt so worn that the cuffs were getting lacey and pants speckled with the paint Odd and I had used to give the porch a new coat three summers back. But then, she was the one who'd help paint the porch, whose elbows had worn out those sleeves. Everything that was mine was hers first, hers more.

She smiled at me, a crooked, uncertain smile. Was that how I smiled sometimes? It was not the smile I recognized from photos or the mirror. She extended her hand across the table and said, "It's good to meet you."

"No!" Fern cried out. "Don't shake hands!"

"What?" I said.

"Why not?" she said.

"The world will explode!" Fern replied.

My other me gave Fern a look, half exasperation, half amusement. "We're clones, not time travelers."

"Besides which," I said, "the world already exploded."

"Except it didn't," she replied in a small voice. "It kept on going."

"What did you *expect* would happen?" I asked her.

I didn't say it unkindly, but I did say it plainly. It seemed to me a fair enough question to ask, but her eyes dropped to her lap and Fern clicked her tongue and behind me the clink of Odd's coffee making paused.

"I didn't expect anything," she said, after a long moment. "I didn't work it out beforehand, and I didn't think about what would happen after. So there. How's that for a sound plan?"

And then she proceeded to tell me the story of how she'd faked her own murder, without meaning to fake her own murder.

She spoke in a lightly ironic voice, as if mocking herself for her own unwitting success, but when she'd finished she sat back and stared hard at the tabletop, and I could see how underneath it all, she was still stunned by what she'd done.

She finished with, "Or rather, my body is here. I'm still inside it. It's me."

And with that, she got up and walked from the room. From the front of the house, the screen door whined opened and closed.

"Should I . . . ? Or maybe you . . . ?" I said. *Go after her*, I meant.

"Leave her be," Odd said.

"Are you sure? Because I'd want someone to—"

"She's not you, Louise." He said it mildly. He'd turned back to the counter.

"She's not, you know," Fern said. And I remembered back in Bar None, the day we'd first become friends, the day I'd stolen her letter, how even then she'd referred to her former self as *my other me*.

"How could we be the same as we were, any of us, after what we've been through?" Fern went on. "That's what's so funny about Gert, about the replication commission, and all the rest of them. We're their cause, the victims they've saved. But we're not just that. We're not just what happened to us. We're people. We react to the world. We change."

"I don't think we're the same as we were," I said. I glanced down the hallway, where she'd disappeared. And I didn't say the rest: *I wouldn't have left them.*

"You figured it out," I said to Fern instead, "that she was alive."

"Impressed?" Fern tilted her head jauntily.

"How'd you do it?"

"Mind like a steel sieve." She tapped her temple. "Wait. Did I say sieve? I meant trap. Mind like a steel trap."

"Fern. How?"

"It was the Luminols, actually," she said. "When Lacey's mom said how it was your murder that convinced everyone to bring us back, I thought, *That's murder as marketing.* So I figured maybe it was really just that: Marketing. A story someone was telling. And if it was a story someone was telling, well, then maybe the murder was just part of the story, made up."

"You *guessed?*"

"But it was easy to guess." Fern looked where I just had, in the direction of the hall. "What she did, it was like something I might do."

"Why didn't you tell me?"

"But I *did* tell you," Fern said.

"You didn't. You left."

"But I left the cat."

"*That* was you telling me?" I clicked my tongue. "Naming your cat after me?"

"So there were two Lous. Clear as can be!" Fern drew herself up. "Really, I can't help it if you can't figure out a simple clue."

"You didn't answer any of my messages."

"Because I didn't think you should come here."

"Why not?"

"Because you'd judge her."

I opened my mouth to say that this wasn't true, but then I

closed it again because she was right. I didn't understand her, my other me. I didn't understand how she could leave her life. Leave them. Leave Silas. Leave *Nova*. She had carried her, had birthed her, had fed her from her body. She had done all the things I hadn't, all the things I'd wished I'd done so that I could feel like Nova's mother. And still she'd taken one step and then another and another and . . . no. It was unfathomable.

Odd came to the table and passed the mugs around. Neither of us had asked for coffee, but we sipped it just the same, and it was what it needed to be, bitter and hot.

"This one turned up a few days ago," Odd nodded at Fern. "Said she knew who was here. I told her she was mistaken. Then she started shouting over my shoulder into the house."

"What?" Fern said. "Too much?"

"Just a touch," Odd replied.

"Well, she heard me anyway. She stepped out in the hall behind him."

"How'd you know she was here?" I asked. "Another guess?"

"No guesses this time. Just some searching and then some blackmail."

"Blackmail!"

Fern shrugged. "First, I spent some time in *Early Evening*, sitting on the trail where you were murdered. Well, *weren't* murdered. Were and weren't. Whatever. I thought she might come back there."

"Angela saw you there."

"Yeah? Well, it was a bust. So then I blackmailed Gert."

"Gert knows," I said slowly. "She does, doesn't she?"

"You know Gert," Fern said, "terrifying in denim."

"She showed up here the day after Louise did," Odd explained. "It was quite a week for answering the door."

"How did she—?"

"Figure it out?" He shrugged. "She made Louise a deal. Stay away. Have a new life. In return, save four other women."

"Save four women. What did she mean?"

It was Fern who answered. "She meant us: Angela, Lacey, Jazz, and me. And you in a way."

"The young mother," I remembered.

"The sympathetic young mother," Fern agreed. "The Luminols were right about that. Gert could use you, your murder. The women with the lipstick throats. The celebrities. All of that was Gert, behind the scenes, stirring things up. And the replication commission, too."

"They faked my murder so they could bring back the rest of you."

"*Lou*," Fern groaned.

"No, of course. Not that." It was the same old story, that they cared about us, that they were saving us. How many times did I have to learn that it was really always about them? I tried again. "They faked my murder to save the replication commission."

They'd been in the middle of a scandal, the wealthy clients, the secret payments, the government oversight that had turned out to be, well, an oversight. And then the politician they'd brought back who'd turned out to be a rapist. There had been an outcry. There'd been talk of shutting down the entire commission. But then the commission had brought us back, saved five murdered women, and made themselves into heroes.

"Murder as marketing," I repeated.

"Everyone loves a dead woman," Fern said. "As long as she's the right kind of dead woman."

"But the searchers *found* me," I said. "My body. There was a body."

"Lou, come on," Fern said. "Gert literally works for a place that clones people. You don't think she can make a corpse?"

Horror ran through me. "You're saying she cloned me, another me, and then—"

"No," Odd said firmly. "A facsimile. A shell."

"An empty," Fern added.

I put my face in my hands. A copy of me with no one inside.

"Can you not . . . can we not call her that?" I asked.

They looked down at the tabletop.

"Silas knows, too," I said, not a question. "I found all these calls from Gert, before my body was even found. Gert must have told Silas the truth."

"*I* told Silas the truth," my other me said.

She was back, standing in the kitchen doorway. If she'd been crying, it didn't show. She retook her seat at the table across from me. Fern and Odd looked between the two of us, and it must have been stunning, eerie, to see the both of us facing each other, a living mirror.

"Stop that," she said to them.

"You told Silas?" I prompted.

"Gert didn't want me to. She said it was an unnecessary complication. Let him think I was murdered like everyone else did. It would be easier for him in the end, she said. But I didn't think so.

That it'd be easier to believe your wife had died in fear, died in pain. I thought he deserved the truth."

So many small things, so many of the things that had made Silas look suspicious, now made sense. The money. Silas had given it to her, her half of their savings, an even split. The detectives who thought Silas was lying about my murder, they were right; he was. *I'm glad you're back*, Silas had said to me, then, *No, let me amend that. I'm glad you're here.* This whole time, Silas *had* been hiding a secret, just not the secret I'd thought he'd been hiding.

"Do you regret it?" I asked her.

"Telling him? No."

"Hurting him, I mean."

"Of course I do."

"And Nova?"

"I left so I *wouldn't* hurt her." She said it in such a way that I could tell she'd said the same thing to herself many times before. "It's better if I go before she remembers me. Better for me to go, if I can't be sure I'll stay."

I thought back to those months after Nova's birth, the desperation mired with depression, the urge to run twinned with the inability to move. It was like a spell that had turned my body to stone but had left my fear untouched so that I'd calcified, a statue suffused with panic. I didn't know how she'd come through it, my other me, how she'd come through that feeling, that time. I only knew how I had. And I *had* come through it. I knew that now, too.

"I needed to leave," she said. "That's what I needed. What I still need. I didn't ever think I could leave. I didn't think I could be that person. But I *am* her now." She looked at me, and her eyes, which were my eyes, which were not my eyes, were steady and clear. "I'm not coming back."

"You have, though," I said. "Come back. To the day care. To the house. You've come back to see Nova. You were in her room."

"She wasn't supposed to do that," Odd said with a cluck of his tongue.

"Yeah," she agreed softly. "I told them I'd stay gone. For good. For Silas's sake, for Nova's. For yours. If people found out what Gert did, what we did, well . . ." She bit her lip, tilted her head. "Guess I'm not so good at keeping my promises."

It occurred to me in that moment that I should be scared of her. She was, after all, the actual murderer, her own and mine.

"You can't take away my life," I told her.

"I didn't come back to take your life," she said. "I gave up that life. I gave it up. I just needed to make sure that you wouldn't—" She broke off.

"That I wouldn't what?"

"That you wouldn't leave, like I did."

"I won't."

"I know," she murmured. "I know."

"We're not the same," I said.

She wasn't crying, but I knew my own face, and I knew how I looked when I was holding back tears.

"I'm going away," she said.

"Going?" I said. "Where?"

"I don't know. We're going to travel first."

"We?"

She glanced at Fern, who smiled back at her, a smile that didn't say *someday, someday soon*, a smile that said *yes, here, yes, now*.

"We'll find somewhere to stay for a while."

"It's what you want?" I asked her. "It's not because you're afraid?"

She lifted her chin. "It's what I want *and* I'm afraid."

I watched her, the woman with my face. Did she look afraid? Funny, I didn't know what fear looked like on my own face, though I'd felt it often enough. What I knew is that she wasn't me. And who could say why? Who could say why her this? And why me that? One of us wanted to go. One of us wanted to stay. One of us had carried Nova, had birthed her. One of us would be Nova's mother. I was Nova's mother.

"Go," I said. I laid my hands on the tabletop, flat on the red. The scuff marks were too faint for me to feel them beneath my palms, but they were there; I knew they were there. "You go and I'll stay here. I'll make sure she's okay. I'll love her for you. I'll love them both for you. And for me."

She reached across the table and I took her hands.

As I'd predicted, the world exploded.

As she'd predicted, the world didn't explode.

"Thank you," she said, and squeezed.

RETURNING

IT'S SO EARLY IT'S DARK WHEN FERN AND I LEAVE.
My hair is wet from the shower, my eyes squeaky from sleep. We
packed the car the night before. Fern's friend promised it had miles
left in it when she'd bought it off of him. I believe it has miles.

Fern slips around me, putting the last items in between the seats,
stowing them here and there, forgetting and then remembering
her jacket. Odd stands on the porch. He doesn't seem to know what
to do with his hands. He keeps moving them from his pockets to
the railing and back to his pockets again. When we finally pull
away, he'll have to figure out what to do with them. He'll lift one
of them and wave goodbye. That's what he'll do.

The sky is turning from black to blue now, the bugs changing
shifts with the birds. Fern comes out of the house with her jacket

bunched in her hand, shakes it above her head like a prize. I have a feeling in my chest, a feeling like I'm going to see the horizon.

Fern tosses me the keys, a twinkle in the air that I reach out and snatch. "You want to drive?" she says.

And I do.

22

WHEN THE AUTO FINALLY PULLED UP TO THE HOUSE, the lights were still on. Silas had waited up for me. Before I'd left Odd's, I'd answered the messages he'd sent to my screen. I'd told him where I was and what I now knew and that I was okay. And that I was coming home.

I found him in Nova's room, sitting on the floor, his back resting against her crib. Her night-light lit the bumpy bridge of his nose and his face, his familiar face.

"Hey, stranger," I said. Because I am the way I am.

"Hey, friend," he replied. Because he is the way he is.

"Is she asleep?" I tiptoed forward and peered over the edge of the crib.

"You want to wake her up?"

"No, no."

"It's okay if you do. Sometimes I wake her up just because I miss her."

I smiled. "I do that, too."

I bent into her crib, close enough to feel the heat off of her skin, to see the threads of her eyelashes, to hear the tiny suck her lips made as she dreamed her dreams of nursing. And the thought intruded that I wasn't able to nurse her, and these were dreams of her, of my other me. But this time the thought didn't twist up my insides. She had given Nova what she could, and now I was here to give her what she would need in the future. My daughter. My husband. We were here, the three of us, these two people and me. We were here together.

Silas and I moved in silent agreement to the bedroom. He sat cross-legged on the bed and I sat facing him. I inched forward until our kneecaps were touching. I felt a jumble of emotions configuring and reconfiguring themselves like the bugs outside Odd's house. Anger and grief and guilt and relief.

I had thought of something else, as the auto had spun back along the same roads it had taken me, like thread rewound upon a spool. From Silas's perspective, I had left him. I had left him and, if even for only a day, had let him believe that I'd been murdered. How had he not hated me for it? But he *hadn't* hated me. He hadn't. He'd cared for me. He'd listened to me. He'd loved me. And what that meant to me was that he knew I wasn't her. He knew she had done that, not me. He saw me as myself. Among my jumble of feelings was hope.

"You lied to me," I said.

"Wheeze—" he began.

"And I lied to you," I said. "Lots. We lied to each other lots and lots."

"Don't forget lots," he added.

"Why did we *do* that?"

"Fear," he said.

"Fucking fear," I agreed. "What were you afraid of?"

"Let's see. That you'd want to leave again."

"I don't," I said.

He swallowed. "You don't?"

"Nope. I want to stay here with you."

"I know you can't promise that you won't ever want to go," he said.

"Neither of us can promise that. But," I said slowly, "I can promise that if I ever *do* feel like I want to go, I'll tell you. Will you tell me?"

He nodded. "I will."

After a pause, he said, "I was also afraid that the truth would hurt you."

"That's funny." I bumped my knees against his. "I was afraid of that, too."

"Maybe," he said, "we could just trust that each other is strong?"

"Good idea," I said. "Because we are."

I ATTENDED one last meeting of the serial killer survivors' group. I arrived late, and when I took my seat in the circle, the others were all talking about what had happened in *Early Evening* the other night, the Angelas slaughtering the Edwards. No one had been able to play the game since then. The company had shut the whole thing down an hour after the hack. All the players, the murderers and the murdered, were spat back into their bodies, into their lives. The next morning, the company had released a statement: The programming had been compromised by an unknown source. The game would be inaccessible until such a time as its integrity could be assured.

"It was you, wasn't it?" Lacey asked Angela. "You messed with the game. You sent everyone that invitation."

"I heard it was hackers," Angela said with an air of perfect innocence.

"Yeah, sure," Jazz said. "Hackers."

"Why would *hackers* do that?" Lacey asked Angela, narrow-eyed. "I mean, in *your opinion*," she said.

"Maybe they were tired of everything playing out the same old way," Angela said as she moved her hair slowly, decorously, behind one shoulder and then the other. "Maybe they wanted a new story. What?" she asked. "Why are you all staring at me?"

"Because you're a goddamn celebrity," Lacey said.

"Hardly," Angela murmured, clearly pleased.

"Lacey, did you end up playing?" I asked.

"I did."

"And?"

She pointed at Angela. "You had an army of yourself! I'd like one of those. An army of Laceys." She sighed. "Do you have any idea what I could do with that?"

"Yes, and it's scary," Angela said.

Lacey laughed at that, the rest of us, too.

I listened to the others talk, about the game, about their weeks, about their families and friends, about their homes and jobs, until the hour was almost up.

As always, Gert turned to me and said, "How about you, Lou? Did you have anything to share this week?"

"Actually I do." I sat on the edge of my pink, pin-tucked chair and looked around the circle at the women's faces. The rhyme began in my head: *Edward Early, Edward Early, hunting in the dark. Edward Early, Edward Early, left Angela in the park. Fern he dropped in the shopping cart. Jasmine he laid on the*—I stopped it. Enough. We weren't there anymore. We weren't them. We certainly weren't a rhyme.

"This is going to be my last meeting," I announced.

Angela and Jazz made noises of protest. Lacey said, "That's an option?"

Gert became very still in her chair. She watched me without moving or changing her expression, which was fixed in a small polite smile. How had Fern described her? Terrifying in denim.

"You've helped me," I said. "All of you. I wouldn't have gotten through these past few months without you. But I had a long talk with, well"—I caught Gert's eye—"with myself, and I figured some things out. I think maybe the group isn't for me right now."

Her smile not shrinking an inch, Gert said, "What *is* for you, Lou?"

"My life," I said firmly. "Just living my life."

She inclined her head. "You should do what's best for you. I hope you know that's why we brought you back. And that's what I've always been trying to achieve, what's best for you, each of you, all of you. I hope that's been clear."

"Like you said, you brought us back."

"That's right," she replied. "I did."

I smiled at her. "And now here we are."

Worry crossed her face. Good. Let her be a little uncomfortable, a little uncertain. They'd brought us back, but that didn't mean they could control us.

"First Fern, now you," Lacey said. "Fuck."

"We'll miss you, Lou!" Angela cried.

"I hope not," I said. "I hope we'll still see each other."

"We'd better," Jasmine said. "Who else is going to help me write *Beyond the Blade: The Jasmine Jacobs Story*?"

"And me to write *Knife Sharpener: The Lacey Adler Chronicles*?" Lacey replied.

"And *Open Wound*, the Angela Reynolds tell-all bestseller!"

"Open wound? Angela, that's disgusting."

Angela shrugged. "Disgusting sells."

"Okay now," Gert began, "if we can just—"

She shouldn't have bothered. We drowned her out.

MR. PEMBERTON HAD BOOKED the first appointment of the day. A lot had happened in the past week, too much to absorb. Still it had nagged at me, the careful questions he'd asked me during our sessions, the story he'd told me about his wife's post-partum depression, and then how I'd found him alone in my Room, how when he'd ported out, he'd called me by my name, a name I'd never told him, a name he wasn't supposed to know.

So it wasn't a total leap when, sitting on the couch across from him, holding his hands in mine, I said, "It's you, isn't it?"

Mr. Pemberton pulled back and blinked at me. But he didn't say *What?* And he didn't say *Who?*

After a moment, the man in the jewel-toned turtleneck flick-ered away, and she was there in his place, my other me, the other half of this story.

"Don't be mad," she said.

"What were you doing all these weeks? Watching me?"

"Making sure."

"Making *sure?*"

She looked down at our entwined arms then back up at me. "Making sure you were okay. Making sure you wouldn't run."

"I told you I won't. I'm here."

"I know. I came back to say goodbye."

"Where are you?" I asked. "Actual you."

"In a hotel room."

"A hotel room where?"

She smiled. "Somewhere."

"So you did it, then. You left."

"I'm on my way."

"Well, I'm on my way, too," I said. "And I'm okay."

She stared at me for a moment, then she hugged me tight. I felt her cheek against my cheek. Her arms, my arms. Her face, my face. Her body, my body, mine.

"Okay," she said.

With that, she flickered out.

And I found I was holding myself.

ACKNOWLEDGMENTS

Members of the support group for survivors of writing a serial-killer novel include:

My editor, Sarah McGrath, who believed in me and who made this book better by miles.

My agent, Doug Stewart, who held my hand, had my back, and championed my work.

Alison Fairbrother, Delia Taylor, Glory Plata, Nora Alice Demick, Viviann Do, and the rest of the Riverhead team.

Ben Browning, Jack Butler, Caspian Dennis, Rich Green, Szilvia Molnar, and a special thanks to Maria Bell, who deserves all the fancy chocolates.

My colleagues and students at Emerson College.

Kate Beutner, Kris Bronstad, Julie Glass, James Hannaham, Rajiv Mohabir, Jessica Treadway, and Novuyo Tshuma, who kept me company through this project, with extra thanks to Kate and Kris, who never left a text unanswered, and to Rajiv, who was there when I wrote the final pages.

My mother, Beth Williams, who read the manuscript twice through when my father couldn't, and my father, Frank Williams, who lived a life filled with books and stories and who will always be with me in the pages.

My dogs, Fia Ginger, who sat with me while I wrote this book (miss you, girl), and Zelda Togarashi, who chewed my wrists through copyedits.

Ulysses Loken, who has my deepest thanks for all the rest.